PARADISE, WV

PARADISE, WV

ROB RUFUS

+ KEYLIGHT
B O O K S
AN IMPRINT
OF TURNER
PUBLISHING

Turner Publishing Company
Nashville, Tennessee
New York, New York
www.turnerpublishing.com

9781684426713 Paperback

9781684426706 Hardback

9781684426720 Ebook

Cover Design: Lucy Kim
Book Design: Meg Reid

Library of Congress Control Number 2021937112

Printed in the United States of America

This one's for you, Mom.

For always being my candle in a world that's more shadow than light.

"Like Socrates once said, all we really know is that we don't know shit."

—Shooter Kane

PARADOS

Michelle Wilcox was sure of two things: it was a hearse, and it was waiting on her.

"*Please*," her friend scoffed. "That ain't no hearse. It's one 'a them old-time limos."

The women debated the make of the car for a good ten minutes. It was parked against the trestle of the overpass that raised I-64 high above the bleak landscape of Paradise, West Virginia. Others wandered through the shadows, searching for their fix, but none seemed to notice the car hidden there in the deeper dark. The moonglow was *just* bright enough to illuminate the long front end, tinted windows, and dark paint job.

This was a special car. A special car for a special occasion. A limo or a hearse.

Michelle strained her eyes…yep, just as she'd thought. The back end stayed raised. It *was* a hearse. A Dead Man's Dodge. A Boneyard Buick. A Corpse Cadillac. A Funeral Ford.

"You think he's buyin' or sellin'?" Michelle asked.

Before she could answer, the back door of the car opened. Just a crack, but enough to see the glow of the dashboard lights, a dim green radiance. The women looked at each other.

"That answers that," her friend said.

"You want it?" Michelle asked.

"Nah, honey, I'm still holdin'. The crypt keeper's all yours."

Michelle scoffed and slapped her friend playfully on the arm before starting toward the special car. It was a long walk for such a short distance. She was jonesing bad, and her nerve endings jumped with every step, sending sharp, anxious pulses through her warring insides.

Then, all of a sudden, she was there. The special car.

It wasn't a hearse after all. It was a plain old sedan.

Michelle sighed. She felt better. She opened the door and slid onto the leather seat.

"Close the door, please," the driver said.

She did. "It's twenty-five for vanilla, forty for 'round the world."

The driver nodded. Shifted. The car started to roll.

"There's a spot up by those trees," Michelle said, pointing.

The driver nodded again. The engine masked the sound of the locks clicking shut.

She felt silly for thinking this was a dead sled. She couldn't help but giggle.

"Something funny?" the driver asked.

"Oh yeah...it's stupid, but 'fore I walked over I *swore* you was drivin' a hearse."

Darkness enveloped them. The doom of night.

The driver smiled.

EPISODE ONE

Chorus:
"Father, what is this hell
you've put me through?"
—Metallica

1

Jane Lusher could move faster than the world. She was always full of nervous energy, and it took a conscious effort to downshift so as not to leave her little brother in the dust. The anxiety pills helped. She took two every morning at breakfast so by the time they left for school, she could usually handle walking at Henry's painfully slow pace.

His left foot dragged across the fallen leaves like a rake—*shhhhhht, shhhhhht*—all the way across their yard. Henry limped because he had a condition called SCFE (*skiffy*, as their grandmother pronounced it), which made the bones in his hip grind together as if they had been fractured. When the siblings reached the road, Henry stopped to pick the wet leaves off his shoe. Then they crossed to the other side of the street and ducked the fence into Parthenon Place, the trailer park that was their shortcut to Shady Spring High School.

"Named after the Parthenon," Mammaw said once, "'cause every trailer in Paradise has its own Greek tragedy playing out inside."

The words rang true for the entire state. Opioids had sunk their claws into the hide of West Virginia, and they continued to push deeper, unwilling to relent until they merged with the state's internal makeup and became forcefully ingrained into its very DNA. It would take years for the rest of America to notice, and even longer for America to care. But native sons and daughters didn't need the nightly news to tell them a cavalcade of misery had descended upon their land.

Parthenon Place was Jane's personal barometer to measure the spread of the plague. Every morning, she would note if another neighbor had literally lost their home to drugs, their trailer replaced by a telling rectangle of mud and septic muck.

"Bomp, bomp, bomp," Henry sang, "another one bites the dust." He pointed to another bare patch of earth.

"I know," she nodded. "This whole place is just...sad."

"You know what *ain't* sad? You know what's badass?"

Henry popped the collar of his jean jacket and spun around so she could once again see what their grandmother had cross-stitched onto the back. It wasn't uncommon for Mammaw to make Henry's clothes (bootleg band shirts mostly, being a metalhead was *expensive*), but she'd outdone herself by stitching the name of his favorite Motörhead song—ORGASMA-TRON—onto his jacket.

"You're right." Jane smiled. "It's really cool."

"Hell yeah, it is. Badass as fuck."

She looked away and admired the landscape beyond the trailers. Hills and dense forest surrounded the town on all sides, nestling it beneath a warm canopy of reds and oranges and yellows. But those trees would soon be bare and foreboding, like bones jutting from a shallow grave, a landscape of mud, blood, and shit.

"I'm goin' to see Dad on Saturday," Henry told her.

"Yeah. I'll pass."

"I figured," he said.

"I'm working. You *know* I'm working."

Henry replied with a sullen nod. A moment passed. Jane wrapped her arm around his shoulders and pulled him close. She had to walk even slower, but found she didn't mind.

The shortcut let out on Grant Avenue, where they stopped to wait for the light. They were quite a pair when standing side by side. Henry wore a Cannibal Corpse shirt under his jean jacket and let his long hair fall over his face like Cousin Itt from *The Addams Family.* Jane kept her hair short, like their mother had styled hers before the chemo. Jane was tall and strong, though her athletic physique was hidden beneath a shapeless US women's soccer sweatshirt.

"Can you read that?" Henry asked, pointing to a flyer stapled to the crooked telephone pole across the street. "Maybe it's for, like, a concert... shit, *tell me* it's for a concert."

Jane squinted. "Um, it says 'best...'" Her words trailed off.

"Best what?"

Jane didn't answer. She was laser-focused on the flyer.

The light changed. The traffic stopped. Jane pulled her gym bag higher up on her shoulder and rushed across the street. Her gait verged on a full-on lunge as she sped over the pavement toward the telephone pole. She reached it. She read:

BEST KILL EVER!

LIVE

The new touring true crime podcast!

SATURDAY, OCTOBER 15, 2011

EPISODE: THE BLIND SPOT SLASHER

Bear Road Shopping Center
Paradise, West Virginia

POP-UP MURDER MUSEUM!   HALLOWEEN COSTUME CONTEST!
BEER/FOOD VENDERS   RAFFLES! PRIZES!

@BESTKILLEVER @CASTAWAYPOD #BESTKILLEVER

It hit her like a gut punch. Jane thought she might puke. She read it again and then ripped the flyer from the pole. Staples and wood chips flew. Henry limped up the curb behind her. She handed the flyer to him. He read and reread.

"What the fuck is a podcast?" he finally said.

"It's a radio show on the internet," Jane explained. "People listen on their phones."

"What about a pop-up murder museum?"

"I don't know," she said. "I don't *wanna* know."

Henry wadded the flyer into a ball and threw it out in the street.

"Litterbug," she said.

"Blame the asshole that put it up. If he were here, I'd shove *him* into traffic instead."

She scoffed. "Come on, tough guy."

They set off again. A vacant-eyed man watched them from the stoop of the corner house. It was one of the many drug dens on that block. They pretended not to notice and turned right.

"You think people are gonna go to that podcast thing?" Henry asked.

"No way," she said. "No one would waste their Saturday watching a radio show."

Her voice fell flat when they reached the school. Flyers were taped to the walls of the outdoor concourse, stapled to telephone poles, shoved beneath windshield wipers. Flyers and flyers and flyers and flyers and flyers and flyers. It was advertisement by blitzkrieg.

The morning schoolyard cliques maneuvered around the flyers. Talking about them. Laughing about them. Taking pictures of them with their phones so they wouldn't forget.

Jane rushed forward without a word. Henry followed as fast as he could. She ripped a flyer from the hands of a freshman on her way to the telephone poles. The kid threw his hands up in protest, but didn't have the guts to open his mouth. Henry reached Jane at the third pole, so she let him do the honors. He ripped the flyer off the rotting wood as the morning's first warning bell rang.

The sound of the bell cut their schoolmates' attention. They forgot about the flyers and funneled inside as if snapped out of group hypnosis. Jane motioned for Henry to follow the herd.

"You sure?" he asked.

"Yeah. I'll get 'em down quicker if I do it myself."

"OK." He wadded up the flyer and shoved it into his jacket pocket.

They sighed in unison. Jane was a senior. Henry was a sophomore. They wouldn't see each other again until school was out and soccer practice was over.

"Love you, Ass Face," she said.

"Love you, Butt Breath," he replied.

Jane smiled, then jogged to the next telephone pole. She tore off the flyer then went on to the next, glancing back at her brother as she crossed the street. Henry labored up the steps of the school, pushing his way into the building as the second bell rang.

Another day in Paradise began. The Lusher siblings were already late.

No one said shit about Henry's jacket. He got no comments or condemnations. No one seemed to notice it at all. By the time fourth period rolled around, he was desperate for a reaction. He spent half of study block peacocking around the library, trying to get a rise out of the librarian, Ms. Vaughn. If he could just offend *her* delicate sensibilities, every kid in earshot would take note.

Back and forth, back and forth, before her desk he walked...but no dice.

Crestfallen, Henry headed to the folding table that served as the school's computer lab. All four of the desktop PCs were in use. He hated the first come, first served situation and thought it was unfair since most of his classmates could use their phones to get online. He sat at a nearby table to wait out the websurfers. He unzipped the small compartment of his backpack and removed a mildewed paperback called *Dancing with Death*, a Shooter Kane classic. Henry leaned back and opened the book to where he last left off:

> She pursed her crimson lips as I pulled the trigger. Ginger's eyes registered shock, which didn't shock me a bit. High-class dames like her never imagine their last kiss will be with the barrel of a gun...

Henry heard movement. He looked up—the boy at the third computer had logged out. Henry shoved the book into his bag and hurried to the station, cautious of quicker classmates looking to snag the spot. He made it to the chair unimpeded and sat down before the screen.

School computers were meant for schoolwork, but Henry had to cut corners. Running an online business wasn't easy when you lived an offline existence. He made sure the coast was clear, logged on to the computer, opened the browser, and typed "www.justiceforharlan.org".

Henry scrolled past his own photo, past the pictures of his sister, the pictures of his parents. He went to the footer menu so he could log in as the webmaster. Once on the administration page, he checked his messages (two new ones, both hate mail) and then went to the retail store. His eyebrows cocked when he saw the sales figures. *Fifteen shirts since last week? Really?*

The uptick had to be because of that podcast thing.

He wrote down the sizing and shipping information for each order so he could fulfill them at home. Once he was done, he checked the clock—ten minutes of class left. He reached into his pocket, pulled out the wadded flyer, and smoothed it on his thigh. "Best Kill Ever," he muttered. He typed it into the browser. Dozens of results came up.

He went to the podcast homepage, which featured a picture of a pretty woman and a pretty man drinking white wine in front of two microphones, having a blast. Photos of famous serial killers were overlaid behind them. Beneath the photo, there was a list of tour dates. Twenty-seven stops.

He clicked on the "live taping" link listed for West Virginia and read the episode summary for Paradise:

> On this episode of *Best Kill Ever*, Remy and Laci deep-dive into the case of the *Blind Spot Slasher*! BSS, aka Harlan Lusher, is thought to have killed up to twelve people, making him the most infamous serial killer in Appalachian history. Cults, corpses, carnage—this story has it all! Mature audiences only. A live Q and A with the victims' families will follow the taping, and

our pop-up Murder Museum is an interactive glimpse
into the mind of madness. Plus: vendors, raffles, games,
and a Halloween costume contest!

Henry grimaced. His sudden queasiness surprised him.

So much time had passed, but he still wasn't used to reading
about his father.

Jane dreaded locker rooms. She considered forced public nudity
the most outdated form of teenage torture. She changed into
her sports bra without removing her sweatshirt, craned her
torso into the locker to put on a T-shirt, and then nearly stepped
inside it to change from jeans to soccer shorts. The footfalls of
after-school escapees echoed through the vents like scattering
rats.

Jane had managed to get through the day without dwelling on
the podcast, which was good because she hadn't needed to take
another buspirone. Jane didn't like to take her anxiety meds
before practice. She was too serious about soccer to risk stifling
her performance.

She was a great player, always had been, but got unruly when
she was stressed. Even in Peewee League, she took wild chances
whenever the fear of losing crept in. That's why her dad nick-
named her Calamity Jane—she would do anything to keep from
losing.

Yet it was loss that defined her. She lost her dad six years ago,
when he was framed for killing those women. She lost everything else when the civil litigations started. She lost her place
in the world when they moved from Charleston to Paradise and

crammed into her mother's childhood home. She lost her mom two years later to cancer. She lost. She lost. She lost.

But on the field, she still had control. Had a chance to win. That's why she pushed herself so ruthlessly. That's why she abstained from her meds. That's why she stayed switchblade sharp.

Jane shut the locker and sat down on the bench to lace her cleats. It wasn't until she stood up that she noticed Carrie Clemmons and Ramona Sutter loitering at the end of the row. Carrie wore Adidas shorts and a matching sports bra. Ramona had on a similar annoyingly cute outfit. It was obvious they were waiting on her. They couldn't contain their giggles.

Jane dropped her eyes as she tried to move past them.

"Hi, Jane!" Carrie said, stepping in front of her.

"Hey," Jane said. "We better get out there."

"Sure," Carrie nodded, "but I was wondering, do you know who put up those flyers?"

Ramona stepped next to her friend. Their eyes glowed. Their glee was sickening.

"I don't know what you're talkin' about," Jane muttered. "Now come on—"

"Did *you* put them up?" Carrie asked. "Does your family get a royalty check whenever someone mentions your psycho-killer fuck of a dad and the crack whores he chopped up into—"

"Clemmons! Sutter!"

All three girls jumped. Coach Harris stood behind them. They hadn't seen her enter.

"Five laps," Coach Harris ordered. "Go."

"But—" Carrie started.

The coach shot up a silencing hand. Carrie and Ramona seemed to physically shrink as they slunk past her and rushed out the door. Coach Harris stepped forward before Jane could follow suit. She towered over the girl—all the girls—and was likely a Viking queen in her past life. She gripped Jane's shoulders, imparting no sympathy, only strength, as she glared down. "Listen to me," she ordered. "I *guarantee* WVU and Marshall will make offers by next month. The scout from Concord hinted at a full ride, too. That's three scholarships to choose from, three tickets outta here...*If*," she paused, tightening her grip, "you don't let anyone get in your head and mess up your game."

"I know," said Jane, sighing.

"No, you don't," she said, squeezing again, "but I've seen it before. People like Carrie and Ramona will do anything they can to keep you down. They resent you because they know that, when they're older, the only interesting thing about their boring lives will be that they once got to play on the same soccer team as *you*."

Jane nodded. Her nerves calmed. The coach let her go.

"OK," Coach Harris said. "Are you still Jane Lusher?"

"Yes, ma'am," she muttered.

"Then get your skinny butt out on that field and do some damage."

Jane did just that.

2

Otis Perkins sat on the porch of the dilapidated home his parents rented on the west end of Paradise. His eyes raced across the pages of his latest true crime book, *Black Dahlia Avenger.* He had started the book a little over two hours ago and was nearing the end.

His ability to speed-read was often viewed as a cheap parlor trick. Even those who knew he was gifted, knew he'd skipped three grades and would soon be attending Duke on scholarship, had a hard time believing that a fifteen-year-old possessed such an odd talent.

For Otis, speed-reading was more than a gift. It was a blessing. He'd read *dozens* of true crime books over the past two years— cold cases solved, serial killers captured—and justice was the indomitable lifeblood flowing through each. Every book served as a brick in the mental fortress he'd built to stop the inverse narrative from bombarding him twenty-four hours a day.

The opposite story was *his* story, where crime struck blindly, justice went unserved, and victims suffered in perpetuity. That story began two years earlier, when Otis was thirteen.

His family lived in Huntington back then. They had a nice house of white brick on Fifth Street Hill overlooking Ritter Park. His father, Fred Perkins, was one of the most respected engineers in the state. He oversaw operations at G&O Railways downtown.

Life was small-town simple for the Perkins family. The local news had yet to pick up on the spike in overdose deaths, and the uptick in crime seemed as far from their day-to-day lives as a foreign war.

But then, one evening as Otis helped his mom with dinner, they got the call: Fred Perkins had been mugged while leaving work and savagely beaten within an inch of his life.

Broken ribs. Nose. Jaw. Misaligned vertebra. Four stab wounds. A punctured lung.

He spent three weeks in the hospital.

No arrests were ever made. No one was ever punished.

No one but Fred Perkins, who was weaned from morphine to oxycodone a few days before the doctors sent him home from the hospital. He developed an addiction almost instantly.

He lost his job within the year. The bank took their house soon after. The family floated between friends and relatives for a while, but it always ended in disaster. Fred Perkins the addict had a habit of burning bridges thoroughly and completely.

Even after he completed rehab, no one from their past was willing to forgive. No one empathized with the wrongs Fred had suffered. No second chances were granted. That's how true crime slowly became Otis Perkins's true north; it kept him open to the possibility that justice—no matter how delayed—was not always denied.

BING-bing! BING-bing! BING—

Otis finished the last two sentences of his book and closed it with a sigh. It was one of the most compelling stories he'd ever read. He reached into his pocket and pulled out his iPhone. He turned off the alarm and checked the clock: 2:30. Time for his dreaded ride. He put down the book as he stood and walked to the side of the house where his bicycle leaned.

Otis hated exercise of any kind, but a recent article about adolescent heart disease had his mom worried about his lack of physical activity. She made Otis promise to be active at least an hour a day. He begrudgingly started biking—the only exercise where coasting was possible.

He fastened his helmet, loosening the strap beneath his chin before kicking the kickstand back. The tires of the Cannondale buckled a bit when he climbed on. Otis had a body type department store salesclerks described as *husky*—he was broad-shouldered, heavy, and compact with a pinkish complexion that made him look a little like a fire hydrant with a pulse.

He pushed off the gravel, nursing the brake while letting the incline of their driveway do the work. He coasted down to the empty street, then pedaled off into the sad, strange landscape.

Otis hated Paradise. He often felt his family had been hurled into *The Twilight Zone*—an alternate dimension he hardly recognized. It was a dimension where his genius father grinded out night shifts at the coal yard, a dimension where Otis homeschooled himself while his mom worked days at the Piggly Wiggly. Otis clung to the sense of unease he felt in this new reality, because what scared him more than *anything* was that Paradise could someday feel like home.

Somewhere in the distance, a high, lonesome train whistle whined. The sound hurt his heart more than any sedentary lifestyle could. Cold tears rimmed his eyes. He blamed the chill in the air and pedaled harder. His chest and legs began to hurt. His throat began to burn. Otis labored for another block before pulling to the side of the road for a breather.

He put his feet down and leaned on a stop sign. He watched other kids walking out of the high school farther down the block. They innately formed the same cliché cliques as back in Huntington. Otis never had many friends, and homeschooling brought that number down to zero. But he could weather the solitude until next year, when he'd be North Carolina bound.

He would make friends at Duke, young intellectuals and brainiacs with common interests.

Suddenly, a girl caught his eye. Walking alone, shuffling down the sidewalk in a near limp, she held her backpack in front of her and gave an unimpeded view of the embroidery on her jacket.

Orgasmatron? Is that some Transformer I've never heard of?

He thought about it for a second then gripped the handlebars and pushed on. He made a left to avoid the traffic on Grant, huffing and puffing two more blocks before coasting to yet another stop at the abandoned K&P Station. Half a dozen flyers were taped to the boards that covered the windows. Otis leaned his bike against a dry pump and walked to the advertising spread. The corner flyer flapped in the breeze. The tape had come lose. Otis smoothed it back against the board unconsciously as he read the flyer.

A podcast is doing an episode HERE? I wonder . . . crap, is this the one where they make fun of everything? I hate those—

"Hey! Big Man!"

Otis barely had time to register the voice before the rock hit his shoulder. He tripped forward, slamming his head into the board before collapsing onto his side. If Otis hadn't been wearing his bike helmet, he would've been knocked out cold.

His eyes darted in every direction while he tried to compute what had happened. Then he saw the girl with the limp moving across the lot toward him. It took a few seconds for Otis to realize she was actually a *he*—and that he held a handful of rocks.

"You dumb motherfucker," he said, sneering. "You thought you could plaster those up without nothin' happening to you?"

"What?" Otis sputtered.

"The flyers! I *saw you* puttin' them up!"

"Wait!" Otis pleaded, holding his hands out before him. "I wasn't, I didn't, I was just looking at them! I swear! I *swear*! I hate that freakin' podcast! I would never!"

Otis trembled, struggling to catch his breath. He didn't know why the boy was angry. All he knew was that, when he dropped his arsenal of rocks, it was the most beautiful avalanche ever.

"Shit, dude," the boy sighed. "Sorry. I thought you were advertising."

"Honest...mistake," Otis wheezed.

He offered his hand, and Otis took it. The boy helped him up.

"I'm Henry," he said, dusting Otis off a little.

"Otis Perkins. Nice—well, not nice, but...glad to meet you."

"So, you've heard of this shit before?" Henry asked again, nodding at the flyers.

"Yes. I'm what you might call a student on the subject of true crime...lots of true crime podcasts have been popping up lately. But this is the worst...it's *beyond* distasteful."

"How come?"

"Because they don't take it seriously, any of it. They make jokes about the crimes, *real crimes* that hurt *real people*. They hide behind sarcasm as they profit off the horror of the victims while simultaneously lauding their perpetrators. I think it's disgusting."

"Barf-worthy for sure," Henry said.

Otis looked at the flyers. "Still, I'm surprised *any* podcast would come here."

Henry didn't comment. Otis started walking back to his bike. Henry walked with him. Otis didn't feel threatened anymore. Strangely enough, he felt the need to make his assailant warm up to him, as if he'd come down with a warp-speed case of Stockholm syndrome.

"That's a really cool jacket," Otis offered.

Henry stopped in his tracks. "You a Motörhead fan?"

"Uh . . ." Otis cleared his throat. "Isn't everyone?"

"They *should* be! Lemmy is fuckin' God!"

"Yes, yes, you're right." Otis nodded enthusiastically. "He is a hundred percent God!"

"Big Man," Henry smiled, "you just made my day."

Otis smiled back, blushing.

"Are you more of a metalhead or a punk? 'Cause Motörhead kinda falls between genres."

Otis took a guess. "I am a metalhead."

"Man! I've been waiting forever to meet another metalhead!" Henry slapped Otis on the arm. "You should come over to my house and listen to records with me sometime. I got the best collection in this shit-stain of a city, without a fuckin' doubt."

"I'd love to," Otis said, trying to mute his surprise. "This weekend, maybe?"

"Yeah, awesome. I'm busy Saturday, but Sunday's cool."

"Great!" Otis said, pulling out his iPhone. "Should I text you—"

"Nah," Henry said, "I don't have a cell phone."

"OK, I can DM you on—"

"I don't have any of that crap. Just come over. 431 Lockland. I'll be home all day."

"Oh, uh, sure." Otis nodded, putting the address in his contacts. "How about after lunch?"

"Cool." Henry shrugged. "Good to meet ya, man."

"Great meeting you . . . *man.*"

Henry grinned. Otis mounted his bike and pedaled away.

"Go, man!" Henry yelled behind him. "You were built for speed!"

Otis wasn't sure how to respond. He wondered what a "metalhead" would say.

He pedaled faster . . . he felt good . . . *faster* . . . he felt lucky . . . Otis took a chance.

He stood up on the bike and screamed at the top of his lungs: "*Lenny is God!*"

3

Downtown Paradise consisted of eight blocks and thirty-three build-ings: six bars, five pawn shops, four restaurants, three funeral homes, two banks, Dollar General, Hart's Hardware, the Book Nook, Kool Klips Salon, the Texaco station, and a few gray gov-ernment offices. The rest were vacant or boarded shut. The sad-dest of these was the Showplace Theater, whose ornate sign still rose above State Street though its neon bulbs were dark.

The marquee foretold bleak coming attractions: 4 SALE 4 LEASE 4 RENT.

Across from the theater was a three-story brick building with the words BARKLEY CO. SHERIFF STATION chiseled above the doors. A wooden bench sat to the left of the entrance, and a woman sat upon it with an unlit cigarette pursed between her lips.

Lt. Elena Garcia. She was young for her rank and looked even younger. She wagged the cigarette back and forth with her tongue. She didn't light it, but in a town like Paradise, smoking was still considered the only legitimate reason to take a break at work.

She took her phone from her pocket. Three texts. All from Craig.

> Craig (1:43 p.m.): All Ruby talked about at breakfast is how excited she is ur off on Sunday. It's beautiful, really.
> Craig (2:02 p.m.): It isn't just Ruby, FYI. I'm excited too, been missing u bad. I hate how hard all this has been.
> Craig (2:45 p.m.): Anyway, I know ur on duty. Holler at me when your free with your schedule. Miss U

She sighed. She put her phone away.

She took a pretend drag off the cigarette and looked out at the street.

It was jarring to watch a town die. She thought she'd seen the worst of the burgeoning drug epidemic when she was with Charleston PD. But Charleston was a city, with resources towns like Paradise didn't have. Lt. Garcia had only been with the Barkley County Sheriff Department three months, and she felt powerless to sway or stomach the sheer devastation. Painkillers hit the area like an atom bomb, and she had arrived in time to do nothing but bear witness the slow, painful death of all that survived the initial blast.

"Excuse me, Lieutenant?"

She turned. Sgt. Sean Coffey leaned on the open door of the station house.

"Sheriff is askin' for ya." His mustache curved in an unintentional grin when he spoke.

"Anything serious?" she asked, sliding the phone and cigarette into her pocket.

"No clue." He shrugged. "Just figured you'd wanna know sooner than later."

"Thanks for lookin' out," she said, and stood up.

He held the door for her as she entered the station and then went back to his desk. She was thankful for Coffey. The thing she missed most about being a city cop was having a partner, and he was as close to one as she'd found in Barkley County. Though lower in rank, he possessed qualities much more valuable; his heart stayed in the right place, his nose stayed clean, and his dick stayed in his pants. She couldn't say the same for the rest of her peers. There was a handful of decent officers in the department, but most were morons and power trippers. Key among the latter was Lt. Billings, whose office she passed on her way to see the sheriff.

"Does Connors need to see us?" he called from his desk. A game of computer solitaire reflected off his rimless glasses.

"Me." She shrugged. "I don't know about you."

He scoffed. "Equal opportunity's a bitch."

She flipped him the bird and continued down the hall.

The rank will make all this worth it...the rank will make all this worth it.

She took the county job because they offered her a fast-track promotion. She convinced her fiancé, Craig, that dealing with backwoods bullshit for a few years would raise her rank enough to secure a solid transfer position someplace nice, where they could permanently settle. Craig was self-employed, so he'd stayed behind in Charleston to get their house market-ready and to take care of Ruby, their five-year-old daughter.

Garcia's plan made sense on paper. But three months had passed, and their house still wasn't listed. Craig promised he was getting things in order, but lately she wasn't so sure... whatever. She could cry about her own problems on her own time (in the shower, like an adult).

She pushed the drama to the back of her mind when she reached Sheriff Connors's office. The door was shut. The shades were drawn.

She knocked. Brisk but firm.

"Come on in, Lieutenant."

She took a deep breath and entered. Buck Connors had been sheriff for ten years, though the cigar stench of his office smelled older than the dinosaurs. He was a fat man with thin hair who thought a cowboy hat and muddy boots worked for every occasion. Garcia shut the door. He motioned her to one of the two chairs in front of his desk. She sat down.

"How many years did ya work CPD's drug task force?" Sheriff Connors asked.

"Four years and two months, sir."

"So, you're good with junkies?"

"I have no animus for addicts," she said. "If that's what you mean."

He slid a file across his desk. She picked it up, opened it, and read:

Wilcox, Michelle Anne
D.O.B. 05/02/1994
HEIGHT: 5'1"
WEIGHT: 110 lbs.
ETHNICITY: Caucasian
EYES: Brown
HAIR: Blonde
Priors
12/20/2009—Possession
04/10/2010—Possession

Notes
Narcan administered: 11/01/2010
Narcan administered: 08/16/2011

"My wife's niece," he groaned. "She's been missing over a week. Parents say she's never gone radio silent before, even when she's using. They're assuming the worst. I'm assuming the same. But my wife'll have my ass if I don't get her sister some answers. I figure you might be a softer touch with the hopheads than Billings—"

"I'll find her," she said before he could finish.

"That's what I like to hear." He nodded. "Three officers be enough?"

"Yes, sir. Will Coffey, Kern, and Jones be OK?"

"Works for me." He shrugged. "Start poundin' pavement."

"I won't let you down, sir," she said, standing.

"I wouldn't either."

She took his meaning.

4

Otis was pushing it. The run-in with Henry had thrown his bike ride off schedule. By the time he saw their dilapidating Victorian rental, night was already coming down hard.

He panted like a sick dog as he forced the bike up the incline of the drive. His mouth hung open in a gaping O of exhaustion, but Otis was smiling inside. He hadn't expected to make friends in Paradise, but something clicked between him and Henry outside that old K&P Station.

Otis decided not to tell his parents yet. He needed time to workshop a friendship origin story that didn't involve assault. His mom would be home from work soon, and he expected to find his father having a cup of coffee at the kitchen table, fueling up for the midnight shift.

Otis pushed harder, until one last pedal thrust got him onto the plateau where their house sat. He dismounted, breathing hard, and leaned his bike against the bricks in its usual spot.

"Otis!" his father called from behind him.

Otis turned. Fred Perkins stood in their neighbor's yard wearing a heavy Carhartt jacket over a wifebeater and pajama pants. He was shoving leaves into a black trash bag. Otis started toward him, confused. His father tied the bag off, picked up a rake, and walked to his son.

"Have a nice ride?" he asked, setting the bag against the front gate.

"Sure," Otis said. "Why are you raking the neighbor's leaves?"

He wrapped his arm around Otis's broad shoulders as they walked to their house.

"I was having a hard time sleeping. My back's been acting up worse than usual."

"Those new meds don't help?"

"Not much," he said, "but Kristin, my sponsor, says that when her pain gets really bad, she does something nice for someone else. She swears it helps, so I thought I'd give that a try. Hence, I was raking the leaves out of Miss Cranston's yard... fine, upstanding fella that I am."

Otis chuckled. "I hope it helped."

"I believe it did," he said, and leaned the rake next to the bike. "Now, enough about my good deed. When can I expect my next briefing?"

"I'm ready when you are."

"Then come on," he smiled, "I still have some time."

Otis nodded. They walked onto the porch and into the old house. The underlying stench of mold loomed beneath the smell of his mom's Glade PlugIns. His father tossed his jacket on the recliner and walked slowly up the stairs. Otis followed.

His mom graded most of his schoolwork, but book reports were different. Making Otis write a paper on every book he speed-read would be onerous. So instead, his father tasked Otis with "briefings" twice a week—succinct verbal summaries of his latest literary conquest. The briefings were to be given while his father readied for work. Otis enjoyed their odd ritual; it was one of the only chances they had to spend time together during the week.

They entered his parents' room. His father went into the bathroom and turned on the faucet. He held his hand beneath the water until it warmed, then splashed it onto his face. From the bathroom door where Otis stood, he could see the scar beneath his father's right shoulder: one of the four spots a stranger stabbed him after robbing him blind.

"Today's book is called *Black Dahlia Avenger*," Otis said. "It's part memoir, part case study, part true crime exposé. It was written by Steve Hodel, a decorated LAPD detective."

"Black Dahlia? They made a movie about that, right?" He sprayed a dollop of shaving cream into his palm and began lathering his face. "She had a smile carved on her face?"

"Yes"—Otis nodded—"which is the least degrading thing the killer did to her, in my opinion. Elizabeth Short. She was tortured and killed in the winter of '47, then her mutilated body was put on display like a surrealist painting. It's the most famous unsolved murder in Hollywood history . . . and the author claims his father, George Hodel, was the killer."

His father ran his razor beneath the water. He began to shave. "How have I not heard of him, then?"

"He was dead by the time his son pieced it together, and most of the new evidence is circumstantial. But through the lens of abductive reasoning, he makes a heck of a case—"

"Oh," his father exclaimed, "I forgot to tell you! I got you something earlier. You'll find it even more interesting than this Hodel character. Go check my jacket pocket."

Otis hesitated a moment, unsure if he should finish his briefing, then decided his father could press him if he wanted to hear more. He hurried from the bedroom. The stairs played like scales on a squeaky piano as he trampled down them. Otis entered the living room, picked up his father's coat, and began rummaging through the pockets.

Car keys.

Loose change.

A folded piece of paper.

Otis knew what it was as soon as he removed it. He unfolded the flyer on his way back upstairs. When he entered their bedroom, his father's face was as smooth and pink as his own.

Otis held up the flyer. "Is this what you meant?"

"Yeah! Saw it on a telephone pole this morning. I knew you'd find it interesting."

"Thanks," he said, "but I'm not a real big fan of this podcast."

"I meant you'd be interested in the topic, not the show. BSS?"

Otis shrugged. "Should I know the name?"

"If you fancy yourself a budding true crime scholar."

"OK." Otis bit. "Who is he?"

"Our local boogeyman. Paradise was his killing floor."

5

His name was Gravyboat, but those in the know just called him Gravy. The fluffy twelve-year-old bichon was ten pounds overweight and moved at an arthritic pace, but his toylike eyes still sparkled with a lust for life. He was the namesake of bluegrass legend Gravyboat Johnson, with whom his owner had a brief affair in 1978. Her name was Betty Webb, but those in the know just called her Mammaw.

Her eyes had that same youthful glimmer. Her hair was a puff of curly white. She could stand to lose *more* than ten pounds, but the plump stature she shared with her dog gave them the magical appearance of two friendly clouds made of nothing but silver linings.

Mammaw shuffled across the kitchen tile in her leopard-print slippers. She checked the timer on the microwave. Gravy watched his dinner—a frozen hamburger patty—do the nuclear twist inside. The kitchen was small, separated from the living room by a built-in island that served as the dining room table. It was more of a two-bedroom cottage than a house.

Beep, beep, beep!

"Soup's on," Mammaw said as she opened the microwave.

She removed the plate and scraped the hamburger patty into his bowl. Gravy went to town. She smiled, taking a moment to enjoy his enjoyment before washing the plate. With the microwave off, she could hear Henry listening to music in the room that was once her bedroom. She now slept on an air mattress in the living room, which suited her fine. He and Jane deserved the bedrooms. Kids needed their privacy. She was old enough to do whatever she damn well pleased right out in the open.

She poured herself a cup of coffee then opened the "special" drawer beside the utensils. It was where she stored her playing cards, weed, and other treasures of ill repute. The kids knew where she kept her stash, but they had no interest in illegal drugs. They were *true* angel babies, and Mammaw was often amazed that she had any claim to them at all.

The dog bowl scraped against the tile. Gravy was done with his meal.

"Come on, you hungry ol' hippo," she said.

A half-smoked joint and Zippo sat in the middle of a ceramic ashtray. She took them out of the drawer, grabbed her coffee cup, and walked down the short hallway that led to the back porch. She shivered when she opened the door—the wind was harsher than it should've been. The sun was low in the sky, the horizon the color of rotting pumpkins.

Fall had snuck up on her. Everything seemed to, lately.

Mammaw let the dog into the yard to do his business. She set the ashtray on the wooden porch rail that she leaned against. She sipped her coffee, then slid the joint between her lips.

She lit up and took a drag. Her insides warmed a little. She exhaled.

Smoke drifted over the creek behind the yard and vanished into the Halloween horizon.

Henry told her about the boy. Otis. She was hopeful he'd met *someone* in Paradise that would see him as more than a last name. Henry also told her about the flyer. She didn't know what a podcast was, but she knew how terrible it must've been to see those ads posted up everywhere. The town was spiteful, even on its deathbed, and Paradise made sure Henry and Jane knew they'd never be welcome.

"Gravyyyyyyy!"

Mammaw heard Jane call from the road. She took another hit as she watched the dog run to Jane. She still wore her soccer clothes, and the shadows made the contours of her muscles more prominent. Jane knelt in the grass and loved on the dog. There like that, in the gloaming, she was the spitting image of her mother.

Mammaw smiled. Bittersweet.

"Hey," Jane said as she unlatched the porch gate and let Gravy stumble up.

"My little angel baby," Mammaw said, wrapping the girl in a warm embrace.

"How was your day?" Jane asked, letting go.

Mammaw picked up her ashtray and coffee, keeping the joint between her lips.

"Oh, it was fine. How was yours, honey?"

Jane shrugged. Mammaw nodded and hugged her again.

6

Otis couldn't sleep. He'd been lying in the dark for hours, staring at the water-stained ceiling while the white noise app on his phone whooshed mindlessly. His father's tale of a local serial killer intrigued him to the point of insomnia.

His dad hadn't remembered much more than the headlines. A wealthy developer killed and mutilated drug-addicted women he picked up on the roads around Barkley County. The "Blind Spot" moniker came from rumors that the victims' eyes had been carved out.

Now Otis *had* to attend the podcast. He decided not to research BSS on his own until afterward—he would go in cold and give *Best Kill Ever* a chance to redeem themselves.

Otis groaned. He sat up in bed.

He flipped on the bedside lamp, which cast odd shadows across the room. There was a poster of Spider-Man on one wall and a framed print of Albert Einstein on the other. His desk was positioned by the window. Stacks of used books were piled against the wall at the other end of the room—over a hundred books bought for five cents each when the Huntington Public Library liquidated its inventory. Most parents would've refused to haul the bulk of books along when they moved, but Otis's parents were good that way, in spite of everything else.

He tossed the flannel sheets back. His feet touched cold hardwood. Otis went over to the books, scanning spines in search of something that could steal his interest away from BSS.

It was no use. Nothing there was going to trump local boogeyman lore.

Otis couldn't hold out any longer. He sat down at his desk, flipping on the space-heater beneath it to thaw out his feet. He turned on his computer. He squinted when the screen lit up.

He googled "Blind Spot Slasher."

Thousands of results in 0.62 seconds. Harlan James Lusher.

Wikipedia was at the top of the list. A sidebar on the right displayed a photograph of a man in handcuffs being led through a crowd of reporters by police. There was a young boy in the photo walking behind him who seemed to be yelling at the police officers...

"Henry?" Otis said out loud.

The boy in the picture was younger. His hair was shorter. His face was streaked with tears. But the mask of rage beneath them was identical to the one he'd seen coming at him through the parking lot. Otis clicked the tab beside it marked "More Images."

He was bombarded by thumbnails. Mug shots. Crime scenes. Courtrooms.

He changed his search: "Harlan Lusher, family." The results poured in. Otis couldn't believe what he was seeing: Henry Lusher. Fifteen. The Blind Spot Slasher's only son.

It was more that true crime coincidence. It was kismet.

"Killer kismet," Otis muttered to the empty room.

He sat with that for a moment. Then he hunkered down and got to work.

7

The hallway was more chaotic on Fridays. Students slacked, gabbed, and grab-assed through the break that came before the fifth period bell. But for Henry—whose next class was at the opposite end of the building—that break was a serious point of stress. His prick of an algebra teacher, Mr. Daniels, knew all about his hip condition but still wrote him up whenever he was late to class.

No exemptions given. No one cares. Welcome to existence.

Henry maneuvered past a group of basketball players that were crowded around his locker. He twisted the three-number combo and pulled the wobbly tin door free. He replaced his health and English I book with one called *Introduction to Algebra* and a binder full of scribbled worksheets. He shut the locker and pressed his head against it.

His hip hurt worse than usual, and he wished he had a cell phone so he could call Mammaw and ask for a ride. His longing for technology vanished a millisecond later, when Carrie

Clemmons and Ramona Sutter came through the gym doors, laughing like hyenas with a Cujo-level case of rabies, backs arched as if they were walking some invisible red carpet.

He wondered if they laughed that way when they bullied his sister online. Did they share the same sick smiles back when they suggested Jane kill herself on social media?

I'm gonna shut you up one day, he thought. *You'll never see me comin'...*

He averted his eyes as they passed him.

The hallways started to clear out. Henry pushed forward.

Pushing was all he could do. Push through the day. Keep going straight through Sunday morning, when the podcast would be ancient history and everything would chill out. By the time Big Man came over, Henry wouldn't have a care in the world.

The thought made him smile. He was excited to hang with Otis. Henry never had luck making friends in Paradise, but things would be different this time. After all, Otis was a metal-head, and if they could relate on a musical level, they could forge a true understanding.

Music was magic that way.

It could soothe the pain of loneliness, that utterly savage beast.

8

Garcia stabbed her pointer nail into the cuticle of her thumb to keep from falling asleep. The passenger seat of the unmarked Crown Vic wasn't exactly the lap of luxury, but after three days of pulling doubles, it may as well have been a California king.

They still hadn't found Michelle Wilcox, and they were running out of places to search. She kept deputies Jones and Kern stationed at the I-64 overpass. The tent camp beneath it served as an open-air market for addicts and hustlers. The deputies kept their distance, watching with binoculars.

She and Sgt. Coffey did the legwork. They combed Paradise proper, and by Friday they'd worked their way to the outer edges of the perimeter. They had hit parks, rest stops, vacant lots, abandoned buildings, every holler in the county line. They had exactly nothing to show for it.

Now they just had one spot left on their list—the Grisham Glass Factory.

Garcia sent Coffey into Tudor's to get them some coffees before setting out. She watched from the passenger window as he left the café with a tray of large Styrofoam cups. Though they both wore their civvies (her in a black-and-white flannel and cowboy boots, him in jeans, a blue polo shirt, and a faded denim jacket), Coffey still looked like a cop to her.

That, or an angry blueberry...

She chuckled at the thought as she reached across the driver's seat and opened his door.

"Mr. Coffey with the coffee," he said. He ducked into the car and handed her the tray.

"Thanks," she said. "Grisham Glass is next."

He nodded and turned the engine over. They rolled out.

Garcia found the ebb and flow of the car's blown shocks oddly soothing. She stabbed her thumb again. *Wake up!* She pulled the tab on one of the cups and chugged strong black coffee.

"You really think she went all the way to Grisham?" he asked.

"I dunno. But I heard girls have been working it ever since Harmon Street got raided. I can't imagine they get much business out in the sticks. I figure one might talk out of boredom."

"You're wise beyond your years, ma'am."

"Desperate's more like it," she said. "I'm not ready to tell the sheriff his niece is dust in the wind."

Coffey nodded. The Crown Vic picked up speed. They turned onto one of the many unnamed backroads that scarred the landscape. Garcia watched the wilting wilderness roll by. She counted dead deer on the side on the road. Four Bambis in, her attention shifted to a fenced-in dirt road on her right. The sign above it was faded, barely legible in the late afternoon glow: LORDSVILLE LOVES YOU! There were cabin-like buildings visible beyond the fence.

"Lordsville loves you," she said.

"Spooky, ain't it?"

"What is it," she asked, "some kinda Bible camp?"

"You've never heard of Lordsville?"

"Nope."

"Damn. I keep forgettin' you just moved here. How 'bout Pearl Jolley, you heard of her?"

"Jolley as in *Mayor* Jolley?" she asked.

"He's her cousin...whole family's a power-hungry lot. Her daddy was a swingin' dick in the senate. Pearl, or *Sister* Jolley as she calls herself, is the batshit-crazy black sheep. She opened Lordsville sometime in the seventies. It was kinda like a hillbilly Jonestown."

"Bullshit," Garcia scoffed.

"I'm lyin' I'm dyin'." He shrugged. "It was one of those stupid 'live off the land' communes...basically a cult. But when I was a kid, Sister Jolley was like a rock star 'round town. She'd have these huge revivals...lotta snake handling, poison-drinking craziness."

"A cult," she mused. "The place looks abandoned to me."

"Suspect it is. A fire took half the place down, back in the eighties. Lotta people died. I reckon membership slumped afer that...ashes to ashes, nuts to nuts."

"Did Sister Jolley die?" Garcia asked.

"Nah. Her son did though, along with twenty or thirty others."

"Goddamn."

"Weren't more than a handful of survivors. Funny though, one of them was another local celebrity..." he said, pausing for dramatic effect, "serial killer Harlan Lusher."

"Jesus! How do I not know this?"

He shrugged. "You must not read the oddities section of the news."

She looked out the back window of the car. She watched the sign disappear.

"Think Michelle Wilcox found Jesus?" she asked.

"No way," he said. "No local would step foot in that place, high as hell or stone sober."

She nodded. He drove on.

Ten miles later, the abandoned glass factory came into view. Three blocks of houses lined the ridge beyond it. In the sunset glare, it looked like a friendly, middle-class neighborhood. But as they got closer, the empty driveways, tarp-covered roofs, and boarded-up windows came into focus—painfully common markers of a painfully American landscape.

When they reached the factory, Coffey slowed the car to a creep. The building had the aura of an empty grave. The soot-colored walls were covered in bad graffiti. Nearly all of the windows were broken, and the shattered glass of the glass factory said all there was to say.

"Should we go in and check for squatters?" Coffey asked.

"No," she said. "Drive up to that row of houses, there."

He nodded. They crept down the block of broken homes. Nothing. Coffey turned left and hit the next block. They cruised the crushed community. Nada. He turned onto the third and final street—bingo.

A woman loitered near the dead-end sign posted at the end of the block.

"Park," Garcia said.

He pulled over. She grabbed her coffee and took a second cup from the tray.

"Keep eyes on me," she ordered. "But wait here unless I signal you."

He nodded. She nodded back. She got out.

Garcia sat the coffees on the hood of the car so she could adjust her belt holster. She moved the gun from her hip to the back of her jeans, where her flannel shirt would cover it. Her badge was already tucked in her pocket, out of sight.

Garcia started down the block. Every house looked uninhabitable. Black mold covered the porches. Burweed and henbit poisoned the yards. The woman at the end of the street was the only sign of life, though it was likely there were others in the house nearest her, watching. Garcia took a deep, purposeful breath and crossed to the dark end of the street.

The dead-end woman was just a girl. Twenty, *maybe*. The armpits of her Mickey Mouse T-shirt were stained yellow. Her shorts were too short for the weather. She leaned on the sign where the sidewalk ended and watched Garcia approach.

"Yo, J.Lo," the girl called, "you lost?"

"No." Garcia smiled. "I don't think so."

"Hmm." She shrugged. "Right on . . . you tryin' to go bumper-to-bumper with me, then?"

"I've been sworn to celibacy. But this coffee's hot if you want it."

The girl shrugged again and took the cup. She pulled the tab and drank greedily.

"Thanks," she sighed. "I needed that."

"My pleasure," Garcia said.

"So, you a nun or something?"

"Basically," Garcia said. She offered her hand. "I'm Elena."

"Sissy," the girl said, and shook it.

Garcia pulled three snapshots of Michelle Wilcox from her pocket as Sissy chugged caffeine. "I'm out here looking for a friend of mine. Her name's Michelle—"

Sissy held up a halting hand. She looked at the house apprehensively. She bit her lip.

"Sorry. I ain't supposed to talk to no one who ain't payin'."

Garcia nodded calmly. She sipped her coffee. Sissy did the same. The wind picked up.

"I can't give you money," Garcia said a moment later, "but I have something else."

She reached into her pocket and removed a NARCAN inhaler. Sissy gulped audibly.

"You know what this is?" Garcia asked. "It can counteract a heroin overdose—"

"I...I don't need that," Sissy muttered.

"But your friends might. No need to call 911 next time a bad batch goes around."

Sissy bit her lip again, harder. She reached out for the NARCAN spray.

"What the fuck, Sissy?" a voice yelled from the house.

Sissy jerked her hand away from the NARCAN. Garcia slid it back into her pocket and focused on the thin, shirtless man strutting angrily across the yard toward them.

Clock his rebel flag tattoo.

Clock his dilated pupils.

Clock the knife in his waistband.

"We were just talking," Garcia said calmly when he reached the sidewalk.

"Sissy ain't got shit to say about shit," he snapped.

"Fair enough." Garcia nodded, handing him the photographs.

"Then let me ask you. I'm looking for my friend, Michelle Wilcox. Have you seen her around anywhere?"

His eyes widened, then arched. "You a cop?"

"She's a *nun*, Gary!" Sissy blurted out.

He shot her a look, then turned back to Garcia. He was all sorts of confused.

"I can pay if I need to." Garcia shrugged. "I just want to find my friend."

"Never seen no one pay to *talk* to a bitch," he scoffed. "Pay 'em to shut up, maybe."

"First time for everything," Garcia said, commanding her lips to form a smile.

"Ten bucks for ten minutes," he said.

Garcia nodded. She pulled out her wallet and gave him two fives. He pondered on them for a moment then gave her back the photos. There was a skip in his step as he walked back to the house, as if he'd just made the best deal since George Parker sold the Brooklyn Bridge.

Garcia put her wallet away. She waited until he was inside to give Sissy the NARCAN.

"Thanks," Sissy said. Her voice had gone shaky.

"I can give you a ride outta here . . . get you somewhere safe—"

"No!" she snapped. "I'm OK." She took the photos. She looked at them carefully.

The first was from a church picnic. The second was a senior portrait. The third was a candid of Michelle Wilcox partying somewhere sad. Sissy's eyes focused on the third photo.

"I've seen her before. Down at the overpass."

"When?" Garcia asked.

"Week or two ago," she said. Her hand shook horribly when she handed the photos back.

Garcia clocked it. "What is it, Sissy?"

"Your friend...I, I think...I think she might be dead. She got in the car..."

"What car?" Garcia pressed. "What happened to the girl in the photo?"

Sissy's eyes dropped down. Her entire body shook. Garcia waited for her to compose herself, but when Sissy spoke again, her voice regressed to the tone of a child in trouble.

"The black car. The one Steph got in. My friend. Last winter. They found her dead a week later...I think *your* friend got in that same car."

Garcia was stunned. *This isn't an overdose. This is something else. Something worse.*

"What was your friend's last name?" she asked.

"Jackson," Sissy said, "or Jenkins. Somethin' with a J."

"What kind of car did they get into, Sissy?"

"A big one," Sissy muttered, "black or dark gray...I'm real sorry. I hope I'm wrong about it. I hope she didn't get her eyes x-ed out."

Garcia tensed. "What do you mean, x-ed out?"

"When they found Steph's body...the killer had carved out her eyes."

9

For the first time since the move, Otis forewent his schoolwork and opted for an education of another kind. For the rest of the week, he spent his days (and most of his nights) researching the case of Harlan Lusher.

Otis was both amazed and disturbed by all the information he could find online. He read old newspaper articles and watched old footage. He read the court transcripts and scanned official documents. He looked at crime-scene photos of a dead girl stabbed through the eye.

YouTube fed him an assortment of conspiracies. Reddit held even more. He went through all of them, read every thread and subthread. He even stomached the comment sections, which were often as disturbing as the content of the articles themselves.

The Blind Spot Slasher. The Skeleton Man.

He couldn't stop thinking about Harlan Lusher.

It wasn't just that he had an upcoming playdate with one of Lusher's children. It wasn't because the murders happened locally, or because they were noteworthy enough to bring a big-city podcast calling. It wasn't even because he had serious doubts about Lusher's guilt.

His fixation came from a deeper place. He had read so many tales of justice delayed and denied. But in those stories—as in *his* story—justice was denied to the victims, not the accused. Harlan Lusher's story was different. It was the first time Otis honestly empathized with victims on both sides of the line. Because the Lusher children were victims whether their father was guilty or not, and when he saw the photographs of them crying at the sentencing, he felt tears swell for his own father, who had served a three-year sentence in a prison of another kind.

When he studied the pictures of Henry Lusher, Otis saw himself.

So, he dove deep into the case; weighing evidence, playing angles, doing all the things he wished he could have done for his own father years ago.

He still hadn't told his parents what he was doing or why he was doing it.

He still hadn't told them about Henry.

He walked into his parents' bedroom Friday afternoon, due for another book report. His father stood shirtless at their bathroom sink, checking the water temperature. Fred Perkins had gained weight since getting clean, and he was looking more like his son every day.

"Someone owes me a briefing," he said.

"I know...but I've only read one book this week."

His father turned to him, surprised.

"It's kind of your fault," Otis said. "I haven't been able to stop reading about the Blind Spot Slasher. I keep delving deeper into the case...so I was wondering if I could maybe brief you on that, in lieu of a book."

"Hmm, all right." His father nodded. He picked up the can of Barbasol and sprayed shaving cream into his hand.

"Harlan Lusher," Otis started, "was convicted of three murders and suspected in at least nine more. He preyed on female drug addicts, women on the fringe of society. He got the nickname 'Blind Spot Slasher' because his alleged victims were stabbed through the eyes. *The Charleston Gazette* also called him 'The Skeleton Man' for a while."

"Skeleton Man? How'd they come up with that one?"

"Acid," Otis said. "The killer used acid to dispose of the victims' remains."

His father shivered. "I did not know that."

"Did you know he had a twin sister?"

"Really?"

"Mm-hmm. Her name was Hazel." Otis said. "I should probably start at the beginning, so the story makes more sense."

His father nodded and went back to lathering his cheeks.

"Harlan and Hazel's parents, Mary and Evington Lusher, grew up on a pumpkin farm outside of town. From everything I read, their lives were normal until Evington abandoned them. When the twins were six, Mary moved the family to the Lordsville Christian Commune—"

"Ah, that's right!" Fred Perkins said, nearly laughing. He picked up his razor and ran it under the water. "I forgot Lusher was part of that cult. How completely diabolical."

"I couldn't find much information on Lordsville," Otis said. "I'm hoping the podcast tomorrow will fill in more details on that. But Harlan's family lived there for a decade, right up until The Fire of 1984."

"I remember that. Lots of people died."

"Harlan was one of the only survivors. Most of the other members, including his mother and sister, were killed in the blaze."

He raised his chin to shave his neck. "That's what set him off, huh?"

"That's how the DA's expert witness spun it. But I don't buy her theory. Harlan Lusher went to military school after the fire. He went to college, got married, had a family...not to mention became extremely successful developing lodging for mining operations...I have a hard time believing anyone could manage that in the throes a trauma-induced psychotic break."

"Point taken," his father said. "So, when did he turn into Ted Bundy?"

"November 2004," Otis said. "A woman named Sheena Wiseman was reported missing. She was last seen leaving a Halloween party and getting into a truck with LUSHER DEVEL-OPMENTS painted on the side. Harlan Lusher was questioned, but he had an alibi. He and his family were at their church's Halloween trunk-or-treat celebration. Numerous witnesses confirmed it.

"Still, they impounded his work truck and found traces of blood in the back. They searched his house and all of his development properties...they found Sheena Wiseman's body in one of his model cabins."

"They called it the Love Shack, or something?"

Otis nodded. His father washed the cream from his face and turned the faucet off.

"Sheena Wiseman was stabbed through the eyes. Partial skeletons of eleven other women were rotting in a mass open grave."

His father wiped his face with a towel. "But you don't think he did it?"

Otis shrugged. His father walked past him and opened the top drawer of his dresser. He began changing into his work clothes. Otis paced in front of the bathroom and laid things out.

"His prints were at the scene...but of course they were. They found a partial DNA match on the victim's clothing, but the defense said it matched one in every five hundred people. I'm honestly shocked he was ever convicted. I think knowing he grew up in a cult poisoned the jury's ability to think abductively."

"His defense team should've hired you," his father said with a grin.

Otis blushed. He didn't disagree.

"So, what *do* you think happened?"

"I have a few theories," Otis said. "I'll tell you more about them after the podcast."

"My son, the private eye," his father said proudly. "Never expected that flyer to throw you into the case headfirst."

"Well," Otis admitted, "I was, uh, actually *thrown* into it even before that. I happened to meet his son, Henry, the other day when I was riding my bike."

His dad's face went from content to concerned. "Harlan Lusher's kid?"

"Yeah, just...randomly. I had no idea who he was. But he was really...he was neat."

"You met *Harlan Lusher's* son," he reiterated, "and you think he's neat?"

"Yes," Otis nodded. "He invited me over to listen to heavy metal on Sunday—"

His father shook his head. "I don't think so, Otis. I'm sorry, but no."

"I thought you'd be *happy* I made a friend."

"You're about to make a *ton* of friends at Duke. I don't think it's a good idea for you to start hanging around someone like—"

"Like what?" Otis said, more assertively than he intended. "Henry can understand me in a way those kids won't. What are the chances I meet a freshman that knows what it's like to watch their father get tossed to the . . . to the . . ."

His head dropped. He couldn't finish. He shut his eyes.

He felt his father's strong hands grip his shoulders and squeeze.

"OK," he said softly. "OK . . . but let me be the one to tell your mother."

10

TGIF meant *work, work, work* at Mammaw's house.

Henry sat at the table, scribbling shipping addresses from his notebook onto the faces of the mailers. He would call out a size, then Jane would sift through the three cardboard boxes of T-shirts until she found one corresponding. If Henry said nothing else, Jane tossed the shirt to him. If Henry said "autographed," she tossed it across the table to Mammaw. Mammaw forged her son-in-law's signature, then handed the shirt to Henry. Gravy waddled around, supervising.

They did this every Friday night, fulfilling orders with expert precision as *Dateline* played on the TV. That week was a record sales week. Twenty-six orders came in. Henry knew the spike was because of the podcast—media attention brought the weirdos out of the woodwork.

It had taken Henry all of a year to convince his family they had no choice but to accept said weirdos as their customer base. Their website—www.justiceforharlan.org—had been started by his mom during the trial. Back then, she sold JUSTICE FOR HARLAN T-shirts to raise funds for a private investigator. But her effort was an overall failure; the hate mail and death threats received muted the handful of donations.

Things got worse when the civil suits started. Lusher Developments, LLC, folded faster than a house of cards on a train trestle. The Lushers lost all of their savings, then all of their assets, then all of their everything. They suddenly found themselves poor—like, *West Virginia* poor—and they were ill-equipped to adapt to the harsh conditions of their new environment.

But then, around the time they moved in with Mammaw, the offers started coming in: $500 for an autographed eye exam chart, $200 if Harlan would leave a scary voice mail on an answering machine, etc. Henry was the only one in the family able to look past his disgust and see the financial possibilities; there was an entire subculture of serial killer superfans chomping at the bit for a taste of his dad. In their world, Harlan Lusher was a rock star. They didn't care if he was guilty or innocent. They just thought he was cool.

Henry convinced his family that these gore-obsessed groupies were a cash cow. So they changed the T-shirt graphics, they started offering autographs, they upped their prices . . . and little by little, it worked. Harlan's "fans" found their way to the website and money trickled in. They raised nearly enough to cover the retainer of a big-time private investigation firm . . .

But then their mom got sick. Cancer.

Ruiner of dreams. Turner of fortunes. Destroyer of hopes.

Hiring a private eye seemed almost frivolous after that. Harlan made them put the money they'd raised toward her medical care. They did as he asked. They bought the best treatment they could—but they couldn't buy her more time.

Still, the webstore stayed open, and the money went to household expenses. Between the shirts, Jane's job, and Mammaw's SSI check, they could (usually) keep the lights on and the fridge stocked with food.

"Need a large," Henry said.

Jane dug through a box and tossed him a shirt that said HARLAN LUSHER FAN CLUB.

Henry folded it, put it in the mailer, and sealed it shut. Mammaw finished the autograph she was forging and slid the shirt over to Henry.

"Looks good," he said, and packed it. He looked over his checklist and then gave them both a satisfied nod. "That's all of 'em."

"How much did we make?" Jane asked.

"Almost fifteen hundred dolla-dolla bills, y'all!"

Her face puckered, nauseated by the thought.

"We gotta take it where we can get it, baby," Mammaw cooed.

"I know, just—" She scoffed at herself and stood up. "Whatever. I'm just glad this shitty week's almost over."

"And we survived it," Henry added. "Who woulda thought?"

Jane laughed sadly. She bent down and picked up the nearest box of shirts and carried it to the closet where they were stored. Henry tossed the mailers into the large Tupperware container they used to carry orders into the post office. He and Mammaw would stop there in the morning on their way to the Salem Hill Correctional Center.

Jane came back for the next box. Mammaw took the third, walking behind her.

"Sure ya don't wanna come tomorrow?" Mammaw asked.

"Sure that I've gotta work," Jane said, unloading the box.

They'd had the conversation a hundred times. Jane insisted that she loved her dad, that she held no suspicions or ill will. She spoke to him on the phone once a week, but she refused to go to the prison. Jane told Henry and Mammaw that seeing him at the trial was hard enough; she feared a prison uniform would soil her image of him entirely. She needed her dad—in her mind, her heart—to remain her dad. Not a convict. Not a killer. Not a prisoner. Her dad.

Henry didn't really understand her position. He visited his dad every week. They always made sure to put Jane on the visitation list in case she changed her mind. He heard Mammaw remind Jane of this as she handed her the final box.

Jane put it in closet and shut the door.

11

Henry did the hard part alone. Mammaw stayed in the waiting room as he limped through the halls of the Salem Hill Correctional Center. He had to strain to keep up with the escort guard.

Squeaking tile. Harsh fluorescents. The smell of Lysol, piss, and sour sweat.

Echoes of anger and boredom seeped through the air vents above him like noxious gas.

His escort stopped. Henry almost bumped him.

The door in front of them screamed like an air-raid siren and then opened.

The guard led Henry into the visitation room. There were ten stations separated by metal dividers. The guard walked him past the first seven stations. Henry side-eye spied on the other visitors talking to convicts through unbreakable plexiglass. It was then that he decided not to tell his dad about the podcast. What good would bad news do in a place like this?

The guard stopped him at station eight. Henry sat down in the metal chair. The seat on the other side of the glass was empty. The guard left him there, alone.

BAAAAAHHB! CLICK. CRANK.

The door on the opposite side of the glass opened. Harlan Lusher was led into the room by two guards. He'd lost weight, Henry noticed, and looked rather pale. But he was smiling the biggest smile a man in shackles could manage. Henry smiled back, bittersweet. Harlan sat down across from his son. They picked up their respective phones.

"My beautiful boy," he said, "you're a sight for sore eyes."

"Same to you, Dad. You're lookin' trim. You been running?"

He nodded. "More, now that it's cooled."

"Cool," Henry said lamely. "How, uh, is everything goin' in here?"

"It's been an eventful week," he said. "Guess who visited me Tuesday."

"Who?"

"Travis and Cybill Adkins, Tasha Adkins's parents."

Tasha Adkins. One of the three women he was framed for murdering.

"They came to forgive me," Harlan continued. "They want to move on with their lives. What an amazing family they must be. The strength it would take to offer that, the grace..."

"What'd you say?" Henry urged.

"I told them I can't accept absolution for something I didn't do. Travis Adkins didn't take that very well...understandable, I guess. But Cybill, I think she believed me. I think she could tell I was being sincere."

"Shame she didn't have that change of heart before they took our house—"

"Hey," Harlan snapped, "your mother would slap you silly if she heard you say that. They did what the DA told them to do. I have no ill will toward them. We've *all* been put through the ringer. But Mrs. Nesbitt assures me that they're almost done with their investigation, and then we'll get a new trial, and they'll get me out of here. The families of those victims will realize I'm not the monster they were looking for...I have a feeling they'll make things right."

"Mrs. Nesbitt?" Henry asked, his tone hopeful. Mrs. Nesbitt was a lawyer with Operation Deliverance, a nonprofit group dedicated to overturning wrongful convictions. They'd been reviewing his dad's case for months. "What's new on that front?"

"Their investigators are on the verge of tying Pearl Jolley directly to the murders. They just need to verify some things—"

"Holy...crap! What'd they find out?!"

"Nothing new," Harlan said. "Information about Lordsville my old lawyers wouldn't introduce at trial. They were afraid the cult stuff would distract from the facts of the case."

"What information?" Henry asked, nearly begging.

"Things you're too young to know, son. Bad things they did to us...to Hazel..." His voice trailed off, and his eyes went somewhere far away. It happened whenever Hazel came up. Henry knew no misfortune could crack his father's fractured heart like the loss of his sister.

"Hey," Harlan said, suddenly snapping back. "How's Janey doing? Last time we talked, she said her coach expects her to get offered a scholarship."

"Yeah." Henry nodded. "More than one, I think. She's still killin' it, playing ten times harder than everyone else."

"She was always intense on the field, wasn't she? I can still see her back in Peewee League, number nineteen with a bullet. And now..." Harlan didn't finish. He just smiled, shaking his head at the wonder of it all.

Jane rode her bike downtown. The four-mile haul was easy compared to soccer practice. Her legs hummed in harmony as the bike chain revolved. She'd hardly broken a sweat when she turned left on Union, slowing and switching gears. No traffic. She pedaled past the neon welcome signs of The Sugar Shack and TJ's Pub, which were already packed with day-drinking roughnecks.

The signage beyond the strip of bars wasn't quite as inviting: CLOSED. CONDEMNED. STAY OUT. She passed the old theater. The old record shop. The old jewelry store. She could feel the town dying off piece by piece, like municipal leprosy. A toe here, a nipple there, a thumb, a nostril, a tongue. It was an ugly goddamn way to expire.

The Book Nook was one exception. It was a healthy appendage of Paradise, one of the few businesses that wasn't in some stage of decomposition. It was also the only place willing to give Jane a job. The shop's owner, Suzie Summers, had become a true ally to her over the years.

Jane eased on the breaks as she reached the awning of the store. She hopped off her bike and chained it to the rotted tree sticking up from the sidewalk. She stretched her calves and then walked across the street to Tudor's Café so she could buy Ms. Summers a cup of coffee. She did this every day before work; it was an affordable way to show her appreciation.

The restaurant was packed. Waitresses hustled from booth to booth, taking orders and refilling drinks. Jane pushed her way to the lunch counter and motioned to the waitress.

"Two large black coffees to go," she said over the noise. The waitress nodded.

She wasn't supposed to drink coffee (it exacerbated her anxiety), but she needed caffeine to make it through another boring shift at the shop. The Book Nook was Ms. Summers's passion—she hosted book clubs, story times, even lived upstairs to be closer to the business, but they had few paying customers. Ms. Summers made her money selling rare books to collectors online. It was the only reason her store hadn't gone bust with all the others.

Suddenly, Jane felt eyes on her. She scanned the room until she spotted Carrie Clemmons and Ramona Sutter in the booth beside the bathroom. Two other girls from school, Trudy Wright and Billie Jean Hamlow, sat on the opposite side of the table. All four girls were staring at her.

Carrie Clemmons waved. She used all five fingers, as if she were playing scales on the piano. Jane waved back, and the girls busted into a laughing fit.

"Two fifty," a cigarette-scarred voice said.

Jane turned back to the counter. The waitress held her to-go cups.

Jane threw three dollars on the counter, grabbed the coffees, and hurried out the door. She steadied her breathing as she crossed the street. She imagined Coach Harris telling her not to let Carrie get in her head: *Are you still Jane Lusher? Then get your skinny butt out on that field.*

She paused beneath the awning of the Book Nook, took a

beat, then entered the shop. She felt better as soon as she was inside, enveloped by stories of struggle and sadness that all seemed to turn out OK. It was the one place in town where happy endings were still within reach.

Ms. Summers stood at the counter, reading the jacket of a new hardcover. The woman was striking, even in her sixties. She wore bright, flowy clothes, and her dark hair was streaked with silver, not gray. As Jane walked over, the sun reflected off the green tint of Ms. Summers's glasses. Jane knew she wore dark glasses to deflect from what the kids at school called a "wonky eye." But there was nothing wonky about Ms. Summers. She was beautiful, and her smile was one of the few things Jane would miss about Paradise if a scholarship came through.

"The caffeine train has arrived," Jane said.

"Thank God," Ms. Summers sighed. She put the book down and took the cup. "It's been *so* slow, especially for a Saturday."

"It's still early. We could pick up."

The door opened, as if on cue, and a middle-aged woman walked into the store. She looked around for other customers before approaching the counter.

Ms. Summers smiled at her. "Hey there, Kayla. Help you with anything today?"

"Um, maybe," she said timidly. "I just finished the *A Million Dirty Secrets* series, and I've read all the E. L. James books...do you have anything that's more, um, adventurous?"

Ms. Summers's smile widened. "Follow me. I think I have just the thing."

Jane watched the women head to the back of the store, where they shelved a small selection of books they playfully referred to as "horny housewife lit." Jane took her place behind the counter. She sipped her coffee and picked up the book Ms. Summers had been looking at.

The Past Is Dead & Other Miracles by Donovan Shelby. She liked the title.

She flipped it over to read the back jacket. This time, she didn't hear the door open.

"Hey, Jane!" Carrie Clemmons said. Her friendly tone was sharp enough to draw blood.

Jane looked up from the book. Carrie and Ramona were strolling toward her, smiling. Trudy and Billie Jean Hamlow hung back and pretended to browse.

"Hey," Jane said flatly. "Can I help you find anything?"

"I just wanna apologize," Carrie said. "I was a mega-bitch the other day. I'm sorry."

"Yeah." Ramona nodded. "We're, like, *really* sorry."

"It's...um, it's fine."

"No, it's not," Carrie said sincerely. "I've tried to think of a way to make up for it all week...and yesterday it came to me. I know how Coach Harris has been pulling for you with those college scouts, which is really nice of her since you're so poor and stuff. That got me brainstorming on a way that I could help you out, too...so I did."

Jane didn't respond. Ramona's smile widened.

"I let those schools know all the press they'd get for recruiting you," Carrie continued. "I mean, after all, you're not just a good player...you're *famous*." She pulled a flyer from her purse and set it on the counter. "So, I invited every one of the scouts to this podcast taping."

"Coach Harris never locks her office," Ramona explained. "It was *super* easy to find their e-mails. You should totally come and mingle tonight. It'll be a *prime* networking oppor—"

Her words cut off the second Jane shoved Carrie with enough force to send her flailing. Carrie winged her shoulder on the sharp edge of the travel section before falling on her ass in front of the horror and sci-fi novels. Her three friends froze. Jane walked past Ramona to where Carrie lay. Ms. Summers hurried over to see what the commotion was.

Jane knelt beside Carrie. "Bitch," she whispered, without knowing what she was saying. "You have ten seconds to get out of here before I *end* you. Got it?"

Carrie's jaw dropped. Jane stood, crossed her arms, and began to count. Carrie stumbled to her feet and grabbed her purse. Trudy tried to help her catch her balance, but Carrie shoved her away. Trudy, Ramona, and Billie Jean hurried out the door. Carrie followed, but her eyes were fixed on Jane.

"You're as crazy as your dad," she spat as she backed through the door.

"Four," Jane said, "three, two..."

Carrie rushed to the sidewalk and closed the door behind her. Ms. Summers gave Jane a moment to settle down before approaching. She laid a gentle hand on the girl's trembling arm.

"Jane," she whispered. "They're gone. You're OK, now. You're OK."

The tears came with a shudder. Jane couldn't stop crying. She couldn't stop shaking. Ms. Summers embraced her, cooing comfort, petting her hair. It just made Jane cry harder. She heard the door chime again as the horny housewife ducked out of the shop. She was alone with Ms. Summers. She was cared for. She was safe. Slowly, her breath began to calm.

"Shaw wrote that 'hatred is the coward's revenge for being intimidated.'" Ms. Summers whispered. "Those girls just proved his point. They're cruel because they're scared of you."

A shudder shot through Jane. Her words were nearly unintelligible.

"Sometimes I'm scared of me, too."

12

The killer had carved her eyes out.

The words haunted Elena Garcia's sleep. But in the dream, Sissy was no longer standing at the dead end of a dead street. Sissy was standing at the foot of her bed. Sissy had gaping black holes for eyes and blood running down her cheeks like thick mascara tears. Sissy repeated the words over and over, not as a mantra but a warning: *The killer had carved her eyes out...*

Needless to say, Garcia slept for shit.

Sissy's comment reminded Garcia of the one thing she knew about Barkley County before becoming a resident: their blood-stained claim to fame, the Blind Spot Slasher. She hadn't mentioned Sissy's comments or the connection to Sgt. Coffey. Due diligence was due before she saddled her colleague with what was likely a rumor or a drug-induced fantasy.

She was supposed to report to Sheriff Connors as soon as she arrived at the station on Saturday, but instead, Garcia fueled up on caffeine and hit her desk. She logged in to her computer and searched the homicide database for Sissy's friend, Steph J-*something*.

She looked twelve months out—nothing.

Twenty-four months out—nada.

She changed tactics. She expanded the search beyond homicides. She perused the J's.

She hit pay dirt...maybe.

Jenson, Stephanie Gale
D.O.B. 05/02/1980   D.O.D. 12/02/2009
HEIGHT: 5'6"
WEIGHT: 132 lbs.
ETHNICITY: African American
EYES: Brown
HAIR: Brown
Priors
04/04/2008—Solicitation
06/15/2008—Possession
11/01/2009—Possession
Cause of Death
Overdose of Narcotics: NHI

NHI meant "no humans involved." NHI meant no murder. No mutilation. No boogeyman.

It must have been a rumor. Sissy must have been wrong, or high, or all of the above. Finding anything more on Steph Jenson was unlikely; accidental and natural deaths didn't warrant storage of supplemental information, since too much data tended to back up their antiquated computer system. But Garcia got lucky—there was a photo from the scene.

She clicked on the thumbnail. It downloaded at slug speed.

Steph Jenson slowly revealed herself: *A body in a wooded area. Face up in the dirt. No jacket, even in December. Sweatpants. A T-shirt. The cold makes her skin look like ivory. Track marks on both arms, and around both ankles. Dozens of bloody lacerations zigzag the place where her eyes should be.*

Garcia shivered as if the cold from the photograph was seeping through the screen. She went back to the girl's profile. She read and reread. She checked the log: Submitted by: Dep. Coffey on 12/02/2009.

Garcia spun around in her chair. Coffey was in early too. He sat kicked back at his desk, talking on the phone. It didn't look important. She waved him over. He hung up and hustled. She stood and offered him her chair.

"Take a look at this," she said.

He sat down. He leaned in. He looked over the photo.

"You remember her?" Garcia asked.

"Yes, ma'am," he said. "It was my first DB. Terrible."

"You remember the lacerations around her eyes?" she asked.

"Of course." He nodded.

"Then why does your report say NHI? You don't think humans were involved in cutting up this girl's face?"

Coffey looked around to see who was in earshot. She leaned down close.

"I called it in as a homicide," he whispered. "But once the drug charges came up on her sheet, Sheriff Connors sent everyone home but the EMTs. He said any DBs with drug pops on their records were to be written up NHI. Department policy."

"But didn't this remind you of the Blind Spot Slasher?"

"Of course it did. First thought that popped into my head was 'oh God...he's back'."

Sheriff Connors was clipping his fingernails when Garcia entered his office. She held Steph Jenson's file and crime-scene photo at her side. She cleared her throat.

Sheriff Connors didn't look up. "Started to think you'd gone missing too, Lieutenant."

"Sorry for the delay, sir," she said. "I was following up on a lead."

He brushed the dead nails into his palm, then swirled his chair around to dump them into the wastebasket. He swirled back and looked Garcia up and down. She was still standing.

"Well," he urged, "did the lead pan out?"

She sat the paperwork on his desk. "This is Steph Jenson. Last seen getting into a black sedan at the I-64 overpass. A week ago, a witness saw Michelle Wilcox get into the *same* car."

Sheriff Connors picked up the paperwork. He leaned back and read. "At the overpass?"

"Yes, sir." She nodded.

"This report says Jenson was an overdose."

"Stating the obvious," Garcia said, "Steph Jenson sustained numerous facial lacerations before her death. Around her eyes, specifically. Doesn't that remind you of Harlan Lusher?"

He looked up. "Is Lt. Billings in yet?"

"I think I saw him in his—"

"Billings!" Sheriff Connors yelled through the open door.

Garcia groaned. She turned as Lt. Billings's shiny head bobbled toward them.

"Yes, sir?" he said, entering.

"Billings worked the Lusher case," Sheriff Connors said to Garcia. "Take a look at this photo. See if anything jumps out."

Billings sat down. Garcia did too, uninvited. Sheriff Connors handed him the photo.

"Who's the beauty queen?" Billings asked.

The sheriff yucked. Billings read the file.

"Does that remind you of the Blind Spot Slasher?" she asked.

"No," he said, turning to her. "Lusher never dumped his bodies. He dissolved them in vats of chemicals. Plus, the 'Blind Spot' moniker wasn't as significant as the press made it out to be. The eyes were probably one of the many things that perverted bastard toyed with..."

"But that's an assumption," she countered. "Maybe cutting the eyes *was* significant—"

"Stabbing," Billings corrected. "His victims were stabbed through *one* eye at an upward angle hard enough to fracture the skull. Any other wounds were secondary." He pointed to the photo. "These look like superficial lacerations. Scratch marks. Could've been an animal."

"Hell, if she was high enough she coulda done it herself," the sheriff added.

"Still," Garcia said, "can you get me her autopsy report? I can't find it in the system. I have Coffey getting me a list of NHIs and I'd like something more to compare them with—"

"There was no autopsy," the sheriff said. "Track marks speak for themselves."

Billings gave her back the photo. "You think BSS is still out there?"

"I'm not saying that," she urged. "But this could be some sort of copycat, or...look, if Michelle Wilcox got into the same car, then she's in danger. *Period.* We need to find her—"

"We?" Sheriff Connors said. "Didn't I put *you* in charge of that?"

"Yes, sir," Garcia said surely, taking the cue. She got up and walked out of the office, fully focused on keeping a steady stride to deny them the satisfaction of hearing her stomp away.

Coffey was waiting at her desk.

"What'd the sheriff say?"

The way she dropped into her chair answered his question. She tossed the crime-scene photo onto a stack of paperwork and groaned, frustrated. She rubbed her face. She looked at him.

"Tell Jones and Kern to start doing one-on-one interviews at the overpass, anyone who'll talk to them. Tell them to ask about a dark sedan that cruises the area for girls."

"Yes, ma'am." He nodded. "And I got those numbers for ya . . . two-hundred-some bodies were classified NHI in the last three years."

"Shit," she groaned. "You got plans tonight?"

"Why?"

"I need you to help me prove myself wrong."

13

Saturdays were hard for Henry. After a morning of shipping T-shirts to creeps and an afternoon at the prison, he usually spent the rest of the day sulking in bed or throwing rocks into the creek. But that Saturday evening was devoted to getting his bedroom ready for Sunday.

Henry pulled his comics out and stacked them on the floor. He put *Batman vs. Spawn* at the top of the pile. His Shooter Kane books were beside them, along with some other pulp favorites. Otis seemed like one smart motherfucker, so Henry hoped his mass of reading material would show he was on the level.

Once the books were displayed, Henry moved on to music. When he invited Otis to listen to his record collection, what he'd meant was his assortment of cassette tapes. Henry got his music at the local flea market, where used CDs cost a dollar but cassettes were only twenty-five cents. He knew it was lame to listen to tapes in 2011, of course. Downloading was the thing. But he didn't have an iPhone, or an iPod, or a computer. Thankfully,

Henry knew his collection was good enough to make the format inconsequential.

He went to the dresser where his boombox sat, the altar at which he worshiped. He arranged all thirty-four tapes around the stereo, piling them like totems to the gods of metal. Then he opened the cassette tray to make sure something deadly was in the chamber . . . shit, of course there was.

Metallica. *Ride the Lightning*. Side B.

Henry shut the tray. He was about to press play and thrash out to "Trapped Under Ice" when he heard the front door open and slam. Then came the unmistakable sound of Jane stomping dramatically across the hardwood and on to the tile. Muffled conversation followed.

A moment later, he heard her bedroom door open. Slam.

Henry sighed. He couldn't play music if she was upset. The walls were too thin.

He surveyed the room. It looked good. Cool. Badass. Feng Shui as all fuck.

Henry was ready for company.

Satisfied, he went into the living room to see what the drama was about. Gravy sat on the couch. The dog stuck his tongue out at Henry as if waving hello. Henry responded in kind. Then he turned to Mammaw, who stood frowning at the flyer in her hands.

"What's up?" he asked, walking over.

"Janey ain't feelin' so good," she said softly. "Some girls brought this into her work to torture her."

"This *fucking* podcast," Henry growled. "Who was it? Did she—"

"Honey," Mammaw said, placing a hand on his shoulder, "let's leave it be for now."

"Yeah...OK."

"She's goin' to bed early. Maybe we should do the same. Tomorrow'll be a fresh start."

Henry nodded. "Maybe you're right."

"I'll go ahead and put dinner on, then."

She set the flyer on the table and waddled into the kitchen. Drawers opened and shut. Pots and pans clattered and clanked. Henry was fixated on the flyer.

He grabbed it, wadding it into a ball as he walked back to his room.

He shut the door. Locked it. Threw the flyer at the trash can. Missed.

He needed to calm down. He grabbed his book and lay across the bed. He tried to read. He couldn't concentrate. He shut the book and stared at the dangerous girl on the cover.

He wondered what Shooter Kane would do if someone messed with *his* sister.

He wondered how Shooter Kane would handle a podcast messing with *his* life.

Henry got up. He picked the flyer off the floor. He uncrumpled it.

He read it again, more critically. He scanned the details with new eyes.

If they wanna gawk at the blood and gore, he thought, *maybe they should see how it feels to be stuck with it. Maybe these apathetic assholes should spend a night in our world so they see how entertaining it* really *is*.

He reread the flyer. *Costume contest.* If he could find a costume that camouflaged his limp, his odds of pulling something off without getting spotted were pretty good. He read the flyer again. *Bear Road Shopping Center*. It was too far to walk. He'd have to take Mammaw's car. He'd only "borrowed" her car once before, and his fear of being pulled over made it the most joyless joyride in history.

But you ain't in the joy business anymore, he imagined Shooter Kane saying. *You're in the payback business...and business is about to boom.*

Corny, but it was something.

Shooter Kane would do *something*.

Henry thought it over for a moment. Then he shook off his nerves and got to work on a costume. He didn't have much time to throw one together. He hoped he could come up with a good one. He hoped he had the guts not to chicken out. He hoped Mammaw had coffee brewing.

It was gonna be one long fucking night.

14

Otis rode in the shotgun seat of their '96 Lincoln Continental. It was gunmetal gray with a burgundy leather interior, a sleek sled his father managed to avoid selling in darker times. It survived for sentimental reasons—the car was where Otis's parents shared their first kiss. The mental image grossed Otis out, but he was still glad they had kept it. It was one of the few things tethering them to their old lives.

Otis flipped on the seat warmer, hoping it would bring his color up. He hadn't had much time to put an outfit together, so he worked with what the good Lord gave him and made his rosy complexion the key component of his Halloween costume; he turned a red T-shirt inside out and drew the mischievous smile of the Kool-Aid Man on it.

The car turned on to Bear Road. A few blocks later, they reached the strip mall. The stores were mostly abandoned, and it looked like the podcast event was relegated to the parking lot.

"Thanks again for bringing me," Otis said.

"My pleasure," his father smiled. "Nothing I'd rather do on my night off than pal around with you. Plus, I have to admit, you've piqued my curiosity."

Rows of cars were parked along a grassy knoll beyond the lights of the parking lot. They pulled into a space near the tree line. His father killed the engine and stretched his neck.

Otis got out. He could hear "Monster Mash" playing from a sound system closer to the vendors and carnival games that bordered the pavement. A collapsible stage was set up in the middle of it all, and a few fans stood in awe of the two empty chairs and microphones. Dozens of vampires, zombies, and witches loitered while waiting for the show to start.

His father locked the car, and they walked toward the festivities. They passed a man sitting on a parking curb drinking a beer. He wore a shirt that said HARLAN LUSHER FAN CLUB.

His father checked his watch. "We've got some time. Want a corn dog or anything?"

"No," Otis said. "Let's check out the Murder Museum."

He scanned the scene—*there*. A line of people were waiting outside an abandoned store. A poster board secured above the doors read MURDER MUSEUM. He directed his father through the growing crowd. Most everyone drank beer from orange plastic cups. Otis passed some girls his age and sighed longingly.

"Who the heck sells that stuff?" his father asked, nodding to another FAN CLUB T-shirt.

"The internet," Otis said. "It's an open market for horrible things."

They took their place in line outside the museum. The song ended. "Werewolves of London" *a-ooooohhhhh*'d over the PA. The lined moved quickly, and soon Otis and his father reached a woman in a folding chair holding a cashbox. Her shirt said BEST KILL EVER, and beneath it VOLUNTEER.

"Ten dollars," she said, "cash only."

"Oh," Otis muttered. "Sorry I, uh, thought it was free."

His father took out his wallet and leafed through it.

"It's OK," Otis whispered. "Twenty bucks is too much. Really. Let's forget it."

His father ignored him. He handed the woman two fives. It was the only cash he had.

"Go check it out," his father said, smiling. "I expect a full briefing later."

"Thanks," Otis sighed. The volunteer ushered him in.

Otis stepped through the blacked-out glass doors. Room dividers turned the empty store into a makeshift labyrinth. It reminded him of a haunted house done on the cheap. The first room was nothing but a lobby of sorts; the wall facing the entrance doors displayed a blown-up photo of the Lusher family. Otis noted Henry smiling. Above the photo, a sign read MAKING A MONSTER.

He moved into the next room. It was full of photographs and artifacts from Harlan Lusher's early life. Index cards had been tacked under each one as informative placards.

"Harlan Lusher and twin sister, Hazel, at play. 1974."

"The Lusher family Bible. Last in possession of Harlan Lusher."

"Harlan and Hazel Lusher's matching jackets. 1976."

Otis stared at the red and blue Bugs Bunny jackets hanging side by side behind the display glass. He wondered how someone was able to get their hands on them.

The internet, his internal voice echoed back.

He scoffed at himself and moved along. A hallway led to an opening. The sign above it read LORDSVILLE LOVES YOU! A poster board was tacked to his left. Otis read the explainer: "Lordsville is a secretive religious community in Barkley County, West Virginia, founded by divisive pastor Pearl Jolley. The Lusher family moved to Lordsville in 1974. Criminal psychologists believe Lordsville opened the door to Harlan Lusher's dark impulses and fantasies."

Otis stepped into the room.

Photos covered the wall. The first showed a beautiful woman of about twenty-five standing with an older man, shaking hands with LBJ. The explainer read: "Pearl Jolley with her father, West Virginia State Senator Buford Jolley, meeting President Lyndon B. Johnson. 1965."

The next photo. Pearl Jolley, older, standing on the stage of a small church. A gold medallion around her neck featured three burning crosses. The congregation was on their feet before her. She was soaked with sweat, singing or screaming or speaking in tongues. She held two large copperhead snakes above her head. The explainer read: "Pearl Jolley started preaching in the early 1970s and soon began referring to herself as Sister Jolley. Her riotous, controversial sermons included snake handling, ingesting poison, conjuring spirits, and sacrificing animals."

Otis moved to the next display, a recruitment pamphlet for Lordsville, which read: "You are already in HELL! You just don't know it yet! LORDSVILLE CHRISTIAN COMMUNITY. Live among the righteous! Join our self-sustaining sanctuary today!"

The next photo was a group shot. Twenty-some people lined up in front of the chain-link fence that surrounded Lordsville. The card: "Lordsville members outside the gates of the commune. 1983. Pearl Jolley stands with her son, Dean. The Lusher family stands at the end of the line."

Otis moved to the next display. It was a collage of pictures—the aftermath of the Lordsville fire. Some of the photos he'd seen, some (of charred bodies, for instance) he hadn't. Suddenly, laughter boomed right behind him. Otis turned. Two meatheads were *ew*gling the photo of Pearl Jolley with LBJ. They were dressed as Spartans from the movie *300*, sans honor. They toasted Solo cups. Beer foam hit Otis's shoulder. He gave up on the display and moved on.

The next hallway was narrower than the others, and the items exhibited were sparse.

Photos: Harlan in the army. The Lushers' wedding day. Harlan playing with his kids.

Encased in glass: A Lusher Developments, LLC, business card and hard hat.

Then, Otis stepped into the final room.

It was a Disneyland version of the Love Shack—a replica of the cabin where the Blind Spot Slasher's victims were found. Plastic chemical drums labeled ACID crowded the left corner. To the right was "the death pit," a dirt pile filled with plastic bones and rubber skulls. Directly in front of him was a mattress doused in what he hoped was fake blood.

The walls were decorated with blown-up crime-scene photos.

There's the real death pit, charred bones piled high like a dragon's den...

There's Sheena Wiseman, still wearing her Little Mermaid Halloween costume...

There's Sheena Wiseman, young and dead, sprawled across the mattress...

There's a close-up of the bloody gash where one of her eyes used to be...

Otis cut his own eyes away before the gore made him barf. He looked for the exit. He found something much more exciting—a long knife sparkling beneath a glass display case. The knife was thin, like a small sword or an ice pick. It had a black leather grip and a squared-off base. The rusty blade was at least twelve inches long.

He hurried to it. He sped-read the caption: "One of the four knives found at the crime scene. This knife is identical to the one that killed Sheena Wiseman. All four blades were later identified as ritual knives Pearl Jolley used to sacrifice animals at Lordsville. Jolley said the knives went missing after The Fire of 1984. This led to rumors that Harlan Lusher intentionally set the Lordsville fire."

"Holy crappers," Otis gasped.

He studied the knife, committing each millimeter to memory, then he saw something. He squinted at the base of the blade, where the rust spots were the worst. There was something engraved on it, but he couldn't make it out. He got out his iPhone, turned off the flash, and snapped a photo. He looked at the screen. He zoomed in.

The hair on his neck sprang up. His mouth went dry.

He turned and ran back through the room, charging into the narrow hall.

"Watch it, lard ass!" one of the Spartans yelled as Otis pushed through them.

He paid no mind. He reached the section dedicated to Lordsville. He found the photo of Pearl Jolley handling snakes. He zeroed in on her medallion. He held up his phone.

He compared the pictures. His eyes went back and forth, back and forth, and back again.

The lines on the blade. The lines on the medallion.

They were identical engravings.

Three burning crosses. All in a row.

Otis looked into the wild eyes of Sister Jolley, captured there in the throes of some great revelation. He saw madness in them, as venomous as the snakes she held over her head. The fact that this woman hadn't been a serious suspect made him question the entire investigation.

The DA had stuck to the narrative that Harlen Lusher stole the murder weapon from Lordsville. But what evidence was that based on? The word of a silver-spoon-sucking psycho who could have started that church fire herself?

Otis no longer cared about the podcast. He knew enough about Harlan Lusher. Now he needed to learn about Lordsville, about Pearl Jolley and her crest of burning crosses.

He found the exit and pushed into the night.

The crowd gathered in front of the stage. His father was leaning on an empty display window, stretching his back. Otis hated the sight of his father in pain for numerous reasons.

"How was it?" he asked as Otis approached.

"Freaky. I'll tell you on the way home. We can leave now if you're hurting. I don't really care about the—"

Eeeeeeek! Amplifier feedback cut him off.

A bald man with a laminate around his neck adjusted the microphones on stage. A row of VIP seating was positioned side stage. The people sitting there seemed out of place—older than most of the crowd, none of them in costume. They looked tired and overwhelmed.

A young, fit, wealthy-looking couple walked out from behind the stage. They shook hands with the VIPs and then went to the microphones hand in hand. The crowd applauded.

"We may as well watch for a bit." His father shrugged.

Otis nodded. They moved to the back of the crowd. The applause died down. The couple took their seats. The bald guy handed them each a glass of white wine and then went to the front of the stage.

"We're live once I count to five! Lemme hear a big West Virginia welcome! One! Two!" He used his fingers to count three-four-five then pointed at the crowd. They cheered enthusiastically. A red ON AIR sign buzzed to life. He walked offstage. The hosts grinned. The show began.

"Hey, guys! I'm Laci Johnson—"

"And I'm Remy Johnson! Are you ready for another episode of—"

"Best! Kill! Eveeeeeeer!" they both screeched.

The crowd clapped dutifully.

"If you aren't familiar with the show," Remy said, "we take a deep dive into the most gruesome murders ever committed in our own hilarious—*respectful*—and totally sassy way!"

"I've never heard 'respectful' and 'sassy' used as dual adjectives," his father whispered.

Otis chucked. The couple onstage toasted each other.

"Tonight, we're coming to you *live* from West Virginia," Laci said, "a place famous for coal mining, moonshine, and *murder*."

"Honey," Remy quipped, "if I lived *this* far from a Jamba Juice, I'd kill someone, too!"

A few members of the crowd chuckled. The others looked confused.

"Tonight's episode is about Harlan Lusher," Laci said, "better known as the Blind Spot Slasher. He's thought to have murdered at *least* twelve people. But before we start, we have a special treat for our listeners...the victims' families are here for an exclusive Q and A! Let's all give them a round of applause!"

She and Remy applauded the VIPs. The crowd clapped, gawked, hooted, and hollered. The family members squirmed in their seats.

"You know what's *scarier* than Harlan Lusher?" Remy said. "A bad night's sleep. Which is why we're proud to have Pillow Talk as one of our sponsors. Their custom pillows did wonders for us both! Their patented memory foam technology was first developed for NASA, and it's out of this world! Use promo code 'slasher' to receive forty percent off your order."

"Now," Laci said, "back to the show."

"Can we leave?" Otis asked.

His father nodded. They turned their backs to the stage and walked away. Once they cleared the parking lot, the hosts' sassiness grew faint. A group of teenage girls in revealing costumes passed them, going the opposite direction. Otis tried not to stare or trip over his feet.

"I can't wait for Remy to start in on that bitch," a girl dressed as a sexy nun said.

His father shot her a look, then continued on. A moment later, they reached the car.

"Are all podcasts like that?" he asked, as he unlocked the Lincoln.

"True crime series are a relatively new trend," Otis said, "but most seem to be headed in a similar direction. It's pretty freakin' gross."

They got in the car. His father groaned, stretched his neck, and started the engine. Otis buckled up. As they rolled past the row of parked cars, a dark figure dashed out in front of them.

"Look out!" Otis yelled.

Brakes slammed. They jerked forward. Otis and his father looked up—there was a hunchback in their headlights. A long, boil-covered nose protruded from the figure's black hood. The hunchback held up an apologetic hand before lurching into the dark.

"We almost creamed Quasimodo," his father said.

"I think that's Igor. Isn't he the one with the limp?"

15

They were outed as cops immediately. The driver hadn't even parked beneath the overpass when they came into view—standing near the trestle on the opposite side of the road, speaking with one of the girls who wasn't *the* girl. They weren't in uniform, but were clearly law enforcement. One was even taking notes! Their presence was preposterous. They were beyond out of place.

The driver shifted and pulled away before either one noticed. The car sped faster and faster, back into the black on black. It navigated the empty roads like a sleek and luminous shark.

Hunting. Searching. Seeking.

The driver could sense her but not see her.

The driver knew she was somewhere on the road. The car sped faster.

Seeking. Searching. Hunting.

She was out there, waiting to be found. She was out there, waiting to be judged.

She had gone away from the Bridge of Death.
She had gone to the Land of the Living.
The driver's senses sharpened.
The car cut the night.

EPISODE TWO

Chorus:
"A million hells
Rage inside these veins."
—Danzig

16

Henry woke up tangled in his sheets with a bitch of a headache. Dust particles drifted in front of the band posters and comic book pages papering the walls. He groaned, shoving his face into the pillow, hoping to suffocate himself back to sleep. His mouth was dry. His body was sore.

Payback was fucking exhausting.

Eventually he pushed himself off the mattress. His hip was killing him. Wincing, he limped to the window. He pulled up the shades—Mammaw's car was parked a bit crooked, but he didn't think she'd notice. He scratched the sparse hair on his chest and rehashed the night.

Putting his costume together.

Swiping the car keys after dinner.

Sneaking out of his bedroom window.

How nervous he'd been driving Mammaw's car to the shopping center. How good it felt to stab the steak knife into that first tire. And the next tire. And the next. And the next. And the next. And the next and the next and the next.

The tools of vengeance were spread across the floor. His Igor costume—black hoodie, his sister's rubber witch nose, the throw pillow that hunched his back—lay beside the knife. He picked his jeans up off the floor and fished Mammaw's keys from the back pocket. He put them beside his stereo, threw his clothes in the hamper, and kicked the rubber nose beneath his bed. He set the knife beside the keys and tossed the pillow back on the bed.

Suddenly, his doorknob turned. Mammaw stuck her fluffy head into his room.

Henry sprang in front of his dresser to block the knife and keys from view.

"Breakfast is ready, sweetie."

"Cool, cool, cool," he spat out.

"You OK?"

"Mm-hmm." Henry nodded. "Just need some coffee."

"Comin' right up." She winked and then shut the door.

He put on a homemade Slayer T-shirt and slid the keys into the pocket of his sweatpants so he could put them back when Mammaw was occupied. He hid the knife in his underwear drawer; he'd move it later. Henry did an idiot check and then forced himself out of the room.

Mammaw and Jane had already started eating. A cup of coffee sat next to a plate that was waiting for him. He eyed it gratefully as he sat down.

"Sorry to start without you," Jane said.

"It's cool. Nothin' worse than cold eggs."

"Amen." Mammaw nodded.

He chugged half of his coffee, then started to eat.

"You go out last night?" Mammaw asked. "I thought I heard ya pitter-pattering around."

"Nah," he said, keeping his eyes on the plate, "just had a hard time gettin' to sleep."

"I had a hard time getting awake," Jane said. "Work's gonna *suck* today."

"You'll feel better in the sunshine, angel," Mammaw said.

She nodded and then stood to refill her cup. Henry watched her. She definitely *looked* better than yesterday, no matter how tired she felt. Her hair was washed and brushed back. The puffiness around her eyes had deflated. *Maybe I should take one of her pills and sleep all day . . .*

"Excited for your playdate?" Jane asked, grinning.

He'd almost forgotten Otis was coming over. "It's not a playdate, dickwad . . . but yeah, it should be cool."

"What's he like?" she asked.

His response came through a mouthful of biscuit. "Otis? He's metal as fuck."

Black Sabbath. Dio. Black Sabbath with Dio. Iron Maiden. Metallica. Slayer. Carcass. Mayhem. Death metal, doom metal, black metal, power metal, speed metal, thrash metal, stoner metal—

"Dang it!" Otis whined as he dropped his head onto his desk.

He needed to leave in an hour if he wanted to make it to Henry's on time. But he'd slept through his alarm and woke up too late to do a comfortable amount of prep work. Now he was trying to cram an entire musical genre into his brain. He'd already lied once by telling him he was a metalhead, and he desperately wanted to avoid being outed as a "poser" (he had the vernacular down, at least).

Even his outfit was suspect. The only black T-shirt Otis owned was from science camp. His hair wasn't long like Henry's, so he brushed it into a sharp V—an odd metal/punk hairstyle the internet called a devillock. It was the best he could do.

Otis forced his head off his desk before he accidentally fell back asleep.

After leaving *Best Kill Ever*, he'd stayed up researching Pearl Jolley and the Lordsville cult. The first thing he did was climb the gilded bark of Pearl Jolley's family tree. He read the claims of Lordsville's religious practices, snake handling, and drug use. He read all about the fire. He watched local news coverage. He watched yellow flames in the black sky. Then he lasered in on an assertion alluded to at the Murder Museum—that Pearl Jolley blamed the fire on Harlan Lusher.

He found a rare interview with Jolley conducted during Lusher's trial. It was with an underground Christian extremist webzine called *Blood & Nails*. Most of what she said was convoluted drug-fueled gibberish, but when asked about Lusher's connection to the fire, she said: "The boy and his sister set fire to their own salvation! They called upon the flames of hell to lick eternity's gate! No verdict but THE VERDICT shall cut this hellspawn down."

Otis deduced from her deranged babbling that she *did* blame him for the fire. Maybe that was her motive. Maybe she framed Harlan Lusher for the BSS murders as payback. She had the means, the connections...but did she have the mental wherewithal?

Otis found it unlikely. He kept digging. He researched the emblem carved on the medallion and ritual knife. Three burning crosses. All in a row. He found nothing on any normal search engine. He had to dive deeper.

Hours of sifting through Reddit posts and YouTube conspiracy videos gave him this: the Trinity of Light.

Three cults within a cult.

In 1974, the FBI began cracking down on the unpredicted number of cults sprouting up around America. The first cult in the FBI's crosshairs was the Church of Ennobled Ascent, an already-infamous cult whose beliefs ranged from the existence of UFOs to the practicality of mass suicide. Their founder, Dr. Benjamin Soto, warned Jolley of the impending government clampdown and suggested they form an alliance: if his church was raided by the FBI, his followers could seek solace at Lordsville and vice versa.

Dr. Soto had already made a similar agreement with Bon Livingston, leader of a religious movement called The Pure outside of Hot Springs, Arkansas. The three of them would act as a power axis in defiance of the federal government. Pearl Jolley allegedly agreed to this arrangement, and the Trinity of Light was formed.

Otis passed out at some point after that.

When he woke up at his desk for the third time in a week, he couldn't deny that his interest in the case had gone beyond mere curiosity. He'd passed some crucial invisble point where interest turned to action. He wasn't working this hard for fun. He was trying to prove that Harlan Lusher was an innocent man.

He was scared to talk to Henry about it. Once Henry learned that Otis was digging through family dirt he might get mad, or worse—he might not want to be friends anymore.

But who wouldn't want to be friends with someone trying to get their dad out of jail?

Otis pondered the question. He left his bedroom and walked

downstairs to the front door. He turned the knob and headed into the crisp, high noon. The answer came. He smiled.

Only a poser. And Henry's not one of those, he's metal as freakin' fudge!

17

Otis Perkins wasn't the only one in Paradise who traded their midnight oil for blood. Lt. Garcia and Sgt. Coffey spent their Saturday night at the station sifting through three years of corpses labeled NHI, looking for any similarities to Steph Jenson's crime scene. Most of the files didn't have photos or autopsy reports, so they had to go off sparse field notes.

They found two NHIs that *might* line up: Joan Kelly Armstrong—"victim has self-inflicted lacerations around the left eye"—and Laura Holly Bernard—"victim appears to have blinded herself after injection."

Garcia kept deputies Kern and Jones at the overpass well after midnight. They got a dozen stories similar to Sissy's tale: a female addict gets into a dark car and vanishes forever.

By the end of the night, Garcia formed a horrible hypothesis: there was a BSS copycat killer in their midst. Coffey agreed with her assessment, but she would need to put together a convincing sales pitch if she wanted Sheriff Connors to bite. It was hard not to jump right into it, but Sunday was her first day off in a month. It was imperative she go to Charleston and spend the day with Craig and Ruby.

She got up early, showered, dressed, filled her thermos, and rushed into the harsh light of morning. Not really morning. Noon. But Garcia was still dead-dog exhausted. She chugged coffee as she crossed the yard and climbed into her truck. She started it and pulled away.

It was a two-hour trek to her old life. She clicked on the XM radio. She found a Nirvana song. She played drums on the steering wheel. The interstate ramp was dead ahead.

Then, her iPhone rang. She checked the screen—Barkley Co. Sheriff.

She killed the music.

"Lt. Garcia," she answered.

"It's Connors," the sheriff said.

Shit. "What's up, sir?"

"You hear about the BSS talk show at the shopping center last night?"

"You mean where everyone got their tires slashed? Yeah, I saw it in the paper. Please say that's not why you're calling on my day off."

"I wish," he sighed, "but no. One of our slashees seems to have disappeared on her walk home. Carrie Clemmons. Seventeen. Senior up at Shady Spring. Guess she didn't wanna wait for Triple A."

"Shit."

"Billings's crew has been combing the area since sunup," he went on. "So far, they've got zilch. CPD has a wrecker on the way to haul her car to the crime lab, but we ain't expecting a lot. So, unless Red Ridin' Hood got lost in the woods, it's looking like an abduction. The folks who threw last night's shindig agreed to stay at the scene for an interview. If they try to stonewall or skedaddle, you have my blessing to detain 'em by any means necessary."

"Sir," she said, in the most submissive tone she could manage, "can't Billings or one of the other officers take their statements? I promised my daughter—"

"You promised Carrie Clemmons when ya put on that badge. Promised her parents, too. If I trusted Billings to do it right, I wouldn't have called. But time is of the goddamn essence, and I need the sharpest eyes I've got on this."

It was the first compliment he'd ever given her. It was a gigantic pain in the ass.

"OK," she groaned.

"I'll text you the info." *Click.*

She turned the radio back up before busting a U-turn.

It took her fifteen minutes to get to the strip mall. She spent ten of them on the phone—first with Craig, then with their daughter. The worst part of the call was that neither got mad. They weren't upset because they weren't surprised. Garcia knew enough about parenting to know if you give bad news to a five-year-old and they *don't* throw a fit, you've set painfully low expectations.

She spent the next four minutes hating herself, then allotted the final sixty seconds of the drive to getting her shit together. When she reached the Bear Road Shopping Center, a crew was tearing down the stage and loading it into a windowless van. The parking lot was covered in garbage: half-eaten funnel cakes, broken bottles, cigarette butts, Solo cups rolling about like bright plastic tumbleweeds.

The lawn adjacent to the parking lot was taped off. There were still at least a dozen unclaimed cars. Their deflated tires made it look as if they'd sunk into the dying grass, like there was quicksand beneath it that could swallow a girl up whole.

Garcia nixed the thought. She parked next to CPD's tow truck, which was in the process of loading a silver KIA sedan on to the bed.

She looked at the info Sheriff Connors had texted over:

Buck Connors (10:50 a.m.): Carrie June Clemmons. 17 yr old. Caucasian.

A picture accompanied the text. It was from her Facebook page—Carrie Clemmons the nun, holding a flask, toasting the camera. Laughing. Being stupid. Being seventeen. Being a kid.

She sighed. She got out. The tow truck's pistons squealed as it lifted the Kia.

"That her car?" she yelled over the noise.

"Yup," the tow operator yelled back. "Takin' it to Charleston, directly."

She nodded and then turned to the parking lot. A black Chrysler with rental plates sat at the curb of an empty storefront. Three people leaned against it—a bald man in a black polo and a couple about her age sporting designer loungewear. All three wore gaudy sunglasses. All three were focused on their phones.

Garcia navigated the broken bottles and ketchup-drenched

napkins. She cleared her throat when she approached the Chrysler. None of the them seemed to notice she was there.

"I'm Lt. Elena Garcia," she said loudly. "Barkley County Sheriff's."

The bald man looked up. He shoved his phone into his pocket and offered his hand.

"Michael Torrance," he said.

"You're the promoter?"

"Producer," he corrected.

"I'm Laci Johnson," the woman said, putting her phone in her purse. "This is my husband, Remy."

Remy waved absently. He was still glued to his phone.

"Laci and Remy host the show," Torrance explained. "The promoter left a half hour ago, but I believe he gave his lawyer's information to one of the other officers."

"OK," Garcia said. "Why don't you start by walking me through the event last night."

"Are you familiar with our show?" Torrance asked.

She shook her head—*no*.

"*Best Kill Ever* is a true crime podcast. We travel to the scene of the crimes we cover and discuss them in front of a live audience. Last night's episode was about Harlan Lusher."

"Is that a normal way to do a podcast?" Garcia asked. "Live, on scene?"

"We've had more competition lately," Laci said. "So, we changed to a live format to set the show apart. Q and A sessions with the locals give our listeners a unique perspective."

"Unique perspective," Remy scoffed. "The only guy that asked a question last night burped it in Morse code—"

Garcia ripped his phone from his hand. "Give *me* a unique

perspective on how a teenage girl went missing at *your* show."

"I don't know," he huffed. "It's not my job to know. We had security, the proper permits. This town should be kissing our ass for reminding people it's on the map."

"Shut up," Torrance snapped.

Remy shut up. Laci shook her head in frustration.

"Sorry," Torrance said calmly. "We missed our flight earlier. We're all a bit stressed."

Garcia tossed Remy's phone back to him. He played hot potato and dropped it. She pulled her own iPhone from her pocket and showed them the photo of Carrie Clemmons.

"This photo was taken last night. Did you see her? Think hard, please."

One by one, they shook their heads—*no, no, no.*

"But last night was a mess," Laci sighed. "Everyone was stranded after the show, and then the roads got clogged with rides and tow trucks. I saw a few people walk off, but I don't remember her...I just can't believe this. We've done over thirty shows, and nothing like this has ever..."

She blinked back tears and ran her hands through her hair.

"We can share her photo on social media," Torrance suggested. "Maybe someone will remember something."

"That would be really helpful," Garcia said.

"Better put it up now," Remy added. "The more time passes, the more...well, you know."

Garcia groaned and stretched her neck, which was when she noticed the sign taped over an abandoned storefront. "Murder Museum?"

"Ah, they forgot to take that down," Torrance said, looking at the sign. "We do pop-up museums at most of our shows.

Sometimes we display actual case evidence, but usually we use props to re-create crime scenes and amp up the crowd's experience."

"This one was weird, though," Laci said. "Doing a story on BSS was actually suggested by one of our listeners. He said he had enough memorabilia to fill the pop-up museum himself. But we didn't really consider coming here until he sent us a list of his collectibles...the amount of stuff he had was unsettling."

"He's definitely a BSS superfan." Remy nodded. "We meet a lot of murder memorabilia enthusiasts, and they're all freaks, but he was by far the freakiest."

Garcia's internal sensors screamed and flashed alerts: *superfan* may equal *copycat*.

"Is the, uh, *memorabilia* still here?" she asked.

"No," Torrance said. "He packed it up last night. Eugene Palmer's his name. And I agree, some of the things he displayed seemed questionable...possibly even illegal."

"Such as?" Garcia asked.

"I dunno," Remy said petulantly, "a *knife* from the crime scene."

Garcia's sensors blew a fuse. She tried not to flinch.

"I'll need Mr. Palmer's information," she told Torrance as calmly as she could.

"Of course." He nodded. "Let me check my e-mail. Laci, grab me a pen."

Michael Torrance checked his e-mail. Laci took a green pen from her purse. Garcia handed Torrance her notepad, and he dished out the information. This was it. She felt it, deep down.

He handed the notepad back.

The word SUPERFAN was written in capital letters over the name in green ink.

In her mind, it was spelled C-O-P-Y-C-A-T.

In her mind, it was written in blood.

18

Otis Perkins was the coolest dude Henry ever met. They spent the afternoon listening to timeworn classics—*Paranoid, The Number of the Beast, Holy Diver*—stuff any metalhead worth their salt knew well. Yet Otis had a visceral reaction to the music—he scrunched his face to every solo; he slapped his thighs to every drum fill. Henry found his new friend's passion beautiful—he loved metal *so much* that it hit him like the first time, every time.

Henry never expected someone so metal could be so nice. But Otis didn't make fun of his doily-covered house or drool greedily at the smell of Mammaw's marijuana. He didn't get annoyed by the dog, who latched on to him like a new chew toy. He didn't even comment on the fact that Henry's record collection was a handful of flea market cassettes.

He was smart too. He rambled on about symbolism, and historical references in the lyrics. Henry was halfway convinced he was in the presence of a genious. They were sitting on the floor, rocking out to W.A.S.P.'s self-titled cassette. It spun down to the last track, a cover of "Paint It Black." Otis was *really* into this one. He banged his head with the double-time snare, his devillock bobbing along in time until the song ended with a scream.

"That was great!" he proclaimed, eyes smiling.

"Yeah, man," Henry said. "Great cover."

Otis nodded enthusiastically. Henry got up to put a new tape on. He grabbed *Master of Puppets* and looked over to make sure Otis was cool with it, but he was digging through Henry's stack of paperbacks. Henry put the tape in and turned the volume down for the first time in his life.

"You like pulp?" he asked.

"I'm not sure," Otis said honestly. He picked up a book and read the front—*Death Ride: Murder at One Hundred Miles an Hour.*

"That one's pretty good," Henry said. "You can borrow it if you want."

Otis opened the book to a random page and read aloud:

Candy was like a python in Chanel perfume, and my vision began to go black as her thighs squeezed my neck like a noose. *Ah well,* I thought, *there are worse ways to die.*

Both boys started laughing. Genuine. From way down deep.

"I would *love* to borrow this," Otis said, "I can bring it back tomorrow."

"Shit," Henry scoffed, "keep it as long as ya want. You can't finish it in a day."

"I can." Otis shrugged. "I'm what they'd call a speed-reader.

It's a bit weird, I know."

Henry shook his head in amazement. He leaned on the edge of his bed. "No offense," he said, "but how the fuck can you stand living in Paradise? You fit in even worse than me."

"It hasn't been easy," he admitted, "but it's, um, a temporary situation. My family moved from Huntington after a string of bad luck."

"What happened?"

His eyes and voice lowered. "My father was mugged one night after work...he was stabbed and left for dead."

Henry gasped.

"He survived," Otis added quickly, "but nothing's been the same. He got hooked on the pain medicine his doctor gave him, and that pretty much ruined our lives. We lost everything because of it...no one wanted anything to do with us, even after he got clean. We moved here so he could take a job he's laughably over-qualified for...but it's temporary, like I said." Otis sighed.

"That's brutal, man," Henry said, not knowing what else to say.

"It was...but it's nothing compared to what you've gone through with your father."

Henry tensed. His eyes joined Otis's on the floor. He didn't know Otis knew about his dad.

Both boys were silent. Unmoving. Unblinking. Metallica thrashed into the next song.

"You don't know shit about what I've been through," Henry muttered, almost growling.

"No," Otis said, "but I know your father is innocent, and I think I can help you prove it."

Otis sensed quick movement in his peripheral. He braced for

a punch. But Henry grabbed his shoulders and squeezed—like a comrade, a brother.

The boys locked eyes. Henry grinned and began shaking Otis excitedly.

"Oh man! Oh, shit yeah! I *knew* you were a fuckin' genius!"

19

Haunted houses aren't uncommon sights in dead towns.

Yet something about the Palmer residence chilled Lt. Garcia. Everything about it, really. It was a marrow gray monstrosity with a turret room that cut skyward like a medieval tower. The house had surely been beautiful once, but it now appeared as a corpse set to rot; missing shingles, decaying wood, and boarded windows abounded. The entire house leaned to the left, as if it were curious to see if you were brave or stupid enough to darken the door.

Garcia shook off the heebie-jeebies and got out of her truck. Sgt. Coffey still wasn't there. She took a second to look over the place. She mentally zoomed with her cop-o-vision.

Clock the Plymouth parked beside the house; dark green, passable for black...

The cruiser pulled beside her. She jumped, startled, but played it off.

Coffey got out. "Jesus Christ. Who lives here, Mr. Chicken?"

"Eugene Palmer."

He nodded. "Expecting to need an assist?"

"Doubt it," she said. "No priors. But walking onto private property without my uniform on is a good way to get my ass shot."

He didn't argue. They made their way across a yard that was both dead and overgrown. Rusty wind chimes did their skeleton dance on the porch as they reached the house.

"Smell that mold?" Coffey cringed. "He must be a hoarder or something."

She nodded and then tested the first rotten porch step. It didn't cave in. They walked up.

Coffey knocked with authority. No immediate answer.

Garcia wiped a window clean with her shirttail and peered inside.

"Definitely a hoarder," she said.

She could see the entire living room and part of the dining room. Mildewed newspapers, books, and magazines were stacked throughout. Three TVs were across from the couch, though it looked like only one was plugged in. Rotting garbage. A Costco-size pack of adult diapers.

Ignore that. Find what's important. Garcia's eyes sharpened.

Clock the open first-aid kit . . .

Clock the Faces of Death *VHS on top of the TV . . .*

Clock the killer clown painting in the dining room . . .

Clock the framed photo on the mantel. Who is that girl? She looks familiar . . .

Coffey knocked again. "Eugene Palmer! This is the Barkley County Sheriff's Department. *Please* open the—"

Clamp! Crank! Click! Garcia and Coffey shared a look as

multiple locks unlocked. The door opened. The acne-scarred face of a man peered out at them, confused.

"Eugene Palmer?" Garcia asked.

"Y-y-yeah?" he stammered.

She flashed her badge. "Lt. Garcia, Sheriff's Department. This is Sgt. Coffey. Is it OK if we come in and ask a few questions?"

"I, uh, I c-can come out," he said.

She craned her neck to see into the house as he walked out.

Clock that padlock on the basement door...

Eugene shut the door behind him. He was around thirty, average build, in a brown flannel and blue jeans. He wore a hearing aid in his left ear.

"You live alone?" she asked.

"I do, yes. Mom d-died last y-year."

"Sorry for your loss, Mr. Palmer," Coffey said.

"Thank y you." He smiled. "That's v-very kind. Please, c-call me Eugene."

"What did you do last night, Eugene?" Garcia asked.

"I went to the Bear Creek Shopping Center. I volunteered for th-the p-p-podcast."

"Is that your car down there?" she asked him.

"Y-yes," he said.

"So, your tires weren't slashed?"

"Is *that* what happened? I saw all those p-p-people loitering after the show. Loiterers are always up t-to no good, so I left soon after. I was parked in b-b-back with the other volunteers."

Garcia got out her phone and pulled up the photo of Carrie Clemmons.

"Eugene," she said, handing it to him, "have you ever seen this girl?"

He looked at the picture. "Yes."

Her mouth almost dropped. Coffey shot her a look.

"She plays s-soccer for Shady Spring, right?" Eugene asked, handing back her iPhone.

Garcia didn't answer. "Do your kids go to school there?"

"Oh, I don't have ch-ch-children. But I love soccer. I just go to w-w-watch them play."

"Are you currently employed?" she asked.

"Yes." He nodded. "I run an online s-store, Creepy Collectables. I s-s-sell items of curiosity, r-rare historical artifacts—"

"Like the ones at the Murder Museum?" she pressed.

"Yes," he said, without flinching. "I lent them some things from my c-c-collection."

"Did you see the girl from the photo last night?" Coffey asked.

"I don't think so. I'd remember a n-nun. They've always scared me."

"Did anyone else stick out?" Garcia asked. "Anyone strike you as out of place? Odd?"

He chuckled. "What *isn't* odd about a m-m-murder museum?"

"Where do you get your inventory?" Garcia said briskly, pushing on.

"The internet, p-p-police auctions, and estate sales m-mostly."

"We've been informed you displayed an item from the BSS crime scene," she said. "How did *that* come into your possession? Don't try to tell me the internet."

Eugene shifted his weight. He gulped, big-time. Her phone vibrated. She ignored it.

"Is t-t-that why you're here," he asked. "The knife?"

She stared him down. Coffey's walkie sounded. He went into the yard to answer it.

Eugene scoffed at himself. "I k-knew I shouldn't have t-t-trusted that idiot."

"Who?" Garcia pressed.

"Jeremy. My c-cousin. He worked for county storage up until last year. He knows I'm a collector, and h-he called me one day out of th-th-the blue and said he could get one of the knives. Not *the* knife, but...he wanted my four-wheeler. I t-t-traded him. You're n-n-not gonna take it back, are you? I promise I won't s-sell it. I just like to h-have it here. With me."

"Do you collect keepsakes from all serial killers, or are you just a Harlan Lusher fan?"

"I have a g-g-general interest in serial killers. It's n-n-not as uncommon as you'd th-think. Most of my c-customers are history buffs who buy items because they think serial murderers are anomalies. But in f-f-fact, someone is murdered by a serial k-k-killer once an hour in America. The *real* reason the items are v-v-valuable is, serial killers aren't p-p-p—"

"Eugene," Garcia snapped, "let's get back to Harlan Lusher."

"Sorry," he stammered. "His memorabilia is a big p-part of my c-c-collection. It's nostalgic, in a way...see, m-m-my fascination with serial killers started with him."

"Why was that?"

"Because I went to s-school with one of his victims. Sheena Wiseman. Grew up just a few b-blocks from here. I always l-liked her. I liked her a, a, a lot."

It clicked. "That's the girl on your mantel?"

He nodded. "That's how I like t-t-to remember her. She was such s-s-special person, even after she got m-messed up on the drugs...and she was so b-b-beautiful—"

"*Lieutenant*," Coffey hollered from the yard.

Eugene Palmer realized he was rambling again and shut up.

"Wait here," Garcia ordered, and then walked into the yard.

"Sorry," Coffey said, handing her the walkie-talkie. "Sheriff Connors says it's urgent."

"Keep an eye on Mr. Murder Memorabilia."

He nodded and hurried back to the porch.

"Garcia here," she said into the static.

"Lieutenant," Sheriff Connors said. "Get to the station, post-haste. I got Carrie Clemmons's friends here. They say she was threatened yesterday by Harlan Lusher's daughter."

"Harlan Lusher's daughter?" she said, totally confused.

"Correct. Jane Lusher. The girls all go to school together. I guess Lusher and Clemmons got into it at the bookstore where Lusher works. You're my highest-ranking lady officer, so I need ya here for this interview."

"All due respect, sir, but high-school drama doesn't play. I'm working a lead now that—"

"I don't care if it plays," he said. "One of these girls' daddies is Mayor Jolley's chief of staff. I don't wanna get on his bad side, and you damn sure don't wanna get on mine. Out."

Static. Static. Static. Garcia flipped the walkie-talkie off and trudged back to the porch.

"That's all for now," she said, forcing the words. "Call me if you remember anything."

She handed Eugene one of her business cards. He looked it over and put it in his pocket.

"No p-p-problem," he said.

He started moving toward the door. Garcia shot her hand out, blocking his route.

"One last thing," she said. "Why is there an industrial pad-lock on your basement door?"

"Oh," he cleared his throat. "Rats. The basement's f-f-full of 'em. They can push their way up if I don't keep that d-door locked. I've tried k-k-killing them, but I'm too squeamish."

She dropped her arm and let him pass. He went inside. He slammed the door shut.

Clank! Crank! Clamp!

She and Coffey stood there a moment before walking off the porch.

"Post up at the end of the street," Garcia said as they plodded through the dead yard.

"Wait, you mean you don't trust him?" he replied with a grin.

She wanted to tell him he wasn't funny, but she couldn't find the energy.

20

She cut through the idiot wind. Effortless movement. Reckless speed.

As she reached the top of Cooper Hill, Jane couldn't resist the urge to stand on the pedals. She arched her back and cocked her chin to the autumn sun. The incline did the rest.

Ms. Summers had sent her home early for the second day in a row. This time, though, it was because there were simply no customers. She got to ditch an hour early with pay. Jane was thankful for Ms. Summers's kindness, thankful to be flying down the hill. It felt good not to work so goddamn hard just to get where she was going. It felt good to be unstoppable.

She blew past a brick church on her right. She read the marquee sign: LET US INJECT YOU WITH FORGIVENESS. NOTHING GETS YOU HIGHER THAN JESUS!

She didn't believe in Jesus, but they talked sometimes. So, as the church faded into a blur, she felt the urge to send a short prayer up to the theoretical godhead in the sky.

Lord, forgive me for threatening Carrie the other day. Forgive me for my anger, and help me forgive them for being such assholes. Maybe they know not what they do, or whatever.

Jane scoffed at herself, a little surprised by the prayer. She shifted her focus back to the road as she came upon the intersection. The street—empty. The coast—clear. She lowered herself onto the seat and grinned with excitement. Her momentum slung her across the intersection and down the sharp curve that put her onto Lockland Street.

She laughed from the thrill of it all. The bike kept a steady pace for two blocks, and by the time it slowed, she felt as if a weight had blown off her back. Jane started pedaling again. She decided she really would forgive those girls, whether they wanted it or not. She couldn't take on their baggage; she had enough trouble keeping pace while carrying her own. If she fell behind again, she might be left behind forever.

There was another bike parked on Mammaw's porch, a Cannondale. It was *way* nicer than her rusty pink Huffy with its bobbing handlebar saddlebag she made from a fanny pack. As she leaned her bike against the house, boyish laughter drifted from the back porch.

She smiled. Henry and his new friend must have really hit it off. Good. He would need a friend once she went to college. She stepped off the porch and followed the giggles around the side yard. Leaves crunched beneath her as she walked to the back porch gate.

Henry was midtirade, too wrapped up to notice her. With his hair in his face and his arms flailing, he looked like a homeless man warning of the apocalypse. "But why the hell would they make the batsuit blue and gray?! I've never seen a blue bat in my fuckin' life!"

"The blue ink showed up better on the page," the other boy said surely. "If they were going for realism, Batman's outfit would've been brown, not black, and..."

His voice trailed off when Jane unlatched the gate.

"Sorry to interrupt," she said as she walked onto the porch. "I'm Jane, this dork's sister."

"Otis P-Perkins," he stammered. He shot off the glider and offered his hand.

She took it. They shook. His cheeks went from red to crimson.

"You're home early," Henry said. "Everything OK at work?"

"Mm-hmm." She nodded. "The shop was just deader than dead."

"She works at the bookstore," Henry explained.

"Cool," Otis said. "I didn't even know there was bookstore here."

"The Book Nook," she said. "It's downtown, across from Tudor's. Are you a big reader?"

"You don't even *know*," Henry bragged. "He *speed*-reads. He's the smartest dude in Paradise."

"That's not a very high bar."

Otis laughed bashfully. Jane started toward the back door, but Henry stopped her.

"I'm being for real, sis," Henry said. "His fuckin' IQ is almost genius level."

She looked back at Otis. "Really?"

He smiled his shy-guy smile. He nodded—*aw, shucks.*

"Damn," she said. "Lucky you."

"No," Henry said. "Lucky *us*. Now we've got our own personal Sherlock Holmes!"

"Wait... what?" she asked hesitantly.

"We *finally* found the supersleuth private eye Mom always dreamed of! Think how excited she'd be! Now we have the smartest motherfucker in town looking into Dad's case!"

The hope in his voice stung, and she suddenly felt very tired. She feared his new pal's interest in their dad would make it impossible for a true friendship to blossom. If Henry was a *subject*, he couldn't be a sidekick; it's simply impossible to stand as equals on uneven ground.

"I'm reading up on the case right now," Otis explained. "But from what I've seen, I think your father was wrongfully convicted. I'd love to ask you some questions, if you have time..."

"Rain check," she said curtly. "I need a nap."

"No problem," Otis said. "Anytime will do."

She hugged her brother before going inside.

"Love you, Ass Face."

"Love you, Butt Breath."

She squeezed him once more, then went inside the house.

"Anyway," Henry said, "back to that stupid-ass batsuit..."

Garcia white-knuckled the wheel as she turned onto State Street. She hated Sheriff Connors for calling her away from that haunted house. She hated herself for not bracing Eugene Palmer harder. She hated the Blind Spot Slasher's daughter for being scapegoated and wasting her time. Carrie Clemmons could be in that house. In that basement. In the dark. But there was no chance she'd secure a search warrant unless she could get the sheriff to hear her out.

The station house came up on her right. Garcia drove past it, gunning the engine for three blocks before parking at the curb of the bookstore. The sooner she got this teenage scuffle cleared up, the sooner Sheriff Connors might let her make the case for a warrant.

She slammed the door of the truck and rushed beneath the awning. The sign on the glass read SORRY WE'RE CLOSED, but she sensed movement inside. She tried the door.

It opened—*ding*! Garcia entered. No one in sight.

"Hello?" a feminine voice called from the back.

"Sheriff's Department," Garcia said.

There was a small clatter, then a middle-aged woman appeared. She wore dark glasses and colorful clothing that reminded Garcia of her middle school art teacher.

"Sorry," she said. "I was just closing up."

"It's OK. I'm Lt. Garcia. Are you the manager?"

"Owner," she smiled. "Suzie Summers. Is there something I can help you with?"

"I'm looking for Jane Lusher. Is she around?"

"I just sent her home," Ms. Summers said, now more guarded. "What's this about?"

"There was an incident yesterday between her and another girl—"

"You're here about the flyer?" she asked.

What flyer? "Were you here when it happened, Ms. Summers?"

"Yes…well, I was in the back helping a customer. Jane was working the register when a group of her classmates came in and began picking on her. Apparently one of them gave her a flyer for that Blind Spot Slasher party at the strip mall. When Jane tried to shove it away, the girl tripped. She stumbled and fell over there, about where you're standing."

"Then what happened?' Garcia asked.

"Then they left."

"And what did Jane do?"

"She cried."

Garcia took out her phone. She showed the picture of Carrie Clemmons to Ms. Summers.

"Is this one of the girls who was bullying her?"

"It's the one who fell," Ms. Summers said. "Definitely not a nun, though."

"Thank you," Garcia said, putting her phone away. "I was surprised to learn the Lushers still live in town."

"Nowhere else to go." Ms. Summers shrugged. "No money, no options. Jane and her brother live off Lockland with their grandmother, Betty Webb. Every time I think this town has moved on, something like yesterday happens. Those poor kids...Lord. The Bible says children shouldn't have to pay for the sins of their parents, but it doesn't always work that way."

"No, ma'am. It does not. Thank you for your time."

"Of course."

Garcia left the bookshop without another word. She climbed into her truck and floored it to the station. She parked in the nearly empty lot, got out, and hustled.

She was still tucking in her flannel when she entered the station. She clipped her badge onto her waist as she rushed past the empty reception desk (supplemental staff had Sundays off) and headed to the conference room. She checked her reflection in the hallway window; she hated being out of uniform when she was at work; it put her perceived authority in limbo.

She opened the conference room door. Sheriff Connors sat at the head of the table, as if he were the matron of a Thanksgiving feast. The opposite end of the conference table was claimed by three puffy-eyed teenage girls. A big man in a tight polo shirt loomed over them. He was helping them fill out their official statement. Lt. Billings leaned against the dry-erase board, arms crossed. He nodded to Garcia. She joined him there.

"No, honey," the big guy said to the girl who resembled him the most, "take out the word 'push' and replace it with 'violently body slammed.'"

She erased and corrected.

"Where are the rest of the parents?" Garcia whispered to Billings.

"Thought it best if they let Mr. Sutter TCB."

The girl put down the pen. Her father squeezed her shoulders approvingly. When he noticed Garcia had joined them, he galloped across the room and shot his hand out to her.

"Levi Sutter," he said, "chief of staff for Mayor Jolley."

"Lt. Elena Garcia," she said, and they shook hands.

"This is my daughter Ramona." He motioned toward her. "And this is Ms. Hamlow and Ms. Wright."

Their smiles were shaky and forced.

"Hello, girls," Garcia said, smiling back.

"Does her statement need any more corrections, Levi?" Sheriff Connors asked.

"I don't think so," Mr. Sutter said. He grabbed the paper and proofread it aloud. "On Saturday, October 15, 2011, we entered the Book Nook with Carrie Clemmons to say hello to the cashier, Jane Lusher, whom we play soccer with. The conversation was pleasant until, with no provocation, Jane Lusher violently body slammed Carrie Clemmons to the ground and then threatened to bash her brains in." Mr. Sutter looked to the sheriff.

"Works for me." He shrugged. "You girls sign and print your names at the bottom."

Mr. Sutter gave the form back to his daughter. Ramona began to sign.

"Making false statements is illegal," Garcia said. "You know that, right, girls?"

Ramona Sutter dropped the pen. Billie Jean Hamlow bit her lip.

Garcia flipped her notepad open. "Why don't you tell us about the flyer."

"That's enough," Sheriff Connors said under his breath.

Garcia stayed focused on the girls. "The more time you make us waste, the less likely it is we find your friend alive. So, tell me the truth, did you *actually* hear Jane Lusher threaten to bash her brains in?"

"I mean . . . not, like, *exactly*," Ramona muttered.

"Then let's move on to the podcast taping. Did you notice anyone suspicious? Anyone following Carrie? Why did she walk home alone? Why weren't you with her—"

"Lt. Garcia!" the sheriff barked, standing up. "Hallway. Now."

"Even the smallest detail could help," she said to the girls as she followed the sheriff out.

Sheriff Connors slammed the door shut. They were alone in the hall.

"You're on thin goddamn ice," he snapped.

"Just hear me out, sir," she said. "I have a lead that's *real*. Eugene Palmer, he worked the event last night and admitted to knowing Carrie. He's a full-on creeper *obsessed* with BSS."

"BSS," he scoffed. "You're tryin' to tie this girl's disappearance to that half-assed BSS theory you shit out yesterday? We're talkin' about a high school *student* here, not a junkie."

"I must have misheard you," Mr. Sutter said as he opened the door. "Your deputy isn't talking about the Blind Spot Slasher, is she, Buck?"

"Lieutenant," Garcia corrected, "not deputy. Were you listening through the door?"

"She was talkin' about a separate case," Sheriff Connors said. "Just spitballing theories."

"What's *his* theory?" Garcia asked Sheriff Connors, harsher than she meant to. "Jane Lusher slashed every tire in that parking lot to get Carrie Clemmons alone? You think Lusher *knew* the girl would walk home by herself? Because, unless you suspect her of being a psychic criminal mastermind, we need to put a pin in this and get a warrant for my suspect's house—"

"A warrant is a great idea," Levi Sutter interrupted. "Let's get a warrant for the Lusher's place and do that CSI crap. Which judge should we go with, Buck?"

"Both of you shut up!" Sheriff Connors barked.

Both of them shut up.

"There's no probable cause for a warrant on anyone yet, as far as I can see."

"Sheriff," Garcia pleaded, "respectfully, we *do* have enough for a search warrant. I just need a moment with you to clarify my case—"

"*Enough*, Lieutenant." he said, raising a halting palm. "Go out to reception and get me Betty Webb's number. You can tell me what you've got *after* we speak to the Lusher girl."

She was dumbstruck. Defeated, she started off to the reception desk.

Levi Sutter called after her: "Grab me a coffee while you're up there. Thanks, deputy!"

21

The sex scene was just getting good when the phone started yapping. Mammaw laid her joint in the ashtray, then marked her page and sat the book beside it. She groaned as she got off the couch and made her way into the kitchen.

She pulled the phone off the wall. "This is Mammaw."

"Betty? This is Buck Connors."

"What can I do ya for, Sheriff?" she asked, as polite as she could manage.

"You're gonna hate me for askin', but could ya bring your grandbabies down to the station? I need their help clarifying some things. Shouldn't take more than a few minutes."

"Then clarify what it's about," she said.

"I can't say over the phone, Betty. Likely nothin'."

She heard Henry and his new friend laughing out back. She was touched by the sweetness of the sound. "If it's nothin', it can wait. The kids've got school tomorrow."

"It's gotta be tonight," Sheriff Connors said. "The station's

nearly deserted. We can come there, if you'd prefer. I just figured you wouldn't wanna get the neighbors talking..."

"Appreciate you lookin' out," she sneered. "I reckon we'll be
down soon."

"Thanks, Betty. I really—"

She hung up. "Asshole."

She went back to the table and snuffed out the joint. Marijuana
hadn't made her anxious in decades, but as she waddled to the
back door, every nerve in her body screamed in protest. The kids
were going to be so upset when she told them. Poor Henry. Poor
Jane.

Mammaw stopped at the laundry closet and sprayed herself
down with Febreze, hoping the mist would kill the smell of
smoke by the time they got to the station. She gave her hair a
spritz for good measure, put the bottle back, shut the closet, and
pushed through the back door.

Henry and Otis were leaning on the porch railing, talking
close and watching the creek sparkle, the brown water turning
gold in the sunset. The sound of the screen door muted their
conversation. Gravy got up and trotted to the door. Henry
turned, saw Mammaw, and smiled.

"The weirdest thing just happened," she said. "Sheriff
Connors asked us to meet him at the station right quick, but he
won't tell me why."

A look of dread washed over Henry's face.

"It's nothing *bad* though," she added quickly. "He told me
that much."

She watched Henry's eyes grow bright as he ping-ponged
from worst-case scenario to best-case scenario. "Maybe Dad's
lawyers got his appeal pushed through!"

"Maybe," Mammaw said. "I think we'll have to go see for ourselves."

"Can Otis come?" Henry asked. "He *loves* detective shit."

"I'm not sure if it's appropriate to bring a friend," Mammaw said.

"But," Henry continued, "if it's nothing bad, who cares?"

"Well," she floundered, "guess that's true."

"Wanna come?" Henry asked, turning to Otis. "Might help the investigation."

"I definitely do . . . but I'm afraid it'll annoy your sister if I tag along."

"You boys talk it out," Mammaw said, turning back to the door, "I'll go wake Janey."

She could hear her grandson's childish reassurance as she went back inside.

"Big Man," Henry said, "I may not be as smart as you, but being the only dude in this house has taught me two key truths: girls are *always* annoyed, and it's almost *never* our fault."

Garcia was beyond annoyed. She leaned on the empty reception desk and shot invisible daggers into Levi Sutter's smug grin. She imagined him getting flogged in the street, branded with a scarlet *P* for "pompous prick."

She allowed herself these fantasies because they kept her anger at a simmer, but the longer he hung around, the closer her feelings came to boiling over. She couldn't afford that. If she shot her mouth off again, she might find herself out of a job. But Sutter made it nearly impossible—he'd thrown the investigation off course and put Carrie Clemmons in *more* danger.

Yet he was self-righteous enough to stand with her and Sheriff Connors, as if they were all on the same team.

The girls had signed their bullshit statement and gone home. Billings was leading another search party. Sgt. Coffey was keeping tabs on Eugene Palmer—last time she checked in, he said Palmer hadn't left the house. Coffey could see him watching TV in the living room.

But the girl could still be in there.

She could be in the basement. In the turret room. In a closet.

In a freezer. In a trash bag. In trash bags.

In the dark. In the dirt.

"How should we play this, Buck?" Sutter asked the sheriff.

"Lt. Garcia will interview the girl. I'll speak with the boy myself."

"I'd rather it be one at a time," Sutter said. "So I can be present for both interviews."

"Now come on, Levi," Sheriff Connors sighed. "You know that's against protocol."

"The Clemmons family wants me in the room." He shrugged. "So does Mayor Jolley."

"The Clemmons family wants their daughter home safe," Garcia snapped, "and the faster we do this, the faster we can get back to work. Unless putting on a show for the mayor is more important."

"Oh," Sutter scoffed, "you wanna see a show, huh—"

The front doors of the station opened. Garcia and Sutter shut up.

A snowball of a woman led the children inside. A long-haired boy limped forward. A short-haired girl walked beside him. Both of their eyes were unsure, the bags beneath them heavy.

Garcia was ashamed to be part of the whole sad ordeal. She looked away, not seeing the other boy that walked in behind them, carrying a little white dog.

"I was stupid to get my hopes up," she heard the long-haired boy whisper to his grandmother. "Cops never have good news...shit. This is gonna suck, ain't it, Mammaw?"

Sheriff Connors stepped forward to greet them.

Henry slouched as naturally as he could. Mammaw sat beside him. They faced Sheriff Connors's empty desk. The female officer was interviewing Jane in a different room, but Jane had insisted Mammaw go with Henry. He was glad. When Mammaw held his hand, it was easier to hold his shit together.

He could see the sheriff in the hallway, arguing with the man from the mayor's office. Then Sheriff Connors broke away and stomped angrily toward them. Henry faced forward as the door swung open. Sheriff Connors shut it behind him and sat down at his desk. He hunched forward, looking exhausted, and laced his thick fingers together.

"Sorry for the wait," he said. "Thank you for coming to speak with me, Henry. As I told your grandmother, you aren't in any trouble. Y'all are free to leave at any time. OK?"

"OK," Henry said.

"Great." He cleared his throat. "Did you hear about the event at the Bear Creek Shopping Center last night? The live podcast?"

"Yeah." Henry nodded. "Of course I did. There were flyers all over town."

"You knew the subject at hand was your father?"

"No. My dad wasn't the Blind Spot Slasher."

"But you knew the show was about BSS?"

"Yeah," Henry said.

"Did you go to the podcast?"

"No," Henry said.

"You must have serious willpower, son! It woulda been hard for me to resist."

"Both of 'em stayed home last night," Mammaw confirmed. "I sleep in the living room, and I woulda heard if anyone snuck out."

"What time did you go to bed?" Sheriff Connors asked.

"Around eight, I think," Henry said. Mammaw nodded.

"You always go to bed early on Saturday nights?"

"No," he said. "But we had a long day."

"Because of what happened to your sister at work? You must've been pretty mad."

"Who wouldn't be mad if their sister got bullied?" Henry said. "Between those girls and that podcast...*yeah*, it was a long day, so *yeah*, we all went to bed early."

"You didn't leave at any point during the night?" the sheriff asked.

"No," Henry said.

"And your sister didn't either?"

"I already said she didn't," Mammaw snapped.

"You ever pull pranks on people, Henry? Egg houses? Slash tires? That sorta thing?"

Henry forced his entire existence stonewall still. "No."

"Really?" Sheriff Connors asked. "When I was your age, I loved pullin' pranks. We used to tee-pee the houses of kids we didn't like, sometimes for payback. What do ya think of that?"

"I think it sounds like you were a pretty fucked-up kid," Henry said.

Mammaw laughed harder than she had in years.

Garcia led Jane to the conference room. She attempted to make idle chitchat as they walked the hall. Jane responded sparsely. Garcia couldn't blame her.

They went inside. Jane took a seat. Garcia shut the door and sat next to her.

"Your eyeliner's so cool," Garcia said. "I can never get my wings that even."

"Thanks," Jane said, blushing.

"Sorry we dragged you down here, Jane. You're not in trouble. Neither's your brother."

"OK," Jane said.

"Can you tell me about what happened at the bookstore Saturday afternoon?"

"Oh," she said, a little surprised. "Uh, so there was this stupid live podcast about the BSS murders. Some of the girls on my soccer team don't like me, so they brought a flyer for the podcast into the shop to mess with me...they do that sorta thing a lot."

"Can you tell me their names?" Garcia asked.

"Yeah, sorry. Ramona Sutter, Carrie Clemmons, Trudy Wright...oh, and Billie Jean Hamlow, too. Is that why I'm here? I don't wanna press charges against them or anything."

"What happened after the girls came into the store?" Garcia asked.

"Ms. Summers let me go home. I have pretty bad anxiety sometimes, and, like, that flyer gave me a panic attack. I was kinda a mess. I dunno how I even rode my bike home, honestly."

"I'm sorry they did that to you," Garcia said, sincerely.

"It's OK."

No. It's not. "Once you got home? What then?"

"I told Mammaw what happened, and then I took a Valium. They're prescribed. I don't take them a lot because they make me super drowsy. I went to bed early after that."

"You didn't leave the house all night?" Garcia asked.

"No," Jane said.

"And your brother didn't either?"

"No...can I ask what's going on?"

"Carrie Clemmons went missing last night. We're attempting to retrace her steps."

"What do you mean 'missing'?" Jane asked nervously.

"She never came home from the podcast," Garcia said. "Her friends—"

"Oh my God," Jane gasped, "are they trying to say I did something to her? Are they seriously saying that?"

"No one's accusing you of anything, Jane. We're just establishing a timeline."

"*God,*" Jane moaned. "Everyone at school already hates me."

Garcia tried to avoid a weepy scene by switching topics. "Let's forget the girls for now. Do you know a man named Eugene Palmer? You may have met him at one of your games."

"I don't think so," Jane said.

"He might have bought some things from your family off Craigslist, or at a yard sale."

"Things like what?"

"Memorabilia, for lack of a better word. Items related to your dad."

"Oh. I dunno. My brother deals with those people."

Garcia leaned in. "What people?"

"The ones who buy the T-shirts," she said. "We started selling them to raise money so we could hire a private eye for Dad. Then I got older and realized the people who buy the shirts don't do it because they think he's innocent. They don't *want* him to be innocent. They're really creepy, almost obsessed, like some sick sorta—"

"Fan club?" Garcia spat out, overly eager.

Jane replied with a single nod.

Otis looked. Otis listened. But mainly, Otis lounged. He'd been sitting in the lobby of the station for an hour. He'd already finished the paperback Henry loaned him, and now Gravy was using it as a pillow while he snoozed in the plastic chair beside him. Otis got out his phone. His mom had sent him a check-in text. He didn't want to lie about where he was at, so he didn't respond.

Suddenly—*footsteps*! And a voice, rising.

The man from the mayor's office was storming toward the exit doors, barking into a cell phone. Otis placed a securing hand on Gravy, then shut his eyes and pretended to be asleep. He eavesdropped as the man marched past him.

"Yes, Mr. Mayor, I told Buck you wanted me in the room...I know, but...Channel Five, Channel Two, I'll call the *Gazette* as well...yes, sir, I'm leaving now."

Otis heard the door open. Otis heard the door shut. Otis opened his eyes.

The Mayor? The newspaper? That couldn't have been about Henry and Jane, could it?

No way. His new friends were exciting, but not *that* exciting.

His attention was suddenly severed by his growling stomach.

Otis realized he hadn't eaten since lunch. He wondered if he could find something to snack on around the station while he waited. He stood up. Gravy didn't flinch. Otis lingered a moment to make sure the dog was still asleep and then walked down the foyer of the building.

He couldn't believe he was inside a police station. It was way more boring than he'd imagined. He stopped when he got to the reception desk—all the cubicles in the bullpen were deserted. The only officers he'd seen on duty were now with Henry and Jane. He looked back at the dog, who hadn't stirred. His stomach growled again.

Otis moved forward with a hunger-begotten brazenness. Visions of donuts danced in his head as he crept down the aisle of desks in search of the break room. He passed endless amounts of classified information he'd usually salivate over. He passed the bathrooms and the water fountain, then turned down a hallway. The door at the end of the corridor was open. The light was on. He could smell coffee grounds. It had to be the break room. With coffee came donuts.

Otis hurried down the hall. He was a few feet from the break room when he heard voices inside—one feminine, one masculine, both inflected with a hillbilly huskiness.

"*Mmmmm!* Good Lord done blessed us tonight," the man said. "All dozen's untouched."

"Dibs on that fritter," the woman said.

"Where's everyone at?" the man asked, through a mouthful of food.

Otis's stomach rumbled. He willed it to silence. His curiosity trumped his craving.

"Billings's got everyone on scene at the girl's LKL. Coffey's been pullin' OT for Garcia since last night. Few others too. Has 'em diggin' through NHIs to see if any weren't ODs."

OD. LKL. NHI. OT. Garcia. Billings. Otis memorized the acronyms and names.

"What's she think, if not OD?" he asked.

"Dernt said it's some BSS BS," the woman scoffed. "LT's lookin' for a copycat."

Copycat. The word exploded in Otis's mind like a clear white light.

"Talk about wishful thinkin'." The man laughed. "Personally, I'd be thrilled if BSS came back to deal with these junkies. Someone needs to take out the trash. Better him than me."

"Him who? There ain't no copycat. Ain't no nothin'. LT's lookin' for a needle in a needle stack. Now pass me that chocolate glaze."

"Lemme make sure I've got this straight," Mammaw snapped at Sheriff Connors, cutting him off as he tried to drag Henry along on another fishing expedition. "Ya don't give a damn what those girls did to Janey, but you call *us* in because one of 'em missed her curfew?"

"Betty," Sheriff Connors said, "you must understand why Mr. and Mrs. Clemmons—"

Bark-bark! Bark-bark-bark!

Gravyboat's bark cut him off. They all turned to the door. More barks echoed down the hall from the lobby. Sheriff Connors stood, motioning them to stay put. He flung the door open, and the barks got louder. Then, an authoritative female voice echoed from the same direction.

"Sheriff Connors? It's Amy Saunders, Channel Five News…"

Henry and Mammaw shared a look. They stood up.

Gravy came scurrying down the hall toward them clumsily, feet slip-sliding on the tile. Otis came scurrying after the dog. They both picked up their pace when they saw Henry and Mammaw. Sheriff Connors ushered them out of his office.

"Come on. We'll grab your sister and go out the back before she gets wind of y'all."

"But I'm parked out front," Mammaw said.

The dog reached them first. Henry picked him up. Otis was panting when he arrived.

"Keys," Sheriff Connors said to Mammaw.

She handed them over. The sheriff gave them to Otis. Otis gulped.

"Pull their car around to the alley. Don't let anyone follow you. Don't talk to *anyone*."

Otis looked at Henry. Henry shrugged. Otis set off running back down the hall.

Sheriff Connors steered them in the opposite direction, toward the conference room. Henry held the dog tight and did his best to keep the pace. Mammaw took up the rear.

Lord, can't you cut my angel babies a break? she silently prayed. She kept moving.

She was old enough to know there was no sense waiting for a reply.

22

Black on black shadows cut ominous shapes through downtown in the dark. Mammaw seemed to ignore them and focused on the road. They were two blocks clear of the station before anyone spoke.

"How many news vans were out there?" Henry asked. He sat in the back with Jane and the dog. Otis slid from the driver's side to the shotgun side once he moved the car into the alley.

"Two, I think," he answered, "but it must've been about something else."

"No," Jane muttered, "they were there for us."

Otis cleared his throat. He turned to the back seat. "What were *you* there for?"

"Bullshit," Mammaw, Jane, and Henry said at the exact same time.

"Oh."

"A girl from school didn't come home last night, is all," Henry clarified. "Her parents assume we had somethin' to do with it since we're spawns of the fuckin' antichrist."

"It's not funny," Jane snapped, slapping his shoulder.

Otis turned back to the windshield. He didn't know what to say. So, he did what any teenager does in the face of awkward silence—he took out his phone.

He'd missed two more texts from his mom. Otis finally replied, vaguely saying that extenuating circumstances were to blame for his radio silence. She replied instantly, demanding an address. She was sending his father to pick him up. It was too dark for him to ride home.

Otis texted her their address and then closed his messenger app. He opened his web browser and went to the Sheriff Department's homepage. He found Lt. Garcia, Sgt. Coffey, and the other names he'd overheard in the break room conversation. He recognized Garcia as the woman who'd questioned Jane. Then he looked up acronyms:

Over Time. Last Known Location. No Human Involvement.

He read that the term NHI is most often used in cases of self-harm, or drug-related deaths. Pair that with what the officers said about their lieutenant's copycat theory.

Extrapolate: She has reason to believe some cases classified as NHIs were homicides. These are cases involving drug addicts, which is who the Blind Spot Slasher targeted. Maybe this is the only link between the BSS case and what is happening now . . . or maybe not.

Otis went to the *Charleston Gazette*'s homepage. He pulled statistics and skimmed headlines—drug-related arrests, deaths, and disappearances had increased steadily since Harlan Lusher went away: 3 percent one year, 11 percent the next . . . the articles gave the numbers context:

02/18/2007—Budget Cuts Leave Law Enforcement Overwhelmed

12/03/2009—Highest Number of Missing Persons Reported in State History

Destrapolate: The conditions that allowed the Blind Spot Slasher to thrive have gotten worse since Harlan Lusher was convicted. The BSS victim pool is slowly turning into an ocean. The environment is ripe for another serial killer to emerge. A new serial killer. A Blind Spot Copycat.

But that theory worked off the assumption Harlan Lusher was the Blind Spot Slasher. If Harlan Lusher was innocent...

Restrapolate: Lt. Garcia has it wrong. There is no copycat. The original Blind Spot Slasher is still out there! Still killing. The police simply stopped investigating "drug-related" deaths. No Human Involvement means no investigation. That could mean dozens, hundreds more BSS victims.

Otis looked in the rearview mirror. Henry was resting his head on his sister's shoulder. She went from petting her brother to petting the dog. She locked eyes with Otis in the mirror.

"What is it?" she asked.

"There's been a break in the case."

The shy boy from earlier was gone. Otis was now empowered by the information he held. Jane, Henry, and Mammaw sat at the kitchen table and watched him pace. Gravy followed Otis back and forth, eyes smiling, dirty nails clicking on the tile.

First, Otis told them about his research. Then he laid out his initial theories: (1) their dad was framed by Pearl Jolley or someone connected to Lordsville, and (2) the murders were committed by *two* of their father's employees, who would have access to the truck and the cabin. A killer-team scenario was rare, but it would account for the wild amount of inconsistencies in the case.

Otis explained what the NHI classification meant and how it was used.

Otis told them what he'd overheard: the BSS copycat theory.

Then Otis told them *his* takeaway: the Blind Spot Slasher never stopped killing.

Henry pounded the table, victorious. "Dad had it right all along! Those crazy Christian Lordsville fucks! They were killin' people back then, and they never stopped! I knew it!"

"Maybe," Otis said, "but this copycat investigation just opened a Pandora's box of questions. If BSS is still active, the first thing we should do is focus on old suspects and employees who stayed in the area. This is still his hunting ground, so the killer most likely stayed somewhat local. We need to look into that before we dig into Lordsville. It's the logical approach."

"Dude, are you kidding?" Henry scoffed. "If Jolley blamed Dad for the fire...it's an open-and-shut case. She framed him and got away with it, man."

"And then *kept* killing?" Otis asked. "She must be close to seventy now. If she murdered those women *just* to frame your father, why would she keep killing after they locked him up?"

"I mean..." Henry started, then shrugged.

"What's your father told you about Sister Jolley?" Otis asked. "About Lordsville? I mean insider information, facts, small details I won't be able to find on the internet."

"Not a lot," Jane admitted. "He doesn't like to talk about it."

"Has he ever mentioned anything called the Trinity of Light?" Otis asked.

Jane looked to Henry. They both looked to Mammaw. All three shook their heads.

They looked back to Otis.

"Pearl Jolley allegedly made a pact with two other cults to defend one another if the federal government raided their compounds—"

"Dude!" Henry yelled. "That's like a fucked-up version of the Knights Templar! That's gotta be the key."

Otis didn't exactly disagree, but he had to table it. He knew they wouldn't be able to see the small stuff if they only focused on the strange stuff.

"What do you know about the Knights Templar?" Jane scoffed.

"Like, everything. Grave Digger has a concept album about 'em. Duh."

"Whatever," Jane said, then turned to Otis. "No offense, but if Lt. Garcia is looking into these murders, I think you should tell her what you've found out. She wants to help. We can trust her."

"Are you kidding?" Henry asked. "A pig is a pig."

"Don't be a dick—"

"Don't be a dipshit—"

"Time out!" Mammaw snapped.

She stood up. The kids shut up.

"Y'all play nice," she said. She opened the cabinet and got out a tumbler.

"Look," Otis said calmly, "I need to get a case together if I want Lt. Garcia, or anyone else, to take me seriously. She's focused on this missing person case. She may think a BSS copycat is involved…but that would go against the Blind Spot Slasher's MO. Unless your classmate is an addict, I think these investigations are completely unrelated."

"Then what do you think happened to Carrie?" Jane asked.

"I don't know. But I *do* know we've been given a unique opportunity to find the *real* killer and get your father out of prison. We'll bring the lieutenant into the loop once we have something solid. If her peers dismissed her copycat theory, mine will be even harder to swallow without some rock-solid evidence."

Mammaw poured herself a scotch. She toasted Otis before she drank.

"I'll start digging in the morning," Otis said. "I'll look for similar murders in a hundred-mile radius, then update the old suspect list. Maybe someone has exhibited BSS-like behavior over the last six years."

"But it's Lordsville," Henry groaned, verging on a temper tantrum.

Otis sighed. "Let's talk about Lordsville. If the cult is involved with these murders, if the Trinity of Light still exists, your father's insight could be the key to unlocking that puzzle. Is there any way I could interview him and see if those dots connect?"

Jane shared a look with Henry. Mammaw sipped her scotch.

"I'll call Salem Hill tomorrow and get ya on the visitation list," Henry said.

Otis nodded, straight-faced. Investigators don't smile, even when they're excited.

"We're gonna need to start being more careful," Jane said. "If the *real* Blind Spot Slasher finds out we're looking for him…he could come after us."

A drawer opened. A drawer closed.

"I got six good reasons for him to stay away," Mammaw said. She held a silver .357 Magnum revolver. The six-inch barrel glistened. Otis was speechless. Henry and Jane grinned.

Knock! Knock! Knock!

Otis jumped. Gravy barked. Someone was at the door.

"If you're a reporter, fuck off!" Henry yelled.

"Um, no," the voice said through the door. "It's Fred Perkins. I'm here to pick up Otis."

Mammaw put her drink down and hurried to the door. She slid the revolver into the back of her elastic waistband.

"Hey, honey," she said as she opened the door. She hugged him as if they were family.

"Well, hi there." He chuckled. "I'm Fred Perkins."

"I'm Mammaw," she said, letting go and ushering him inside.

"You must be Henry," he said, offering his hand.

"Yeah," Henry said, shaking it. "Nice to meet you."

"I'm Jane," she said, waving as she stood.

"Fred Perkins." He smiled. He turned to his son. "Let's get you home before Mom has an aneurism."

"Good idea," Otis said. He gave Henry a look. "I'll call you in the morning."

"Cool." Henry nodded. "See ya."

As Mammaw ushered them out the door, the weight of the gun pulled her pants halfway down her butt. Jane and Henry held in their laughter until the door was shut and locked.

"Lord"—Mammaw laughed, hiking up her pants—"I usually wait 'til the second date to drop my drawers!" She sat the gun between her beloved grandchildren and refilled her drink.

"You were right," Jane told Henry, "he's really smart."

"Reminds me of that famous detective," Mammaw said.

"Sherlock Holmes?" Henry asked.

Mammaw shook her head. "Nah, the one that always wears a brown jacket."

"Yeah." He nodded, "Sherlock Holmes."

"I mean the most famous detective there is," she clarified. "From the TV."

"Columbo?" Jane asked.

"No," she insisted, "the one who outsmarts everyone—"

"*Columbo*," Jane and Henry said in unison.

Mammaw lifted a halting hand. She thought for a moment.

"Walker, Texas Ranger," Mammaw announced, satisfied.

Jane and Henry shared a look of bemused exasperation.

"Yeah, Mammaw," Jane said sweetly, "that's Otis to a T."

Otis walked his bicycle to the car. His father moved ahead and opened the trunk.

"Sorry to make you come out so late," Otis said.

"It's OK." His father smiled. "I've been having trouble sleeping anyway. Your friends seem nice, I didn't get any 'serial killers in training' vibes coming off them."

"Yeah." Otis returned the smile. "They're really great."

Otis saw the way his father winced when he picked up the bike and maneuvered it into the trunk. His neck tilted to one side like it used to. The menthol stench of IcyHot stung at Otis's eyes. *He must be really caking it on*, Otis thought. *His pain must be freakin' awful*.

His father shut the trunk. They walked to their respective doors.

"So, are you gonna tell me where you were all night?"

Otis didn't want to tell. They'd had a hard enough time accepting he was hanging with the son of a (wrongfully convicted) serial killer. His parents would never let him leave the house again if they knew he was on a quest to hunt the *real* killer down. But when they got into the car and his father winced again, Otis thought of all the lies his addiction had spurred and all the harm those lies caused. Otis couldn't restart that cycle. He refused to lie to his father.

"I'm helping Henry look into some discrepancies in Harlan Lusher's conviction. They don't have computers or the internet or, frankly, any idea where to start. So, I offered to do some digging. I can't say much more about it right now, because Henry asked me not to. I want to do right by him...to do something nice, like when you raked Miss Cranston's leaves."

His father nodded. He started the car. He backed out and drove toward home.

"I'm proud of you, son. It's good of you to help that poor family. Lord, I can't imagine what those kids have gone through. I hope your research helps. I hope their pain goes away."

"Me too." Otis nodded. "Far as freak away from us all."

EPISODE THREE

Chorus:
"Push the needle in,
face death's sickly grin."
—Black Sabbath

23

Monday. Otis was up before the dawn.

His father hadn't pressed for more details about his research and had even vowed to support his efforts as long as he kept up with his schoolwork. Otis knocked out Monday's studies in the middle of the night so he could get an early start on the investigation.

Six years since Lusher's conviction. Six years of information and misinformation.

Otis dug in. He scoped similar crimes in a hundred-mile radius. The closest match was a string of stabbings in Lexington back in 2008. All of the victims were women. All of the victims were addicts. But the victims were also sexually assaulted, which went against his killer's MO.

Otis switched strategies. Using newspaper articles, public records, and online résumé websites, he compiled a list of people who once worked for Lusher Developments, LLC. He found fourteen ex-employees. He ran down the first six names. Three still lived in the area.

Otis began checking into ex-employee number one, a man named Lynell Boone. Then his iPhone pinged in an unfamiliar tone. He grabbed the phone off his bed. The screen was lit with a notification, a news alert from the *Charleston Gazette* app he'd recently downloaded.

BREAKING NEWS:
Barkley Co. Sheriff confirms body of missing seventeen-year-old female recovered.

His butt hit the bed. He felt light-headed.

Otis clicked on the alert—no article available. The story was still developing.

Be reasonable. Think logically. This was a high school student, not a drug addict. Not easy prey. Not even close to the Blind Spot Slasher's MO. This has nothing to do with your case. Don't let it distract you. Stay on the trail, don't lose the scent, do it for Henry and Jane . . .

"Oh crap," Otis groaned.

Neither of them had smartphones. No up-to-the-second news apps. Otis wasn't even sure their TV worked . . . which meant they probably had no idea she was dead. He had to call them before they left for school. The other kids would already know. Rumors would be spreading.

In the age of the internet, bad news traveled fast.

Henry was scooping a second helping of bacon onto his plate when the telephone rang. Jane and Mammaw's breakfast conversation hit the brakes. He put his plate on the counter and pulled the phone off the cradle. Early bird gets the word.

"Hello?"

"Hi, it's Otis. Sorry for calling so early, but...the girl, your classmate, she's dead. They found her body this morning, I just got a news update. I don't kn—"

Henry dropped the phone.

"What?" Jane and Mammaw asked in unison.

"Turn on the news," he said to his sister. He picked the phone back up.

Jane jumped out of her seat, grabbed the remote, aimed, and fired. A news anchor stood outside the Barkley County Sheriff's Station. The Channel Five icon loomed in the bottom-left corner of the screen. The ticker beside it read: BODY OF MISSING TEEN FOUND NEAR I-64 OVERPASS.

Jane turned the volume up.

"...and we're expecting the press conference to start any minute," the anchor said.

Jane dropped onto the couch as if she'd been gut punched. Mammaw read the ticker and went to sit beside her. Henry brought the phone back to his ear.

"Hello? Hello? Are you still there?" Otis was asking.

"Yeah," he said. "Sorry. Just turned on the TV."

"Should we stay home from school today?" Jane asked Henry.

"You may want to stay home from school today," Otis said into his other ear.

"Yeah," he replied to them both.

"Why don't I come over? We can work on the case." Otis said, striving for positivity. "I've been looking into old suspects, but I'm starting to think that Lordsville may be the only theory with legs."

Before Henry could respond, Sheriff Connors walked out of the station. The camera added ten pounds, twenty years, and a hundred miles. Lt. Garcia and Lt. Billings followed the sheriff's painstaking gallows walk toward the waiting cameras.

"The press conference is starting," Otis said. "I'll call you back after."

"OK," Henry said. He hung up, grabbed his coffee, and sat on Mammaw's still-inflated air mattress. The dog sat beside him. He petted Gravy absently and glared at the screen.

Sheriff Connors stood center stage. Garcia was to his left, Billings to his right. Their uniforms were rumpled, patchy with sweat and coffee stains. Their eyes were somewhere else.

"I'll read a brief statement," Sheriff Connors said. "Then I'll take a few questions."

Cameras flashed. The sheriff took a piece of paper from his pocket and unfolded it.

"At approximately 3:15 a.m.," he read aloud, "a body was discovered between Polk Creek Drive and the I-64 overpass. It has since been identified as seventeen-year-old Carrie June Clemmons, from here in Paradise. Ms. Clemmons had been reported missing earlier in the day. She was last seen on Saturday night at the Bear Road Shopping Center. We encourage anyone with information to come forward, even if it seems insignificant. You can call our station directly, or the anonymous tip line I'll be sharing momentarily. We ask that all of you, *press included*, respect the privacy of the Clemmons family during this tragic time."

"Was she murdered?!" a reporter yelled.

"Was she raped?!" another shouted.

"We're treating this as a homicide," he said. "I can't go into more detail at this time."

"Who found her?"

"I came upon the remains," Billings said.

Sheriff Connors shot him a look—*why the hell are you talking?*

"Sheriff Connors," an anchor called out, "is it true the children of convicted serial killer Harlan Lusher were questioned in relation to the girl's disappearance? Are they suspects?"

A rumble went through the crowd, on screen and at home.

"This is an active investigation," he said. "We're looking at many different leads. I'll take one more question, then we've gotta get back to work." He pointed to a reporter off-screen.

"Should parents in the community worry for their children's safety?"

"As a general rule," he said, "I'd certainly recommend it."

Otis shut his laptop when the press conference ended. He leaned forward, stomach buzzing, trying to grasp what had just happened. They'd mentioned his friends—called them suspects—on the air, and he was having a hard time pinpointing exactly how he felt.

As a friend, he hated to think what the attention would mean for Henry and Jane.

As an investigator, he hated to think how the attention would complicate the case.

But as a loser, he hated how *thrilling* it was to hear them called out. He'd been at the station *with* them, making him infamous by association, and he hated how cool it made him feel.

Otis was about to call Henry back when he remembered it was Monday. Because his father worked the midnight shift, Mondays were the only mornings he was home to have breakfast with the family. Otis decided the callback could wait until after he ate breakfast, since Henry and Jane no doubt had many unfortunate things to discuss among themselves.

As he made his way downstairs, he wondered if he should tell his father about the press conference. But when he crossed through the living room and into the kitchen, he realized it wouldn't be an issue. His mom stood at the counter in her green bathrobe, slicing a banana. A glass of apple juice, a cup of coffee, and some low-fat peanut butter sat on the table. Two poppy seed bagels warmed in the toaster oven. His father was nowhere to be found.

"Good morning," she said, smiling. She carried the banana slices to the table.

"Morning," Otis said. "Where's—"

"Your father will be back any minute," she said, bringing the bagels and joining him.

"But where is he?" he asked. He sipped his apple juice.

"He couldn't get to sleep last night," she said. "His back was hurting him. He gave up around two and went for a drive...he says being in the car helps." She spread peanut butter onto her bagel. "I think this job is starting to take a toll on him physically."

"He left in the middle of the night without telling you where he was going," Otis clarified, "and he still isn't back...why exactly aren't we freaking out, Mom?"

She gave his chubby hand a bless-your-heart pat. "He won't slip up, don't worry. He's better, he's unaddicted now. The man he was in Huntington...that person no longer exists."

"Has he texted you, at least?"

"Did *you* text me when you were with your new pals? No. But did I assume you were up to no good? No. I gave you the benefit of the doubt. Your father deserves the same from us."

"But it worries me. I can't help it."

"I know it's been hard…but God never gives us more than we can handle."

His eyes resisted the urge to roll. He chomped his bagel at lightning speed.

"I should get back to my homework," he said, standing.

Otis washed his dishes and put them on the rack to dry. Then he walked out of the kitchen without saying another word, picking poppy seeds from his teeth as he trudged up the stairs. But instead of going back to his room, he walked into his parents' bedroom.

He didn't want to do it. He resented every step he took. He stopped at their bathroom.

He flipped on the light.

The first thing he noticed was the ibuprofen bottle on the counter. It was one of the big ones, five hundred count, but there were only a few pills inside. He scanned the rest of the room—an empty bottle of Tylenol protruded from the trash can. Two dead sticks of IcyHot kept it company. He turned to the mirror. He sighed. He opened the medicine cabinet.

The orange bottle with the childproof cap sat alone on the center row. Methocarbon—his father's new pain medication—was less addictive but much less effective. Otis took the bottle off the shelf. He checked the refill date and the dosage—*take up to four a day for pain*—then did the math in his head. There should've been between twelve and twenty-four pills left until his next refill.

He opened the bottle and counted. The equation didn't take long.

There were three pills inside.

Otis put the bottle back. Otis closed the medicine cabinet.

Otis walked into the hall and turned toward his room. Then, downstairs, he heard the front door swing open and slam shut.

"Donut man," he heard his father sing. "The donut man has arrived!"

Otis forced himself to go check it out. His father was standing in the kitchen, holding a box of Jolly Pirate Donuts in front of his mom like a door-to-door salesman displaying his wares. "To your left, we have a jelly-filled, which are *finally* back in season..."

She laughed and chose a donut. When she saw Otis, she smiled.

"Your father brought donuts," she said. *I told you he was fine*, she meant.

Otis ignored her. "Mom said your pain got worse last night?"

"It did." His father nodded. "I couldn't get to sleep for the life of me."

"So, where'd you go?" Otis asked.

"I drove around until Jolly Pirate opened. Nothing like fresh donuts. You want one?"

Otis nodded. He took one with strawberry frosting and sprinkles. He locked eyes with his father. He thought he saw faint signs of pupil dilation. "Maybe you should call your doctor."

"I'm going to," his father said. "The office doesn't open for an hour."

"You *really* drove around until the donut shop opened?" Otis prodded as he ate.

"I know it sounds silly, but I wanted to treat you two. Like I said, when your pain gets really bad, sometimes you've just gotta do something good."

"Well...thanks," he muttered.

Otis hurried back upstairs before the conversation continued.

He went into his room and shut the door. He sat on the bed and peered out the window.

His tears came to greet the coming of the day.

24

Garcia walked back to the station in a sleepwalk. Local reporters shouted over each other. Sheriff Connors ignored their questions. Lt. Billings held the door open for them.

Once it shut, the three of them could breathe again.

"I gotta make some calls," Sheriff Connors said. "You two, report to my office in five."

Both lieutenants nodded. Sheriff Connors stormed off. Billings rubbed his eyes; he looked half in the bag and double dead-dog tired. "That went OK, as far as those things go."

"OK?" she scoffed. "Did you not hear that idiot call the Lusher kids out on live TV? Sheriff Connors didn't refute her either. Who knows what kind of hell they're gonna get."

"Yeah," he admitted. "Sucks for the kids, but it works in our favor. The perp will think our attention's elsewhere."

"It *is* elsewhere," she snapped.

"It's called thinking strategically, Garcia. You should try it sometime."

She didn't reply. Billings walked to the cubicle where the tip line was set up. She wanted to take a mock smoke break, but she couldn't go back outside. So she stormed into her backup sanctuary—the bathroom. It stank of lemon-scented cleaner but was blessedly deserted.

Garcia turned on the faucet, cupped her hands, and splashed water onto her face. The cold revived her a little. She dabbed her face with a paper towel then looked at herself in the mirror.

Exhaustion was her most pronounced feature.

She'd gotten about thirty minutes of sleep before the call came in. Sheriff Connors told her the search party found a body. Thank God the civilian volunteers had gone home by then.

"What God?" she imagined the girl's corpse asking. If it still had a mouth.

Garcia longed for a drink or a drug or a lobotomy to erase the image of Carrie Clemmons.

The girl, not even two hundred yards from the road. The girl in the costume she wore when she was a person, not a thing. The dead grass around the dead girl bubbling white from all the bleach. One eyeball hanging from the socket, the other popped like a water balloon—

"Garcia!" Billings yelled through the door.

She jumped. Water splashed onto her uniform. "One minute," she called back.

With the water still running, she shut her eyes and granted herself a moment to recharge. She thought about her daughter. She saw Ruby playing in the leaves, her black hair striking against the colorful foliage, her smile as pure as young love. She had the overwhelming urge to call her—she physically *ached* to hear her little girl's voice—but it was too early, it was too dangerous, and there was still too much to do.

She locked Ruby inside her heart and returned to the business at hand. She cut off the water and looked back at the mirror. Her reflection wasn't as downtrodden as it had been a moment ago. Her "don't fuck with me" je ne sais quoi was back in full force.

Lt. Elena Garcia looked back in control.

She left the bathroom. Billings waited in the hall, holding two fresh cups of coffee. He handed her a mug, and they walked toward Sheriff Connors's office.

"I know things are bleak when you're getting me coffee."

"We need all the energy we can get," he said. "Negative or otherwise."

They toasted to the sentiment. A moment later, they turned the corner that led to the sheriff's office. His door was open. He stood behind his desk massaging his temples. Billings knocked on the doorframe and entered first. Garcia shut it behind her.

"I just spoke with Doc Resnik," the sheriff groaned. "The girl's folks had to be physically restrained after identifying her. They tried to stop Resnik from doin' an autopsy. They're chock-full of sedatives now, sharing a room at St. Mary's."

Billings whistled—*yikes*!

"Does Doctor Resnik have preliminaries yet?" Garcia asked.

"Dead less than twenty-four hours," Sheriff Connors said. "Killed somewhere else and dumped. Total of thirty-one lacerations to the face, head, and neck...thirteen skull fractures, plus a broken nose and jaw from the force of the blows. Her tongue is gone, but she could've bitten it off herself during the struggle. No sign of sexual assault. Body was doused in household cleaning bleach after the fact. He *did* find some skin beneath her fingernails, which he's already sent out for processing. The girl fought back...but she never stood a goddamn chance."

"Well, that ain't good," Billings said.

"Thanks for pointing that out, Lt. Obvious," Sheriff Connors sneered. "Now, where are you at with the tip line? Anything worthwhile coming in?"

"Just a couple prank calls so far," he said. "But it'll pick up once the news circulates. Mathers and Smith are pulling security footage from the credit union and the truck stop on Rosemont. Those are the only cameras within five miles of the shopping center."

Sheriff Connors nodded. He looked to Garcia for an update.

"I've had Jones and Kern canvasing the overpass since last night," she said. "If the girl was there, they would have seen her. They'll have interviewed everyone who frequents the spot by the end of the day. Sgt. Coffey is staking Eugene Palmer's residence, but it's going on twenty-four hours, so I'd like to send Aldridge down there to relieve him —"

"Dammit!" Sheriff Connors yelled. "I told you to pull him off that snipe hunt before ya left the station last night!"

"Sir," she said, her resolve and frustration audible, "Palmer is the only lead we have. He was in the vicinity and is *obsessed* with Harlan Lusher, who killed in a similar fashion. I know there's not a judge in the county who'll issue a warrant without your go-ahead, so I'm *begging*, get me into that house before another girl's murdered for no good reason... *sir*."

Sheriff Connors turned red. His nose flared like a bull. He opened his mouth to lash out, and Garcia braced for it—but he stopped himself. He took what passed for a calming breath.

"So," he said, "you had eyes on Eugene Palmer all night...was there any movement? Did he leave his house at any time to dump the girl's body?"

"No," she admitted, "but he could have moved it earlier—"

"You're grasping, Lieutenant." he said. "If you remove the BSS-worship angle, ya ain't got enough on Eugene Palmer to justify a search warrant."

She looked to Billings for help. He sipped his coffee. She turned back to the sheriff.

"But—"

"Ain't good for nothin' except shit," he snapped.

Billings laughed. She clenched her fists.

"Get me a reason, and I'll get ya a warrant," Sheriff Connors offered. "But for now, y'all get the hell outta my office and get to work. We've got a killer out there runnin' wild...it's time we put this mad dog down."

25

Jane's breath was steady, but her desperation was audible, like a freight train pushing up an incline. Hot pokers stabbed at her calves and thighs. Sandpaper rubbed her lungs raw. Acid inched from her stomach to her throat. Jane hadn't gone running for a week, and she was paying for it now.

The early afternoon sun was strong enough to offset the chill in the air. Still, she stayed out of the shadows as she cut through the vacant lot and into the southern entrance of Parthenon Place. She had to push harder on the gravel, but she didn't mind. This road would lead her home.

She'd mapped out the five-mile run on the fly, forgoing her normal route so she could avoid the school and downtown. If it wasn't for Coach Harris, Jane would be in her bedroom hiding beneath the sheets, zonked on Valium. But the unexpected phone call from her soccer coach challenged Jane to forego her chemical cover and try a different coping strategy.

Coach Harris rang late in the morning, once it was clear Jane wasn't coming to school: *This is real talk, and if you repeat it to anyone, I'll deny every word. What happened to Carrie is horrible, and she didn't deserve it ... but she was a cruel person, Jane. She tormented you in life; don't give her the power to torment you in death. Your scholarship offers will be finalized any day now. This town's full of ghosts—you've got to stay focused if you ever want to leave them behind.*

Coach Harris was right. Carrie would've loved the power to bully from the grave.

Screw that, Jane thought. She kicked into high gear. A trail of dust rose in her wake, a gravely veil to conceal the hopelessness around her. She ran faster, past the last of the trailers, across the road, and into their front yard. She stopped where Mammaw usually parked.

Jane panted. Hard. She webbed her fingers behind her head and arched her back.

"You better get inside before ya get sick," Henry yelled.

She hadn't noticed him sitting on the porch. She staggered forward, legs burning, interlocked hands resting on her wet hair. Henry had a book in his hands and something shiny in his lap. It wasn't until she reached him that she realized it was the gun.

"Jesus," she said, almost tripping. "What are you doin' with that?"

"Don't worry, it's not loaded. Mammaw had to go to a doctor's appointment. Told me to keep watch, scare off any local news nutlickers dumb enough to come to the house."

"At least she didn't tell you to shoot them," Jane said, opening the screen.

"I asked. She figured they ain't worth the bullet."

After her cardiology appointment, Mammaw planned on doing nothing besides running over to the Piggly Wiggly and buying a frozen pizza for the kids. But when she hit the red light on Sixth Avenue, a mere *two blocks* from the sheriff's station, she couldn't resist the urge to give Sheriff Connors the epic ass-ripping he deserved. She cut right on red and floored it down Main Street.

"How dare Connors let them drag our babies through the mud," she asked Gravy, who was enjoying the side-window view, "like they ain't got it hard enough around here."

When she turned on State Street, she saw news vans lining the station house like a barricade. Newscasters and camera crews loitered, spraying hair and smoking cigarettes. There was no way she could get inside the building without making things even worse for the kids.

"Screw 'em all," she said to the dog. Gravy panted in agreement. She honked as she passed the no-talent news hacks to make sure they saw her giving them the finger.

Three blocks later, the news vans dwindled and the sidewalks were empty again. The bookstore was up ahead, and there was a space right in front. Mammaw decided she may as well take the opportunity to thank Ms. Summers for sticking up for Jane. She eased into the space, cracking the windows before killing the engine. She patted Gravyboat on the head.

"Keep an eye on the car, baby. I won't be a minute."

She got out and walked beneath the awning of the Book Nook. An overhead chime announced her. Mammaw found Ms. Summers—whom she'd only met in passing—reading a hardcover at the counter.

"Hi," Mammaw said. "You may not remember me. I'm—"

"Betty." She smiled. "Of course I remember you!"

"The sheriff lady told Jane ya took up for her the other day," Mammaw said, "so I wanted to stop in and tell you how much we all appreciate it."

"Oh, of course," she said. "I care for Jane very much."

"She feels the same way 'bout you. But anyhow, I'll let ya get back to it—just wanted to say thanks."

Before she could turn around, Ms. Summers raised a halting hand.

"Actually, Betty, I'm glad you're here. There's something I need to tell you."

Mammaw's eyebrows arched. Before she could respond, a customer approached the counter with two paperback books. Mammaw stepped back to wait the woman out.

Ms. Summers worked the register. As she rang up the customer, her glasses slid to the tip of her nose. Mammaw couldn't help but be fascinated by her eye. A lazy eye, they used to call it, but it didn't look lazy to her. It looked clouded and dead, the eye of a taxidermy panther.

Early glaucoma, she realized. *Poor woman. I should put her in touch with my dealer . . .*

Ms. Summers bagged the woman's books and bid her goodbye. The door chimed, and they were alone. She adjusted her glasses as Mammaw stepped to the register.

"Thanks for waiting," Ms. Summers said. "So, I wasn't completely honest when I spoke to Lt. Garcia. You should know that Jane really *did* threaten that girl—"

"Nope," Mammaw said without hesitation. "She would never."

"I agree, it was out of character. I've been dwelling on it, and

I think her attitude shift must have been caused by the medication she takes...drugs can turn a friend into a stranger."

"That they can," Mammaw sighed. "Thanks for tellin' me. I'll keep an eye on her."

She patted Ms. Summers's hand amiably and then headed for the door.

"You should consider taking her off those pills," Ms. Summers urged. "They say blood's the great purifier, and I've found our souls grow uneasy when it's tainted. Chemicals aren't good for anyone. Maybe she should get back into the church. I think the Lord could offer a more permanent peace of mind."

"You let me know next time you see him. I'd like to give him a piece of my own."

Exercise was the ultimate act of self-flagellation. But as Otis steered his bike onto Lockland Street, he wasn't sure which sin he should chastise himself for—thinking his father had lied, or thinking he'd ever been telling the truth. He wished it was easier to give him the benefit of the doubt. His father seemed OK at breakfast (when he showed up) and he (said he) was going to call his doctor. Otis told himself to be reasonable. He told himself to calm down. His emotions were getting the better of him and bringing out the worst.

He coasted to 431 and dismounted at the edge of the yard. He fanned his shirt and caught his breath before pushing the bike through the leaf-strewn grass. As he walked it up to the front porch, he found comfort in the fact that he wasn't alone in his failings of temperament. He could hear Henry and Jane bickering through the screen door.

"I'm not sayin' it to be mean!" Jane was yelling. "But you're more reckless than a drunken tornado! How do you think you're gonna storm a cult when you can't even walk!"

Otis leaned his bike on the side post. He could see them through the mesh: Henry pacing around the living room and Jane pacing around the kitchen, both flailing their arms in frustration.

"I'm not being fuckin' reckless—"

Otis knocked on the door.

Henry spun around lightning quick and raised the gun.

Otis saw the barrel of the .357 in death-o-vision.

Jane screamed. Otis screamed concurrently. His shrill squeal cut above her own. Otis stumbled backward and tripped off the porch. The unraked leaves did little to cushion his fall.

The door opened and Henry ran out. Otis reeled.

"Fuck, man! I'm sorry! I thought you were a reporter!"

Henry still held the gun. Otis stammered mumbo jumbo. His heart palpitated off time.

"It isn't loaded," Henry swore. He flung the chamber open. "See?!"

Jane scoffed as she walked out. "Not reckless, huh? Take the damn gun inside, dumbass."

Henry grumbled but went back into the house. Jane stepped between the lawn gnomes to where Otis lay. She wore jeans and a T-shirt. No eyeliner. No shoes. Her hair was wet from the shower. Leaves crunched beneath her toes.

She looked down at him. "Well, you didn't piss yourself, so at least there's that."

He took her hand when she offered it. Touching a girl made Otis more nervous than facing the barrel of a gun. The realization disturbed him. She pulled him up with a grunt.

He caught his balance. Jane brushed the leaves off his back as they went inside.

"I'm sorry, dude," Henry said, limping over with his hands up to show he was unarmed. "These reporters have my head all jacked up. I'm really, *really* sorry, Big Man."

"It's OK," Otis said. "I should expect you to knock me on my butt at *least* once a week."

Henry smiled and gave Otis a comradely slap on the back.

Jane sighed. "Things are getting out of control."

"That's why we need to do somethin' *now*," Henry said, "before they get worse."

"Going to Lordsville and waving a gun around will *make* it worse!" Jane yelled.

Otis sat at the table to avoid getting sucked into their argument. They joined him instead.

"Tell her," Henry pleaded with Otis. "If the *real* BSS killed Carrie, we need to get to Lordsville before they trash the evidence. Pearl Jolley's old, but she ain't dumb."

"No," Jane ordered Otis. "Tell this idiot if BSS is there, we'd be walking into a death trap."

"I'll tell you both *this*…there is a real chance BSS is tied to Lordsville. But we have no indication he's tied to Carrie Clemmons. It would be counterintuitive to link the cases together."

"But they *are* linked," Jane said. "They're linked by us, me and Henry."

Otis couldn't argue. "OK, say BSS *did* kill Carrie. Why? It's totally against his MO."

Henry actually raised his hand. Otis pointed to him.

"Maybe he realized the cops are lookin' for a copycat, so he wanted to switch things up."

"Or maybe he was at the podcast," Jane said, "and hearing our dad get credit for *his* murders made him lose control. Maybe Carrie was just an easy spur-of-the-moment target."

Otis was impressed. He hadn't thought of that.

"It's possible," he said. "If BSS slipped up that bad, it's only a matter of time before he loses control completely. That's why the three of us have got to stay focused. If we want to succeed where the police failed the first time around, we have to resist acting on emotion. We have to stick to the plan, all the way. Our thinking has to be rational, not rushed. OK?"

"OK," Jane said.

"Yeah, yeah," Henry groaned. "You're right. OK."

"Were you able to get me on you father's visitation list?"

"Yeah," Henry said. "Visitation days are Tuesdays and Saturdays. Mammaw can give us a ride on either one. We can also call Dad if that's easier, but it'll be expensive if you wanna talk to him for more than a couple minutes."

"In person would be better," Otis said. "Could we go tomorrow?"

"Sure, man."

"Good. Thank you both for trusting me with this. I'll do my best not to let you down."

His sudden sincerity quieted things.

Jane shifted in her seat. "What if Dad doesn't know anything? What'll we do then? Hide out until someone gets arrested for Carrie's murder? If my attendance drops, I'll get benched. These college scouts might need to see me play again before making a scholarship offer..."

"Don't worry," Henry told her. "If we don't get anything from Dad, Otis will take his theories to the cops, and we'll hope for the best. Won't ya, Big Man?"

"Sure," Otis said, "straight to Lt. Garcia. As soon as we talk to your father."

"You'll still get your scholarship, drama queen. Give him a chance to do his thing."

"OK." Jane nodded. "You're right. No point in having our own Walker, Texas Ranger, if we don't give him room to work."

"Thank ya kindly, ma'am," Otis said, attempting a redneck drawl.

Henry laughed. Jane laughed. Otis smiled and begrudgingly admitted his father had been honest about one thing: the best way to relieve your pain was relieving the pain of others.

But good deeds—like good drugs—are a temporary comfort.

The higher the crest, the steeper the comedown.

Below him, the darkness loomed.

26

How much dirt is enough dirt to warrant a warrant?

Garcia hunched over the desk, her frustration lit by the glow of the computer screen. She ran a hand through her unwashed hair. She sipped her two hundredth cup of coffee. She brooded.

She *needed* that warrant.

She *needed* into Eugene Palmer's house.

All other investigative avenues were blurs in her mind—she had to see inside the haunted house before she could consider other possibilities, other suspects, other narratives. If she was still with CPD, she already would've kicked in his door. But Garcia had sacrificed too much for her rank to risk losing it on a violation. She needed a clean solve...yet the case was a mess.

She followed up with Carrie Clemmons's friends, and none had seen Eugene Palmer at the podcast. He had no priors. No family. Nothing but a small inheritance and an online store—Creepy Collectables. She checked it out. He sold trinkets from killers and victims alike. Funeral pamphlets, rare items (a turtleneck worn by Ted Bundy listed for $1,050.00, plus shipping).

THINK! He lives in a haunted house. There must be other ways inside. THINK!

Think hidden passages, think secret doors...

Think obvious ones.

"Thank you for seeing me, Mr. Lusher."

"Happy I could pencil you in."

Garcia smiled politely. Harlan Lusher smiled back. They sat across from each other in Salem Hill's one-on-one interview room. A guard was posted outside. Lusher was in shackles.

"You and Jane have the same smile," she said.

"My daughter?" His ankle restraints scratched the cement floor as he shot upright.

"I met her, and your son," she said. "They seem like sweet kids."

"I'm sorry, *how* exactly do you know them?"

"One of their schoolmates was murdered on Saturday, a girl on Jane's soccer team. She and the victim supposedly got into an altercation a few hours before—"

"Jane would never hurt anyone!"

"I agree." Garcia nodded. "But the victim was stabbed through the eyes..."

Clock the genuine distress on his face...

He may be a psycho killer, but at least he loves his kids.

"Obviously," she continued, "the sooner I clear her and your son, the better for all of us."

"What can I do?" he urged. "How can I help?"

"Do you ever get fan mail? People asking about the specifics of your crimes?"

"I couldn't *give* specifics," he snapped. "I'm innocent. I didn't kill anyone."

"But you know what I mean."

"I get a lot of disturbing letters from a lot of disturbed people. I rarely bother reading them, and I never write back."

"Have you ever been contacted by a man named Eugene Palmer?"

Clock that arched eyebrow. He knows the name . . .

"I complained to Warden O'Neil about that guy months ago," he said. "They finally quit sending his letters through. I'm not sure how they got past the sorting team in the first place."

"He wrote to you?" she asked.

"Continuously—"

"Did he ever ask for advice?" Garcia urged. "Did he ever say he was planning anything?"

"He mentioned the murders, of course. But as far as planning . . . no. I got the impression Eugene is a very sick man. I couldn't make heads or tails of his letters. It was all nonsense."

"Do you still have them?" she asked. She was coming off as overly eager. She didn't care.

"I keep every letter I get. The hate mail too. I alphabetize them by last name, by zip code, by the number of letters *in* each name . . . you've got to get creative to pass the time."

She nodded and then stood to notify the guard.

"Lieutenant . . ."

She turned back to him.

"Please, don't let them do to her what they did to me." His eyes took on a teardrop gleam.

She clocked it then turned away.

Thirty-seven letters in five years. She only had to read three of them over the phone before Sheriff Connors agreed to get the warrant; Eugene's letter about the ideal body type of "flesh slaves" put the sheriff over the fence. He set a meeting with Judge West and expected to have the necessary paperwork signed by the end of the day. The search would be *tonight*.

When Garcia left Salem Hill, she left victorious.

The road back to Paradise took her directly through Charleston. Earlier, she'd been too focused on interview prep to let passing her hometown bother her, but now the gold-flaked dome of the capitol seemed like a beacon highlighting her failures as both a parent and a spouse. She should have come yesterday. She should have been there with Craig and Ruby.

The job held her back just as the job now pushed her through.

"Screw this," she said, and took exit 6 before she could change her mind.

Garcia slowed as she veered off the interstate. She checked the time—five past noon. She felt like she'd *earned* the right to bring her daughter lunch before going back to the station. She merged into traffic and headed toward Ruby's school.

Every street sign read Memory Lane. There, on her left— The Dairy Dip, Ruby's favorite ice-cream shop—and there, one block up—Rocco's Little Italy, where Craig took her on their first date—and there, and there, and there, and there. She pulled into the Frost-Top drive-through and ordered two number twos. She got herself a Diet Coke and ordered Ruby two milkshakes; one for yesterday, one for today. She pulled out of the parking lot with the greasy treasures in tow.

She reached Jefferson Heights Elementary a minute later. The fourth and fifth graders were at recess when she pulled up to the curb. The kids rubbernecked when she got out. She relished the pliable smiles of the girls who watched her walk from the cruiser. The boys wore that "cootie carriers can be cops?" look of astonishment on their faces.

She nodded hello before entering the building.

The high-pitched squeals of children echoed down the halls. The school was decked out for Halloween; ghosts, vampires, werewolves, goblins, and other kid-friendly killers spooked up the décor. A woman speaking with the front office receptionist noticed Garcia enter.

"Can I help you, Officer?" she asked.

"Hi, maybe. I'm Elena Garcia, Ruby Garcia-Jackson's mom. I was in the area and thought I'd pop in and have lunch with her."

"How nice! Ruby's a sweetheart. I'm Miss Kaylan, the librarian."

She extended her hand, but Garcia's were full of food and drink.

"Duh," Miss Kaylan scoffed at herself. "Come on, I bet we can catch Ruby in the lunch line. This is my free period, so y'all are welcome to eat in the library. The cafeteria gets rowdy."

"That would be great," Garcia said. "Thank you so much."

She followed the stranger down the hall of horrors, smiling all the way.

They sat at a reading table, boxed in by small bookshelves meant for small arms. Ruby slurped down her second milkshake. Garcia watched the event as if it were the Second Coming of Christ, eternally awestruck that someone so lovely was born unto someone so lacking.

Ruby's milkshake puttered out. She gave it one last pull and then came up for air with a strawberry burp. Garcia didn't chastise her—that belch was the song of the angels.

"Which did you like best," she asked, "chocolate or strawberry?"

"Chocolate," Ruby said, with a decisive nod. "Strawberry's good, but pink is for girls."

Garcia laughed. She reached across the table and held Ruby's little hands.

"I've missed you so much, chiqui."

"I miss you and Daddy misses you. He's sad all the time."

"We'll be together soon," she sighed. "Tell your daddy I miss him right back—"

"No," she snapped, pulling her hands away. "*You* have to tell him! You have to come home."

Garcia moved to the seat beside her daughter and wrapped an arm around her waist. Ruby resisted for moment, then relented. She burrowed deep into her mother's side.

"I know how hard this is. It's hard for me too. I'll talk to Daddy, and we'll get it worked out. We'll all be back together soon, I promise."

"Will you talk to him today?" Ruby asked. Her voice was muffled by Garcia's shirt.

All responses were inadequate. Garcia focused her attention away to keep herself from crying. She stared at the wall across from them and emotionally regrouped, reading a display that said: SPOOKY STORIES FOR BOYS & GHOULS! The wall was decorated with Halloween book suggestions. *The Legend of*

Sleepy Hollow. Don't Open the Door! Little Red Riding Hood. The Berenstain Bears and the Spooky Old Tree. Stuff like that.

"Hey, chiqui," Garcia said, "remember when we read *Little Red Riding Hood?*"

She felt Ruby nodding—*yes.*

"Well…there's a real wolf, like the wolf in the story, that lives in the woods outside of town. That's why Mommy couldn't come yesterday. It's Mommy's job to find that big bad wolf and stop him before he tricks any girls the way he tricked Red and her grandma."

"Make someone else do it," Ruby whined. "And you come home."

"Mommy wishes she could," Garcia said. "But it's my job to keep the woods safe, for everyone. As soon as I catch this ugly old wolf, we can all be together. Me, you, and Daddy."

"Do you have an ax?" Ruby sniffled, finally looking up at her mom.

"What?" she asked.

"The hunter in the story has a big ax. The hunter who catches the wolf."

"Oh," Garcia said. "Yes, chiqui, Mommy has a big ax."

"Is it really sharp? Sharper than sharp?"

"Baby, it's even sharper than that."

27

Born into existence with no purpose other than to be erased from existence.

The girl was not *the* girl. She was nothing but a child of annihilation.

She was not special. She was not marked.

She was not worthy.

She was a mistake—*no*—a response—*no*—a catharsis—*no*—she was a casualty of rage. The Bridge of Death had been tainted by those nakedly foolish police. They alone were to blame. They'd stopped the driver from finding *her*. They'd forced the driver into the Land of the Living. They'd forced the driver to lose control. They'd forced the driver to take the girl.

Now everything had changed.

Now the world was a dangerous place.

Sundown cast Paradise in the fiery light of judgment. The driver squinted through the tinted windshield and agonized. The reality of the situation was that it was time to disappear.

It was time to go to ground. That was the only option. Control had to be reestablished.

But she *is still out there walking this evil, desperate place!*

Was there a Faustian bargain to be made for the soul of another?

Introspection followed. Raw veracity led to righteous reclamation.

The driver smiled into the horizon. The dusk gleamed redder than Revelations.

A single star appeared in the burning heavens, a virgin jewel of light.

It was a hopeful sign. The driver would find her this time. It was meant to be.

The car hunted the haunted highway, waiting for night to come.

28

The Search turned into the Stakeout. The Stakeout turned into Snooze Central. Garcia leaned on the wheel of the Crown Vic, drinking lukewarm coffee and squinting through the darkness at Eugene Palmer's haunted house. Sgt. Coffey dozed in the kicked-back shotgun seat. Jones and Kern were positioned on the opposite end of the block. Garcia set her cup on the dash. She reached into her pocket and rubbed the warrant between her fingers, feeling the power of it.

The search warrant. She'd finally gotten it—only to learn Sheriff Connors had pulled her surveillance while she was at Salem Hill. Now Eugene Palmer was in the wind.

She wanted to pry open the door, but the sheriff ordered them to wait an hour and see if he showed. Better to nab him while they retained some element of surprise; if this turned into a full-on manhunt, they'd have to call the state troopers and the FBI. Sheriff Connors and Mayor Jolley didn't want any outside interference. They wanted a "big win" under their belts (next year was an election year, after all). It was an asinine move that had the department spread thin.

She checked the time. They'd waited forty-nine minutes.

Suddenly—*Clock that moving shadow. A car, sans headlights, creeping this way . . .*

She nudged Coffey awake. He straightened up and cleared his throat.

"There," she said.

"You think it's him?"

"I think it must be."

It was. The car pulled straight into the yard and parked next to the storm cellar. A shadowed figure got out and moved to the back of the car. The figure opened the trunk.

Garcia radioed Jones and Kern. "That's him. Approach on foot. Don't spook him."

"Yes, ma'am. Over."

She looked at Coffey. He looked at her. They got out.

The night was thick with the smell of burning leaves. The wind whispered in a dead tongue. It was a spookified scene. They eased the doors of the Crown Vic shut and then moved toward the house. Garcia zeroed in on the figure—it had to be Eugene Palmer.

Clock him lifting something big out of the trunk . . .

Something that's about the shape of a body . . .

The jingle of his keys as he walks onto the porch . . .

Now—while he's distracted!

Garcia broke into a jog. Coffey followed suit. She drew her weapon. Coffey did the same.

"Sheriff's Department! Don't move, Mr. Palmer!"

Eugene Palmer didn't turn around. He opened the door. He walked into the house.

"Eugene Palmer! Freeze!" she yelled, louder this time. He shut the door. The lights in the foyer flipped on.

"Goddammit," she groaned, as they reached the yard.

Jones and Kern caught up a moment later, panting.

"What's the word?" Kern asked.

"Cover the back," she said. "Jones, cover the cellar over there. We'll take the porch."

Kern moved out. Jones moved out. She and Coffey moved forward.

The porch light was off. The glow from the foyer filtered through the dirty living room window, barely lighting their way. She posted to the left of the door. He posted up on the right.

She pounded the wood. "Eugene Palmer! This is Lt. Garcia, Sheriff's Department! We have a warrant to search the premises! Open the door!"

Five seconds—nothing.

She pounded harder. She repeated her order. Nothing.

"Fuck this," she said, nodding to Coffey.

He took a step back and squared off to kick the door in.

Then the porch light came on. *Clamp! Crank! Click!* The locks unlocked.

Coffey moved to the side. Their gun safeties clicked off.

When Eugene opened the door, he was fiddling with his hearing aid. He feigned shock at the sight of them, tripping backward over himself. He was unarmed, as far as Garcia could tell. His jeans were unbuttoned. His shoes were unlaced. His T-shirt said HARLAN LUSHER FAN CLUB. The shirt had been autographed.

"Lieutenant?" Eugene stammered. "Can I, I, uh, h-help you?"

"Why didn't you halt when we announced ourselves?" she asked.

"Oh God, I m-m-must not have heard," he stammered. "My hearing aid died while I was out. I just replaced the b-b-battery."

He took the device from his ear and showed them.

She took the warrant from her pocket and showed him. "We have a warrant to search the premises." She pushed him aside before he could respond. She moved through the foyer and into the living room. She flipped on the light.

Coffey whistled for the others and then followed Garcia in. He took Eugene's arm and led him into the living room. The couch was covered in stacks of magazines bundled together— *Lust & Leather, Bound Monthly, Tied & True.*

"Those aren't m-mine," Eugene said. "I mean, technically they are, but I s-s-sell them on the website. They're the *exact* issues Dennis Rader k-k-kept in his hideaway."

Coffey cringed.

"Get comfortable," Garcia said to Eugene.

He sat down beside the magazines as the other officers entered the house. Their noses creased and their faces read G-R-O-S-S as they came into the living room. They holstered their weapons and took in the scene.

"Kern, stay with Mr. Palmer," Garcia ordered. "Jones, you start on this floor. The three of us will sweep the upstairs together once Sgt. Coffey and I clear the basement."

"Don't g-g-go down there," Eugene pled. "There's rats everywhere and they, they could get up here and...th-th-these are priceless collectables, I can't have v-v-vermin crawling all over them! Please, th-this is my *job*, you c-c-can't—"

Garcia ignored him. She walked into the foyer and lifted the padlock on the basement door. She turned back to the living room. Eugene's eyes were bulging.

"Eugene, please open this door."

"I d-don't have a key. The key. I l-l-lost it. I'm sorry."

She nodded to Coffey. He hurried outside. Garcia went back into the living room and sat across from Eugene. Kern put on blue latex gloves and got to work.

"Is this because of th-the knife?" Eugene asked. "It's upst-st-stairs, I can go get it..."

"We'll get to the knife," she said. "But first, tell me why you don't want us down in that basement? This will go a lot easier for you if you start being honest now—"

"Don't touch that!" Eugene squealed suddenly. His eyes were on Kern, who was inspecting the clown painting in the dining room. "That's worth forty thousand dollars. John Wayne Gacy painted it."

"Bullshit," Kern scoffed.

Eugene flinched when he pulled it off the wall to inspect the back.

"Lots of accidents happen during searches," Garcia said. "The less you tell us, the longer we stay, and the clumsier we tend to get. So, tell me about the basement. Tell me about Carrie Clemmons."

"I don't have anything to tell," he muttered.

Coffey entered the house with a flashlight and a crowbar.

Garcia shrugged at Eugene—*tough luck*. She stood up.

"Pop it," she ordered, walking into the hall.

Coffey handed her the flashlight, then dug the curved end of the crowbar beneath the latch. Eugene dropped his head into his hands. The latch snapped with one good heave, sending splinters flying. The door creaked open. The stench of the house magnified. They reeled back.

"Watch him," she reiterated to Jones.

He nodded as he covered his nose and mouth. She put on

her latex gloves. Coffey did the same. She found a light switch. She flipped it—dim amber flickered on somewhere downstairs, illuminating the floor directly below them. The sight made her physically gag.

The basement was littered with rats. Dead rats. Crushed in their traps.

Some of the rats were covered in maggots. Some were nothing but dust and bones.

Garcia turned on the flashlight and started down the stairs. She tuned out the rotting rodents and focused on the rest of the unfinished basement as it came into view.

Clock the tools in the corner...

Clock the door to the right, probably a wine cellar...

Clock the—

Vanity. The overhead bulb reflected off a vanity dresser and the matching full-size mirror beside it. Garcia dodged rat traps as she crossed the room. She could hear Coffey behind her. When she reached the vanity she nearly tripped over her feet, which felt shakier by the step. The vanity mirror was covered in photographs of Sheena Wiseman.

Sheena in high school. Sheena at a party. Sheena dead in her crime-scene photos.

"Holy hell," Coffey whispered. "You were right."

She pointed the flashlight at the wine cellar. Coffey followed her over. Something went *squish* beneath her bootheel. She grimaced and kept going. When she reached the door, she pulled her gun and stepped aside. Coffey nodded. He grabbed the handle and pulled...

Their jaws dropped low enough to reach rat shit.

Three body bags hung from the ceiling. Three full sets of outfits hung beside each one, draped in protective plastic. The first outfit was identical to what Sheena Wiseman wore in one of the photos on the vanity. Coffey pointed to the ground. She lowered the light.

There was a fourth body bag on the floor. Clothing lay beside it, hastily discarded. It was the nun costume Carrie Clemmons breathed her last bloody breath in.

She steadied the light. Coffey stepped into the wine cellar and kneeled beside the bag. He pinched the zipper and pulled—not all the way, just wide enough to see inside.

"Christ!" he screamed. He fell on his butt.

Garcia *willed* herself into the wine cellar. She knelt beside Coffey. She spread open the unzipped portion of the bag.

Red lips parted before her, wordless.

Eye sockets opened before her, blind.

Fair skin glistened before her, lifeless.

She removed one of her gloves and ran her finger across the dead, rubbery lips.

Her hand shook uncontrollably. Her mind struggled to grasp the scene.

In the darkness beneath the staircase, a chorus of rats sang.

29

They were fake. Four full face and body suits made of latex, wearable skin of the female form. Each costume had a different make, a different hairstyle, a different skin tone. The zippers ran down the back of the face masks, cutting between the shoulder blades like funeral jackets.

One of the costumes looked disturbingly similar to Sheena Wiseman. One looked like Michelle Wilcox. Ditto, Steph Jenson. The suit that had been discarded on the floor was a Rubbermaid doppelgänger of Carrie Clemmons. It was surreal. They had to be custom made.

The suits were now at the crime lab in Charleston, along with the coinciding outfits, Eugene Palmer's car, and his black-market ritual knife. The only thing not at the lab was the "Sheena Wiseman" face mask, which Sheriff Buck Connors held in his hands.

It was going on 3:00 a.m. The children were nestled all snug in their beds, while Garcia stood in the observation room with the sheriff and Lt. Billings. She was feeling all sorts of twisted up. Her instincts had proven correct, and it was one fucked-up affirmation.

Eugene Palmer hadn't resisted arrest or asked for a lawyer. He hadn't said a word. They snuck him into the back of the station house to keep the press from catching his scent. Now she watched him through the two-way mirror while Billings researched the bodysuits.

"OK, y'all," he said, squinting at his phone, "Google gave me this... *living dolls*. It seems like a sex thing. There's a bunch of websites that let you customize the skin costumes."

"You're sayin' this is just some kink?" Sheriff Connors asked uncomfortably.

"No," Garcia said. "These costumes may be made for fetishists, but that's not why Eugene collects them. To him, they aren't costumes or sexual objects. They're trophies."

The two men turned to her.

"He was obsessed with Sheena Wiseman," she explained, "but too scared to act on his impulses. Sheena seemed untouchable, until Harlan Lusher proved otherwise... that kind of power must have been intoxicating to Eugene. He already admits it's what spurred his fixation with Lusher. So, when he randomly got a chance to acquire one of Lusher's ritual knives, it must have been like a revelation. How could he *not* see it as destiny urging him to take up the baton?"

"And pick up where Lusher left off?" Billings asked.

"Right." She nodded. "But unlike Lusher, Eugene doesn't have a secondary location to keep his kills. So, my guess is, these latex costumes are stand-in souvenirs. Harlan Lusher kept the bones; this is Eugene's way of keeping the skin."

"Christ on the goddamn cross," Connors said, shivering. "If these are trophies, and one's supposed to be Carrie Clemmons...that leaves three others."

Billings pointed to the mask. "That's Sheena Wiseman."

"Two, then."

"My guess is, the others are Steph Jenson and Michelle Wilcox," Garcia said. "Sorry."

Connors sighed and dropped his head. Garcia looked back at Eugene. He was hunched over the table, shaking slightly. His skin looked waxy and green beneath the harsh florescent lights. Suddenly, Connors's thick hand gripped her shoulder.

She turned. Their eyes locked.

"Fine work, Garcia," he said. "I couldn't see it at first, but...*damn* fine work, girl."

"Here, here," Billings seconded, raising his coffee mug.

"Thanks," she said, and tried not to blush.

"Now," the sheriff said, clearing his throat, "can we pull a confession outta this twerp?"

"Not if he's anything like Harlan Lusher," Billings said.

"Give him a go," Connors told him. "Let's find out."

"I say send in Garcia. She's top cop today."

Garcia wasn't surprised that they *thought* she was a better cop than them, but she was shocked either were willing to admit it. She held out her hand—*gimme*. Connors tossed her the latex mask. She walked into the hall and shut the door behind her. She cut left, toward the interrogation room, summoning psych-up slogans as she walked.

You're badder than Bad Lieutenant...*you're badder* than Bad Lieutenant...

She reached the door. She took a calming breath.

She whispered, "You're badder than bad."

She walked in. Eugene Palmer looked up from the table.

He saw the mask. His eyes dropped back down.

She shut the door and eased over. She played it cool.

"Hello again, Eugene. Do you need anything? Coffee? Soda?"

No answer. She slid into the chair across from him, mask in her lap.

"Is it still OK if I call you Eugene? I hate the formalities involved with crap like this."

"Yes, I, I," he mumbled, "I don't m-mind."

"Great. Thanks. You can call me Elena if you want."

He shifted in his seat. He wouldn't meet her eyes.

"Hey, now," she said, "don't be nervous. I come bearing good news. Your serial killer collection just *doubled* in value! Those letters you sent Harlan Lusher are going to be worth more than Apple stock here in a few years, I bet."

"I d-d-don't understand."

"What's not to understand? It's written right there on your shirt. You, Eugene Palmer, will be known for all time as Harlan Lusher's protégé...or, at the very least, like one of those cheesy tribute bands. Let's call you BSS Lite."

"What?! Huh?! No!" He looked up, eyes bulging. "I'm not anything l-l-like that!"

She slammed the mask on the table. He jerked back as if he'd been punched.

"You were obsessed with Sheena Wiseman," she said. "Or in love, or whatever you told yourself to justify your fixation...but then Harlan Lusher came along and did what you couldn't. *He got the girl.* And you got yourself a new obsession to put in her place."

"No..."

"You studied him," she continued. "You collected his belong-ings as if they had magic powers. Then your cousin came along with the Lordsville knife. That must have been like finding the Holy Grail for you, Eugene!"

"I d-d-didn't," he stammered. "It w-wasn't that way..."

"The knife made it all so clear. You were meant to pick up where your hero left off. So, you hunted addicts, girls on the road. You took them in, you sliced them up, just like Harlan—"

"No!"

"Bullshit, Eugene! You kept your rubber trophies because you don't have the *balls* to keep the real thing! How many girls did you leave out there to rot in the wild? Four? Five? You shouldn't have gone to the podcast. It made you too excitable, made you sloppy. It's *easy* to get away with killing drug addicts. But killing a high school girl...that wasn't so smart—"

"NO! NO! NO! NO!" He pounded his hands on the table, coming halfway out of his seat.

She leaned back. She kept calm. She gave him a moment to settle.

"OK," she said coolly. "Tell me what I got wrong."

He took a shaky breath. He stared at the mask.

"I can't," he muttered. "I'm not even w-w-worthy to speak on it."

His eyes stayed fixed on the mask. Garcia clocked it. She thought it through.

"Would Sheena be able to explain it better?" Garcia whispered.

Eugene nodded, barely. She handed him the mask.

He slid it over his face. Bug eyes filled the dead eyes. The lips shifted into place. He zipped up the back of the mask, and the doll came to life. Garcia gripped her seat to keep from shuddering. She had a feeling the doll noticed, anyway. The dead lips smiled.

"Thank you," the doll said in a gentle, feminine voice. "I feel much better now."

The stutter in Eugene's voice disappeared. His shoulders eased considerably.

"Good," Garcia forced out. "Eugene says you can clear up a few things—"

"It's preposterous to suggest Eugene could follow in Harlan Lusher's footsteps," the doll said. "Mere men cannot simply will themselves to become gods, after all."

"And Harlan Lusher is a god?" Garcia asked.

"Of course. He is one of the Sons of Phlegethon."

"Does Eugene know that?"

"Of course," the doll said again. "He read it in the Zodiac letters. He tried to tell you the day you met. 'Serial killers' are not people. They are Sons of Phlegethon, the rulers of Canto, and they come to this earthly realm to sanctify perfect creatures like me. It is a blessing to be chained to them for eternity. Eugene doesn't want to *be* a god, only to be blessed by one."

"He doesn't want to be Harlan Lusher—"

"He wants to be blessed! To be in the service of the divine . . . but alas, he's not worthy. Not in his grotesque human form. That is why he summons me. Summons us. He dons our skins to become perfect. To become flawless. To become worthy."

"You aren't trophies . . ."

"Together we become worthy!" Eugene's voice began breaking through. The doll. The man. The madness. It all came out in one desperate plea. "Together we are offerings! Flesh slaves worthy of eternity's guilded chains! So we roam the hunting grounds! Calling out to the divine! *Please! K-k-kill us! Kill us now! Please! P-p-please! Oh, benevolent Sons of Phlegethon! Please kill me! Kill us! Embrace us with your doom!!!"*

EPISODE FOUR

Chorus:
"I see Satan coming, honey,
in a big black Cadillac."
—Motörhead

30

Calculus was colorless. Sociology was Snoozeville. Spanish II estaba dos sencillo. Otis was finished with his Tuesday lessons by nine in the morning. It wasn't until recently that he'd recognized the perks of being homeschooled—mainly, freedom. As long as his work got done, he was allowed to do whatever he wanted; it was just that he'd never had a friend in Paradise to do things with. Henry had changed all that. Now, Otis was prepping to meet his *pal* so they could travel to a *prison* and interrogate a convicted freakin' serial *killer*.

Otis ate breakfast and showered, then went back to his room and played the interview out in his mind. He decided to keep his questions broad enough for Harlan to expand on the topics. He wrote them out on a piece of paper, since the guards wouldn't let him bring his iPhone back to the visitation room (they would use Mammaw's old Dictaphone to tape the interview instead). Otis then made a cheat sheet of nonverbal cues that would tell him if his interviewee was lying—looking at the exit, fidgeting, throat clearing, excessive blinking. He'd never interrogated anyone before. He was more excited than he was nervous.

Otis checked the time again. He still had some to kill. He got up to grab his phone from the bed but remembered he'd left it at the breakfast table. But when he walked into the upstairs hall to go get it, his mom's voice gave him pause. It drifted through the open door of her room.

"Maybe he forgot to clock in? He can be very...oh...yes, Mr. Fiorello, I know you took a chance on him. You have my word he would never...I just pray nothing happened to him. It's so violent out there! Oh God, what if...I'm sorry. I don't mean to get so upset..."

Otis forgot about his phone. He slowly walked down the hallway.

"...thank you, Mr. Fiorello. I'll be in touch shortly."

He reached the door as she hung up. She slumped on the edge of the bed in her bathrobe.

Otis stepped into the room. "He didn't go to work last night?"

"Otis," she gasped, "you startled me."

He moved past her, into their bathroom. The orange bottle of painkillers was in the trash, translucent and empty. He walked back to where his mom sat. She looked tired. Sad. Pathetic.

"He didn't go to work?" Otis asked again.

"He missed his shift. I bet his doctor told him to call off, but he forgot to mention it."

"Mom," he sighed, "if that were true, he'd be in bed."

"I'm trying to stay *positive*, OK? I don't want to...oh God. What if he was attacked again?" she muttered. "I should check with the hospitals. St. Mary's, and—"

"You *know* he wasn't attacked!" Otis yelled. "You know

exactly where he is! He's nodded out in his car somewhere. He's acting exactly like he did when he first got pilled out."

"No," she said desperately. "We have to give him the benefit of the doubt. We...no, and I don't appreciate your tone. What happened in Huntington wasn't his fault."

"I'm not talking about what happened in Huntington—I'm talking about Paradise!" Otis yelled. "When does this fall on him? Because you *know* it's gonna fall on us! He's gonna lose *this* job, and we're gonna lose *this* house, and you'll be sitting there acting like everything is—"

She slapped him.

She'd never slapped him. She'd never even spanked him before.

She looked at her son, at her hand, at her son again. The surprise, not the sting, of the slap shut him up. He didn't even feel it. He wore his rage like impenetrable armor. He glared at her.

The irrationality of her denial disgusted him.

He turned and stormed out of the room. She made no attempt to stop him. He huffed downstairs. He paced the living room, clenching and unclenching his fists. He paced the kitchen. He saw his phone on the table—then remembered his plans for the day. Plans that were ruined.

Otis screamed. He knocked over one of the chairs at the kitchen table. It smacked the tile. He threw over another. None of it made him feel better. None of it changed a thing.

He grabbed his phone and trudged back upstairs. He could hear his mom using the chipper tone she always took with receptionists. He ran into his room. He slammed and reslammed the door. Then he dropped into his desk chair, exhausted.

He would never get to interview Harlan Lusher. He knew it. He hated it.

He would never be able to save Henry's father. He couldn't even save his own.

He held back his tears as he dialed. He would give Henry the interview questions and hope he could handle it himself. Otis wondered if he should also give him the nonverbal cues to spot deception but quickly decided there was no point.

Some things are self-evident.

Fathers lie. Sons believe.

Garcia's eyes shot open.

She was on the couch. She must have passed out there at some point in the night. Her eyes burned like hell. Her head throbbed. She groaned as she sat up.

The TV was still on, a game show playing, the volume low. The walls of her living room were bare. Moving boxes were stacked in the corner, unopened. She hadn't seen the point of unpacking any more until Ruby and Craig moved in; no amount of decorating makes an empty house feel like a home.

She forced herself onto her feet and into the kitchen. She got a glass of water, chugged it, and poured herself another. Garcia cursed the whiskey bottle on the counter. She wasn't a big drinker, but last night it had felt necessary. She gulped the water down. She poured a third glass.

She checked the time—10:00 a.m. Her next shift was in five hours, though she didn't feel fit to be on duty. Her equilibrium was misaligned, and now all of her intuitions were in question. She'd been so *sure* Eugene Palmer was her copycat killer.

They still had him in holding. They were still testing his DNA. But he wasn't their guy, and she knew it in her unsettled gut. He was insane and innocent. She was inept and in the weeds. Now she wondered if her theory had been wrong altogether. Maybe none of it was connected. Maybe the woods were *full* of wolves, lone psychotics ravaging one another without reason. Maybe *she* was the one who'd been wasting time while they roamed and hunted freely.

She stumbled down the hall to her bedroom so she could snooze away the booze-blitzed blues. She crawled beneath her covers and lay facedown on the pillowcase her grandmother hand-stitched for her when she was young and full of promise.

Garcia shut her dry eyes and beckoned the sandman.

He was off the clock. She was too anxious to sleep. Something was scratching at the back door of her mind. Something important. She cleared her consciousness and let it ease open—

"The shirt," she said into the pillow.

Eugene Palmer wore a shirt autographed by Harlan Lusher. It *had* to be one of the shirts Henry Lusher sold. If he kept a sales log, she could search his customer database and see exactly how many other BSS superfans were in the area. There could be another Eugene Palmer.

A creepy collector. A copycat. A wolf.

She lay back down. She shut her eyes.

Bloodstained snarls of razor teeth waited in her dreams.

Mammaw played cards as if cheating was in the rule book. Henry had long accepted her sleight of hand as standard practice. His bad odds made the game more exciting, especially when he was holding a near-perfect hand. Now all he needed was a seven and/or the three of hearts. He *never* won when they played Seven Bridge, so when the phone rang, he eagle-eyed Mammaw's hands.

"Cards on the table!" he yelled over the shrill ringer.

"It hurts that ya think I'd cheat." She winked mischievously and laid her cards down.

Henry picked up the phone. "Hello?"

"Hey, it's Otis."

"Hey, man. You still biking over, or should we pick ya up on the way?"

"I can't go," Otis said, his sadness audible. "Not today, anyway. Maybe later this week, or if you think you can handle it, I can give you the interview questions, or...I don't mean to string it out. I'm really sorry, Henry."

What the fuck? Henry wanted to scream. But something was obviously up.

"It's all good," he said, trying for upbeat. "Shit happens. What's going on?"

"Um, just...family stuff," Otis muttered. "My father's having problems with his chronic pain, and I need to stick around so I can help out today. I'd put it off, but...yeah."

No more words were needed. Henry understood.

"How about me and Jane come help *your* ass, for once."

"No, no," Otis sighed. "Thanks, but I need to do this myself."

"Then go ahead and give me the questions," Henry said. "Tell me what to do. I'll handle the investigation today. Consider yourself off the clock, Big Man. You just go do your thing."

"Are you sure?"

"That's what partners are for, ain't it?"

"Partners," Otis mused. "Yes, it is."

Henry could almost hear him smile. There was a rustling on the line, then Otis was back.

"OK. Do you have a pen?"

"Hold up," Henry said. He grabbed the notepad they'd been using as a tally sheet and ripped off the card game. On a blank page he wrote and underlined: SHIT TO ASK. "OK, go."

He gave Mammaw a look that signified the card game was over. She nodded and began gathering the cards to put them away. Otis went through his list quickly. Henry scribbled frantic, disjointed versions of the questions.

Henry didn't notice the front door open. Jane entered, panting and exhausted from another long run. Gravy jumped off the couch and trotted over to lick the sweat from her legs.

"It's OK," Henry said into the phone. "Good luck, partner... over and out."

Henry hung up. He gave Jane a look that broadcast bad news.

"What is it now?" Jane sighed.

"Otis can't do the interview with Dad. He had a family emergency."

Jane sighed. Her shoulders slumped.

"No mopey emo shit today," he ordered. He held up the notepad. "Because I've got all his questions right here. I'm gonna talk to Dad myself. We're gonna get to the bottom of this."

The phone rang again before Jane could reply. Henry grabbed the receiver.

"Change your mind, Big Man?"

Jane got a glass from the cabinet and filled it in the sink. She chugged tap water.

"No," Henry said into the receiver, "I don't *care* if it helps. We can't even go out in public now because of y'all..." He paused to listen. He mouthed to Jane: *Lt. Garcia.* "Fine," he snapped after a moment, "but you've gotta hold up your end...yeah...it's 431 Lockland."

He hung up.

"What does she want?" Jane asked.

"To grill me about our T-shirt business. But she said if I help her out, she'll get the news to report that we had nothin' to do with Carrie Clemmons... so maybe at least we can go back to school and you won't get benched or anything."

"The lady lieutenant's comin' over?" Mammaw asked.

"Yeah." He nodded. "In a few hours."

She got up and began collecting drug paraphernalia and marijuana flakes.

"We should tell her everything," Jane said. "We must have enough to convince her to help us, no matter what Otis thinks."

"I'll make you a deal," Henry said. "I'll tell her what we know and everything that Otis suspects. That way, Miss Piggy will be up to speed if Dad has any new info to add."

"But what's my end of the deal?" Jane asked. "Why are you being weird?"

"Well," he muttered, "I'm being weird 'cause I've gotta stay here and talk to her. But Salem Hill's visiting hours end at four, so, like, there's no way I can do both..."

"No," she said flatly. "I can call Dad, but... I'll, yeah, I can call, but that's it."

"This ain't the kinda shit you can talk about over the phone," Henry said. "Maybe it's better this way. Maybe Dad will tell you the Lordsville stuff that he says I'm too young to hear."

"I'm *not* goin' to that prison! I'm *not* seeing him that way! I'm—"

"If you don't wanna see him in chains, then help us get him out!" Henry yelled.

"No!" Jane yelled back. Then her eyes dropped to the floor

and her voice dropped to a childish mumble. "I won't do it, I won't do it, I won't do it, I won't do it, I won't do it, I..."

"Can't read his stupid handwriting," Jane groaned.

She wore less eyeliner than usual. Dark slacks. One of her mom's church sweaters.

"Lemme see," Mammaw said. Jane held Henry's scribbled notes across the center console. Mammaw took her eyes off the road. "I believe it says 'snake handling'..."

She scoffed and moved the notepad away so Mammaw could focus on driving.

Jane read through the questions again. They were crazy. *This* was crazy.

A lightning storm of nerves swelled inside of her. She wished she had another buspirone pill, though they'd surely reach the exit before the chemicals hit.

There was no time for alleviation. She would be at the prison soon.

31

Garcia almost felt like herself again by the time she turned onto Lockland. The sun was a bit too bright, and she was sweating a bit too much, but the worst of the hangover had passed. She found the white-and-red cottage marked 431 and pulled to the edge of the yard. She checked her uniform to make sure everything was zipped and buttoned, adjusted her shades, and got out.

The breeze felt good. Necessary. She took stock of her surroundings—bleak, even for Paradise—as she walked across the unraked leaves and onto the cement platform that passed for a porch. The pink bicycle reminded her of the one she had when she was a little girl.

Barking commenced before she knocked.

Henry opened the door. He wore a Danzig T-shirt depicting a crucified man with the head of a goat. His hair was in his face, so Garcia couldn't read his expression. The dog ogled her and did an adorable "pet me!" wiggle.

"Hey," Henry said, nice enough. He stepped aside so she could enter.

"Hi, Henry," she said, walking inside. "Thanks again for helping with this."

She bent down to pet the dog. Henry shut the door and sat on the couch.

"Where's Jane and your grandmother?" she asked, joining him.

"They went to visit my dad."

"Oh. Sorry if you had to stay behind on my account. I didn't intend—"

"It's fine," he said curtly. "I just want this to be over."

She nodded. "I called Channel Five, Channel Two, and the *Gazette* to let them know you aren't persons of interest. My contacts promised they would run it, and they will. They're desperate for updates, anyway. I wish Sheriff Connors would've cleared all that up at the press conference."

He scoffed. "Wish in one hand, shit in the other—"

"See which fills up first," she finished.

Henry's dark image and foul language made him seem even younger than he was.

He's just another pissed-off kid, she thought, *and rightly so*.

Suddenly, Gravy hopped between them on the couch.

"You got a smartphone?" Henry asked as he petted the dog. "We don't have internet, so I need it if you wanna see those sales logs."

"Must be hard to run an online store without the internet."

"Yeah, it's a pain," he admitted. "I use the computers at school and stuff."

She pulled out her phone, opened the web browser, and handed it to him. He struggled with the touch screen.

"I hate that keyboard," she said.

"Me too. If this is the future, it's gonna be dumb as fuck."

She started laughing. She couldn't help it. He laughed too.

"You always talk this way to adults?"

"Not always, I guess. But you chase murderers and carry a gun, so I figure cuss words don't faze you. Here." He handed the phone back. "That's the order history. There's the sale dates, there's the shipping addresses..."

"What's this column?" Garcia asked, pointing.

"If it's checked, it means they got their shirt autographed. It costs more."

"How do you manage that?"

"My Mammaw's a hell of a forger."

She laughed again. Smart kid.

"I'm not sure how far back the order history goes," he said, "but you can just stay logged in to the account if you want, so ya won't have to write all that crap down."

"Thanks," she said. She scrolled shipping addresses. She clocked places relatively close: Morgantown, Harpers Ferry, Lexington, Huntington, Pittsburgh, Richmond, Louisville, Charleston, Milton, Ashland, Roanoke, Blue Ridge...

"Do your customers ever ask for things *besides* autographs?"

"Nothin' that would make me think they're a copycat killer."

She reeled back a little. "Why do you think I'm looking for a copycat?"

"It's obvious," he said. "You're just like every other cop, assuming my dad's guilty 'cause twelve dipshits said he was. That's why your case isn't going anywhere—your starting point's wrong. It ain't a BSS copycat you should be lookin' for. It's the genuine fuckin' article."

Is that possible? No way. "You sound pretty sure of yourself."

"Oh, I am." He nodded. "I can even tell ya where the killer's at. Lordsville."

"That's the, uh, the church—"

"Cult," he snapped.

"Right." She got out her notepad and began jotting down his statements. "I heard that your dad grew up at Lordsville. Is that true?"

"Yeah, man. Their psycho leader framed him for all those murders."

"Pearl Jolley? Why would she do that?"

"I think she blames him for the fire, but . . ." He trailed off and shrugged. "Crazy people do crazy shit."

"So, you're saying *Pearl Jolley* is the Blind Spot Slasher?"

"Her, or one of her Knights Templar wannabes," Henry said. "But y'all never looked into it. Not the cops or the DA, all 'cause of her last name . . . trippy, what a last name can do."

"This isn't like on TV. Real police don't give preferential treatment—"

"Yeah?" he snapped. "Then why the fuck are the Paradise powers that be cool with havin' a *death cult* outside of town? And I ain't even told you about the Trinity of Light yet—"

She raised a calming hand. "How do you know all this?"

"We got a private investigator workin' on it. Otis Perkins. Maybe you've heard of him?"

"I don't think so," she said, writing down his name. "Can you have him contact me?"

She handed him her business card. His eyes locked on hers.

"All he'll do is repeat what I said. So, are you gonna wait around for that, or are you gonna go to Lordsville and put an end to this shit before someone else gets slashed?"

"I'm going to follow every lead," Garcia said, "including this. Have your PI call me."

"Yeah . . . I will."

"Great." She put her phone and notepad away as she stood. "Thanks again for the help. Watch the news tonight. They'll clear everything up. I promise."

"OK." Henry nodded. He and Gravy stayed on the couch.

"I'll be in touch," Garcia said. She slid on her sunglasses and went out the door.

Henry watched through the window as Lt. Garcia walked back to her truck.

"She doesn't believe me," he said to the dog.

Then make her believe, he imagined Shooter Kane saying. *Make them all believe.*

He wondered if it had come to that. He watched her drive away.

Garcia reached the station house early but felt the urge to hang back until her shift started. She sat in the cab of her truck, copying the names of standout shirt shoppers and pasting them into an e-mail. She was brain blitzed; her convo with the kid had kicked dirt into the already muddied waters of her mind. That morning, she'd been ready to forget about her copycat theory. After talking to Henry, she felt the urge to move not forward but *backward*—to the original BSS case.

Her self-doubt was simmering. It was a luxury she couldn't afford.

She sent the e-mail to herself and got out of the truck just as Coffey pulled in. He tripped getting out of his Mustang, caught himself, and adjusted his sunglasses. His boyish cowlick announced to the world that he hadn't had time to shower.

"Get any sleep?" she called.

"Nah," he called back. "You?" He leaned against his car and waited on her.

"If I did, I was too drunk to remember," Garcia said.

"I'd take booze brain over this Ambien hangover any day, ma'am."

She patted his back when she reached him, then they lugged themselves into the station.

Lt. Billings was standing alone at the edge of the bullpen. He watched the officers change shifts through half-open eyes. Garcia approached him as Coffey continued to his desk.

"How long you been on?" she asked.

"Since eight. Sheriff called me in to run point 'cause he had a big meeting with the mayor. I'll do a full briefing once the goon squad settles...but you should know, we cut Eugene Palmer loose this morning."

"What!" she yelled.

Eyes peeked up over cubicle walls.

"I know," he sighed. "I told Sheriff Connors we should at *least* wait for the lab results. But Mayor Jolley's worried about a lawsuit over some libtard 'due process' bullshit."

Garcia rubbed her temples as she processed the disappointing development. The last of the fresh officers entered, and Billings switched to bully pulpit mode. He clapped twice for everyone's attention. "Huddle up, children! Got a lot of nothing to brief you on."

Deputies Kern, Washington, Dallas, Smith, Dernt, and Litton joined them. Coffey wandered over with Corporal Thomas. Sgt. Collins hung back.

"First off," Billings said, "for those of you who haven't heard, last night's collar has been cut loose, barring any results we get from the CPD lab."

The officers grumbled and groaned.

"Washington, Litton," Billings said, "get to bracing motel staff. Ask about guests who seem or seemed out of the ordinary. Ask about rushed checkouts, room damage, and so on. Aldridge and Murdock were at it all morning and left a list of spots they've already hit.

"The Clemmons family finally gave us permission to search the girl's e-mail, Facebook, and so on. Corporal Thomas is weeding through it as we speak. Coffey, help him out unless Lt. Garcia needs your assistance. Kern, you're working the tip line."

"Any calls come in last night?" Coffey asked.

"A psychic who said the girl was killed by the ghost of Richard Ramirez."

"Didn't someone call about another missing girl?" Collins asked.

"Oh yeah." Billing shrugged. "Some poor schmuck lookin' for his ex-wife. But that call came in on a burner, and it was disconnected when we tried back. Smith, Dallas, Dernt, accompany Sgt. Collins to Shady Spring High and see if any more of Carrie Clemmons's classmates feel like yappin'. Also, I want all of you to go thank Miss Paula at the front desk for picking up two dozen fresh donuts in an attempt to sweeten your sour-ass moods."

He clapped his hands once more. Collins led his crew to the parking lot, while everyone else rushed to the break room to fuel up on sugar and caffeine before setting to their tasks. Garcia was first to arrive. She grabbed a bear claw, savoring it as she stepped aside to let the others have their fill. She brushed flecks of sugar off her uniform while waiting for Kern to finish pouring a cup of coffee.

"You mind running some names through the system while you're on the tip line?" Garcia asked him. "See if any have priors of note?"

"Sure thing, ma'am," Kern said.

"Great, I'll e-mail them over."

"Still on your copycat kick?" Billings asked. She hadn't noticed him approach.

She brushed the crumbs from her hands before replying. "I'm giving Harlan Lusher's fan club one last look, for old times' sake...and hey, speaking of old times, when you worked the Lusher case, did you look into a connection between him and the Jolley family? You know he grew up on that commune, right?"

"Mm-hmm." Billings nodded. "He lived there until the fire. Pearl Jolley actually claims he started it...but Jolley's certifiable. No one puts stock in her crazy ass."

"When Lusher was arrested, didn't he accuse her of framing him?"

He shrugged. "No one put stock in that either."

"So, the connection between Lordsville and the BSS murders was never investigated?"

Other officers inched over to listen. Billings sensed it. His color was rising.

"Pearl Jolley claims Lusher torched her congregation. Twenty some years later, Harlan Lusher says Pearl Jolley framed him for murdering some junkies. *Both* of them spent a decade on a steady diet of Jesus and psychedelics, and neither had any evidence to back up their claims."

"What about Lusher's parents?" she asked. "Were they ever interviewed? Or the other members of Lordsville? I understand why you dismissed it at the time, but given our current—"

"Look," he snapped, "if I wanna relitigate every mistake I ever made, I'll go home and talk to my goddamn wife. Now how about *all* of you get to work before another girl gets killed?"

The others officers scurried off. Billings pushed past Washington, nearly knocking the half-eaten jelly donut from his hand as he left the break room.

Does the huffing and puffing mean I'm right? Garcia wondered as he stormed away.

"Excuse me, Lieutenant," Litton said. "I, uh, I actually know Harlan Lusher's daddy. Not well, or anything, but we'd chat with him from time to time back when I lived in Newburn County."

"Seriously?"

"Yes, ma'am. Ev Lusher. He's what you'd call the town drunk, though there ain't a town to speak of. He lives in the trailer beside my aunt's. Tewney Ridge. Fifteen minute drive, tops."

She scanned the room for Coffey. He was already filling their thermoses.

The Nikon digital camera Henry got for his ninth birthday still worked, but the shutter made a RoboCop whine that was too loud for his mission. This required super stealth. So, he opted for the disposable camera he found beneath the TV console. Thirteen exposures left. More than enough.

Henry put on his black hoodie and then slid the camera up the left sleeve. He practiced slipping it into his palm to take a photo and then tucking it back. After a few dry runs with the camera, he left it bobbing against his wrist. He went into the kitchen and grabbed the flashlight Mammaw kept over the fridge. He made sure the batteries still worked. Then Henry got the gun.

He took the revolver from the drawer and let it sit in his hand a moment, appreciating the weight and the power, memorizing it. He popped the chamber release—the gun was still unloaded. He got the box of bullets from behind the playing cards and loaded six hollow points.

He tried to flick the chamber of the gun shut, as if he were an old Hollywood cowboy. It didn't work. He pushed it in until it clicked, then shoved the revolver down into the waistband of his jeans. When he zipped up his hoodie, it was impossible to tell he was packing heat.

He wouldn't *need* the gun. All he would need was the camera. That crazy old woman had gone unchecked for so long, she probably left evidence sitting out in the open. Lordsville wasn't expecting anyone to stop, look, or listen. Lordsville wasn't expecting anyone to do a goddamn thing. Lordsville wasn't expecting Henry Lusher—*Shooter Kane* protégé, pulp fiction scholar.

But Henry's punk prose paperbacks taught him a pivotal lesson:

Big reveals were *always* the product of *action*.

He was gonna have to shake things up if he expected the truth to shake loose.

Lordsville was about four miles away. The ride would be hard on his hip, but the pain would be worth it. Henry shoved the flashlight into the pocket of his sweatshirt, grabbed a house key, and wrote a note for Mammaw and Jane on the last piece of notepad paper: "Gone to Lordsville 4 recon. I'll be safe, don't worry. —Henry"

He opened the front door and taped the note above the knocker. Then he went to the couch and kneeled before the dog. Gravyboat's tail wagged. Henry leaned nose-to-wet nose.

"I'd bring ya if I could," Henry said, "but you're just too vicious."

The bichon smiled in agreement. Henry kissed him on his little snout before leaving.

There was already a chill in the air. Henry locked up and then went through the laborious task of mounting Jane's bike. When he lifted his leg over the frame, the butt of the gun shoved into his stomach and the ridged hammer cut his skin.

"Fuck," he spat, wincing and gritting his teeth.

Henry thought for a moment, then unzipped the fanny pack his sister had secured to the handlebars a lifetime ago. He tossed the contents onto the porch—gum, tampons, lip gloss, and other dumb girl crap. He pulled the gun from his pants and shoved it inside; he struggled with the zipper but managed to get the fanny pack nearly shut.

"Close enough for rock 'n' roll," he said, satisfied.

Henry gripped the handlebars. His heart pounded in a spastic dual rhythm as he pedaled. It hurt his hip, but he kept at it until he made it through the yard. The road was easier. The blacktop helped. It still hurt when he pedaled, but at least now he was picking up speed.

Faster, now. Faster. A block down. Two blocks. Another.

The houses ahead were targets, and their jack-o'-lanterns mile markers.

The end of Lockland was coming up. The dogwood tree in the

corner yard was strung with homemade spooks made from napkins and fishing wire. The dead black eyes of the ghosts seemed to watch him pass. Henry nodded hello to them as he pedaled off to face his own.

32

A million dying leaves clung to funereal wood, igniting the hills in a flameless October inferno. As Jane watched the landscape through the car window, she understood why interstate commuters might describe West Virginia as beautiful. But when they got off the Salem Hill exit and came to the first prison checkpoint, all the color drained from her world.

Mammaw eased the car to a stop. An automated metal arm barred the full length of the road. A guard with a gun and a clipboard walked out of the security shed to their left. Mammaw rolled down her window and got her ID from her purse. Jane's license was already out.

The guard looked over their credentials, checked his checklist, mumbled something into his walkie-talkie, and then buzzed them through. The security arm lifted. Mammaw accelerated.

"Don't be nervous, baby," she said, taking Jane's left hand into her right.

As if to mock the sentiment, barbed-wire fencing rose out

of nowhere. Spiked coils lined both sides of the road. They passed two towers outfitted with floodlights. Sexless centurions strapped with automatic rifles looked down on them.

"What if Dad doesn't recognize me?" Jane asked.

"Blood recognizes blood," Mammaw said.

"But, like, what if he's mad because I never visit?"

"Shit," she scoffed, "no man could *ever* be mad at you! Let alone Harlan. You're an angel bringin' your poor daddy what he needs most...a little hope."

The road ahead was blocked by a three-layer automatic fencing unit. This barricade was twice as tall as the fence lining the road. A harsh alarm announced them. Jane flinched as the security gates slid open on their rollers, granting her an unimpeded view of the government-green fortress known as Salem Hill Correctional Center. Two armed guards motioned the car forward. Mammaw drove slowly, taking a right at a weather-faded sign that read VISITOR PARKING.

The gravel lot was nearly empty. Mammaw took a space in front.

"Mammaw," Jane said, nearly whispering, "what if I think he looks guilty?"

She shifted into park and killed the engine.

"Everyone here looks guilty," she said, turning to her granddaughter. "Put a man in a jumpsuit, chain 'em up, throw 'em in a cage like an animal...that's enough to make Jesus H. look like Jack the Ripper. Know what I mean?"

Like her brother before her, Jane did the hard part alone. Anxious energy spasmed through her with every metallic echo:

sounds of cells opening and closing, doors locking, unlocking, and slamming. She had no idea if there were other visitors in the stalls; she kept her eyes fastened to the broad back of the escort guard. He led her to the second station. She sat down.

The bench. The dirty glass. The two-way phone.

It was just like on TV.

BAAAAAHHB! CLICK. CRANK.

Two linebacker-size guards emerged on the opposite side of the glass, sandwiching a smaller man between them. The guard walking point moved against the wall. That's when she finally saw him.

"Daddy," she gasped, without realizing it.

His smile was bright enough to white out the blue uniform, the chains, the guards, the inmates, and the prison itself. His smile was the smile of her father. His smile was everything.

As Harlan sat down across from her, she clutched the list of questions like a talisman powerful enough to right all the wrongs done to him. They picked up their respective phones.

"My God," he said, "you look just like your mother."

"Dad, I've missed—" was all she got out before the tears came.

"Shhhh," he said, "it's OK. It's OK."

"No, it isn't," she sniffled. "I'm so sorry…I'm sorry I don't visit. I was just, just, I was afraid this place would make you look different…change how I see you in my heart."

"Janey, you know I understand."

"Still," she muttered, wiping her eyes, "please don't think I don't miss you. I do. I miss you, every day."

"I miss you every day too."

He touched the glass. She touched it back. She clamped down her sobs.

"So, *do* I look different?" he asked.

"No," she said. "I just see my dad."

"Good," he smiled. "But you…I can't get over how much you've grown up!"

"I guess so." She blushed. "But, Dad, I came today because I need to talk to you about—"

"Your teammate getting murdered?"

"How do you know about that?" she asked, arching back.

"A sheriff questioned me about it. She thinks it could be a Blind Spot copycat, and she wanted my help. I'm so sorry about what's happened…it's all so terrible, so awful."

"I know," Jane said. "But that's not why I'm here. Me and Henry were *finally* able to get an investigator, and he thinks whoever framed you is still out there killing. He doesn't think it's a copycat killer, he thinks it's BSS—"

"Still killing," he mumbled, awestruck. "Five, six years later…"

"If we can prove it, we can get you out of here."

"That would be…" He sighed, smiled, and shook his head. "My amazing kids."

"We believe in you, Dad," she assured him. "We always have. Henry said your new lawyer's investigating Lordsville, and that's great. But we need to know why for *our* investigation, and he said you wouldn't tell him."

"The details aren't appropriate for a boy his age."

"I get that," she said. "But our investigator needs to know everything. He gave me a list of questions to ask, but first you need to tell *me* whatever it was you wouldn't tell Henry."

"But, honey—"

"I'm all grown up, remember? You just said so. I wanna help, and this is the only way I can. Mammaw gave me her tape recorder. I won't play it for anyone but the investigator. OK?"

"I just..." he sighed.

"Come on, Dad. Please. You've gotta trust me."

"I trust you, Janey. I just wanted to protect you both from the past, our past—"

"You can't protect us while you're in here," she said. "We need you *out*, Dad."

He sighed again. He looked at his hands. Jane took the recorder from her pocket.

"I'll have to start at the beginning," he finally said.

Jane nodded. She turned the Dictaphone on and held it to the receiver as he spoke.

"My father left us when we were young," he said. "Momma, she was unwell. Mentally. Certainly not fit to be taking care of Hazel and me by herself. She couldn't work. Couldn't provide. So, when she met Pearl Jolley, she sold the farm to buy our way onto the commune. She thought Lordsville would give the three of us a better life."

"What was Lordsville like?" Jane asked.

"Hazel and I loved it at first," he admitted. "There was room to play, lots of animals—they had dogs, sheep, cows, horses, barn cats, you name it. And the effect Pearl Jolley, *Sister* Jolley, had on Momma was unbelievable. For the first time in our lives, Momma was happy. For the first time, she was sweet to us, motherly. Of course, we were too young to understand that her mood improved because she was on drugs. Everyone there was. Sister Jolley demanded it. Hallucinogens, amphetamines...but we thought she was a magic lady. And we loved Sister Jolley, because she made Momma love *us*." He ran a hand over his face and sighed.

"Can you tell me about the"—she looked at her notes—"religious rituals and rights?"

"Well at first, I just remember a lot of speaking in tongues. Sister Jolley didn't start sacrificing animals until we'd been there a good while. Then she came up with something she called the new communion...that's when Lordsville turned into a really dark place.

"Sister Jolley made everyone take psychedelics before they could enter the chapel. Even the kids. Every day. We didn't understand that it was all a hallucination...everything we saw in that chapel, every word she said...we thought it was real. All her prophecies, her rituals...when she brought the snakes into it, no one questioned her at all."

"Snake handling?" Jane asked. "That's when preachers hold them without getting bit?"

"Usually. But for Sister Jolley, it was the opposite. In her mind, serpents were in league with the devil. So, if they bit you, it was because you had the Holy Spirit inside. Once she'd had that epiphany, you could only stay at Lordsville if you were a Blood Bought Believer."

"I don't know what that means," Jane said.

"Neither did I, until I found Momma with a needle in her arm. Sister Jolley had all the adults injecting themselves with snake venom to build up a tolerance."

"Dad! That's..." She didn't know what to say.

"It was just the beginning," he said. "One day, she brought a shipping crate into the chapel full of a dozen copperheads. She called it the Snake Pit. Sometimes, she'd make the adults go to the Snake Pit and prove they were filled with the Holy Spirit. They would handle the snakes until they got bit...and when they did, 'cause they *always* did, the whole congregation would celebrate. Momma got bit on the cheek one time...how she cherished that scar...Lord, it was madness. But after a while it just seemed...normal. Momma made us start injecting venom when we turned fifteen. Wasn't long after when Sister Jolley called us to the Snake Pit."

"Did you go?"

"Didn't have a choice. I went first, and when I got snake-bit...*God*, I was relieved." He held up his right arm. There was a faint scar four inches above his wrist. She wondered how she'd never noticed it.

"Hazel came up after me. She was shaking something awful when Sister Jolley wrapped a copperhead across her shoul-ders...but then, nothing happened. So she put another snake in Hazel's arms, like so...then another at her feet...she put all those snakes around Hazel, but they wouldn't strike. That snake curled around her shoulders as if they were long-lost friends."

Tewney Ridge was way back in the backwoods, a plot of mud on a creek bank with about a dozen mobile homes, many of which looked abandoned. Garcia tensed as she steered the cruiser down the uneven road. A few bumps later, they came to the last trailer in the park. It was a baby-blue vintage number with trash bags taped over the windows.

"You sure this is it?" Garcia asked.

Coffey checked his GPS. "Unfortunately, ma'am."

They got out and trudged through the mud toward the front door. They weren't halfway there when it swung open. A scare-crow of a man stumbled out. His skin was the shade of liver failure. His green eyes were uneven. He reminded Garcia of an unsettling surrealist painting.

"Y'all must be lost," he said.

"Evington Lusher?" Garcia asked. "I'm Lt. Garcia, this is Sgt. Coffey, Barkley County Sher—"

"This *ain't* Barkley County," he snapped. "I don't gotta tell ya my name."

"We come in peace, Mr. Lusher," she assured him. "We just have a few questions."

"About?"

"Lordsville."

He stared at them. Hard. He began grumbling to himself. Garcia waited patiently.

"All right," he finally scoffed, "but I gotta get me a drink if y'all wanna dig that up."

He disappeared into the trailer.

"Hair of the dog, ma'am?" Coffey joked.

She shook her head and started forward. He followed. The detachable stairs of the trailer creaked beneath her footfalls. The interior was nothing but shadow; the entire place was lit only by a bare bulb above the sauce-stained stove top. The smell of booze, mold, and mustard bombarded her nostrils. Her stomach clenched. Ev Lusher sat in the booth that wrapped around his small table. He poured a shot of Old Crow into a mason jar. Garcia slid in beside him.

"Offer ya one?" he asked.

She declined. Coffey stayed by the fridge. He kept his shades on as he watched Ev Lusher drink greedily and then pour himself another. Garcia took out her notepad.

"Let's start from the start," she said. "Your wife, Mary, moved the twins to Lordsville after the two of you separated, correct?"

He scoffed. "Double wrong from the get-go. When Mary took the kids to that nuthouse, she wasn't *my* Mary no more." He took a drink. He killed the glass. "Second thing is, Hazel and Harlan weren't twins...they were triplets."

Garcia wrote it down, trying to make sense of it. He poured another drink.

"Mr. Lusher—" she started.

"Lady," he snapped, "if you wanna hear the story, I gotta tell it how I gotta tell it."

She nodded.

"Mary and me was twelve when we met. Schoolyard sweethearts and all that. Married after graduation. I'd never known anyone like her. She was old-fashioned, even for me...but Lord, that girl was special. An artist. She used to paint, write poems, little stories...but artsy people often got a touch of the melancholy. Y'all ever heard that?"

"I have," Garcia said.

"She had it damn bad. Mary got what she called 'episodes.' She'd stay in bed for days at a time, go nearly comatose. Sometimes she'd say things, troubling things that were scary as all hell. Truth is, I'd been thinking of leaving her till I found out she was pregnant...then, soon as she got that news, her episodes stopped. She was happier than I'd ever seen her. I swear, I thought that baby was just the blessing we needed.

"Mary was fixed on doin' a home birth—old-fashioned, like I said—but when the doc found out we was havin' triplets, she advised against it. Twins are complicated births, and triplets is worse. Dangerous. But Mary refused to listen."

He finished the drink. He poured another. He drank. He continued his story.

"A midwife, a basin, and my worthless ass was all Mary had, all she wanted. She gave birth there in the living room. Her spirits was soaring all night, she was just so damn happy.

"Hazel came first, near midnight. Harlan came a minute later. I had to slap him on the ass to make sure he was breathing. I held one in each arm, like this, while I waited on number three. Mary was pushin' and pushin'. I didn't know nothin' was wrong until the midwife screamed...that's when I realized the girl was born dead. Strangled by the umbilical cord...our girl."

He drank. He rubbed his eyes. Garcia didn't interrupt the process.

"Mary wouldn't let go," he continued. "She was sure the baby'd wake up the way Harlan did. She rocked it for hours, wouldn't pay no mind to her *living* children. It was sick, it...ugh. But the midwife told me to leave her, she said Mary needed to *process*.

"So, I tended to our two babies all night, kept 'em away from Mary while she 'processed' the stillbirth. I put 'em to bed, Harlan and Hazel, the first night in their crib...built it myself out of"—he sighed—"any rate, eventually I passed out. Woke up around sunrise. Mary was asleep beside me in bed. The midwife was gone, so I thought everything was OK.

"I got up and went to check on the babies, and...the stillborn child was lying in that crib between Hazel and Harlan. Hazel was *cuddling* with it. It was blue, all puffy, and—"

"Jesus Christ," Coffey gasped.

Ev nodded. "I wrapped the corpse in my favorite shirt and buried her near the barn, 'side the stump of that same damn tree I'd built their crib from...sat on that stump and drank for hours. Didn't know what else to do. Drank until time wasn't nothin' to me. Drank till I near forgot...then I heard the babies crying. I think I cried, too, before I went back inside.

"Then I found Mary rockin' the two of 'em like everything was fine. She didn't say nothin' about the stillbirth. It was like it never happened. I figured maybe things was OK, after all.

"Months went by. A year. Everyone thought Mary was doin' real good. She was writing again, workin' the farm, takin' care of the kids...but I could tell somethin' was broken deep down inside that woman. Her eyes got darker. I mean it. Went from brown to tar black. I was scared as hell of her, but I stayed as long as I could...I did, I swear I did."

"When did you leave?" Garcia asked.

"When they was two. Wasn't somethin' I planned. The day started like any other day, but when I came in for lunch, I found Mary reading one of her poems to the kids. I stood at the door to listen...good goddamn crucified Christ, it still gives me nightmares. And that's when I left, that very moment. I left my own goddamn kids like the no-good coward I am."

"You have nightmares about a poem?" Garcia clarified.

He nodded. He took a drink.

"Do you remember how it went?" she asked.

He nodded again. He killed the glass and sat it down hard.

He cleared his throat, then recited: "Three dead babies all in a row, walk through the Valley of the Shadow. Three dead babies holding hands, they all want to sing but only two can. The third dead baby tried and tried, but then she let the devil inside. Three dead babies until there were two...now is the devil in *you* or *you* or *you* or *you* or *you* or *you*—"

Time moved differently inside the prison. The milliseconds between words stretched out like wasted years. And it had been years, hadn't it? Last time Jane had seen her father, she'd been a little girl and spoken to as such. Now he spoke to her like a woman. Now he told the truth.

"When the snakes didn't bite Hazel," he continued, "even Sister Jolley was stunned. She'd preach about it all the time, of course, but it had never actually *happened*."

"So, what did she do?" Jane asked.

"Went to pray on it. She took Momma along with her, which scared Hazel even worse. I mean, Hazel cried for *days*. She was sure something terrible was going to happen. But I promised her that everything would be OK. I really thought it would..."

He put the phone down to wipe his eyes. He picked it back up.

"They grabbed us a few days later. Both of us. Momma took Hazel. Two big men held me so I couldn't stop what was happening, though I had no idea what it was. Still, I struggled, we both did, but they dragged us to the chapel like we were disobedient dogs.

"When we got there, Momma gave Hazel twice as much 'communion' as usual. But those men were too busy trying to keep ahold of me to think about giving me the drugs...that's the only reason I'm sure I *saw* what I saw."

"What did you see?" Jane asked hesitantly.

"An *exorcism*," he said. "That's what Sister Jolley called it. She had built a wooden cross with arm, head, and leg restraints. It was positioned right behind the Snake Pit. Her and Momma strapped Hazel to the cross. Sister Jolley's son, Dean, dragged in the iron firepit from our picnic area and sat it next to Hazel while more men came to hold me back.

"Sister Jolley told the congregation that Hazel had the devil in her blood. She said that Momma always suspected it, and the serpents confirmed it. The Lord told Sister Jolley she could *exorcise* the demon by blinding him and tricking him back to hell."

Jane leaned in close. The phone was slick with her sweat.

"Sister Jolley went outside," he continued, "then Momma ripped off Hazel's shirt and gagged her with it. Sister Jolley came back with a calf from the stockade, and they chained it inside the firepit. That animal knew what was happening before I did...Sister Jolley brandished her ritual knife. But instead of killing the calf, she moved t-to...she moved to Hazel. She grabbed her hair, my sister's hair, and she stabbed her through th-th-the right eye. As Hazel screamed, Momma covered the calf in lighter fluid and burned it alive there beside her.

"I must've gone into shock. I thought Hazel was dead. There was so much blood, so much screaming, and she wasn't...she didn't flinch when Sister Jolley pulled the knife out.

"The congregation, men and women who'd raised us, they *cheered*. Sister Jolley *commanded* the devil to flow from Hazel, to follow the screams of misery back into hell. The poor calf kept wailing...those flames danced all the way to the bone...still, it kept crying...longer than should've been possible...and I swear...it sounded just like a newborn child."

Evington Lusher excused himself and went outside to urinate. Coffey leaned down to the table and quietly conferred with his superior officer.

"How much of that story ya think's true?" he asked.

"Enough to turn his life from that to this," Garcia said.

The steps outside squealed. Ev Lusher stumbled back in, zipping up his jeans.

"Sorry 'bout that," he muttered, sitting. "Bladder ain't what it used to be."

"Totally fine," Garcia said. "Let's pick up—"

"When I took off? It's the great shame of my life, leavin' them kids with her..."

"Was that the last time you saw your wife and daughter?"

"No." Ev poured himself another drink.

Garcia couldn't blame him. She waited patiently.

"I hit the road for a decade or more. Did odd jobs, roofing mostly. But I got clean for a while and started feelin' regretful...you know the drill. I heard Mary and the kids were living at Lordsville. I hated myself just enough to go out there and see how bad off I'd left 'em."

"What was Lordsville like?"

"At first, I thought that place was sweet deliverance. Mary greeted me at the gate and I could see a difference right off...she looked healthy, and she was *happy* to see me! Mary thanked me for leaving, believe it or not. She said it forced her to shed her skin of suffering...that's how she put it. She said she'd been reborn...but she also said I wasn't allowed to see my kids until I saw that woman first."

"Pearl Jolley?" Garcia asked.

He nodded. "She was stranger than a skankhouse skunk. High on who the hell knows. Had needle marks runnin' all down her arms. We talked awhile, but she just rambled...I finally got sick of waiting and went lookin' for the kids myself. That's when I realized it wasn't just Jolley, it was *everyone*. They was all on drugs. I passed people drooling on themselves like zombies. But I didn't care about none of that. I just wanted to see the damn kids."

"Did you?" Garcia asked.

"Mm-hmm," he rasped, before killing his drink. "They was at the creek bed, skippin' stones. Harlan didn't even recognize me. He introduced himself when I came over, like I was a stranger.

He asked if I was joining the church. I told him I was thinking on it...but then he grabbed me by the arm, hard, and he
whispered...'*run*.'

"Harlan's eyes told me I was in danger, but I didn't know from
what. So, I start lookin' around like a madman...then I realized
Hazel hadn't moved an inch. Not even a flinch.

"So, I walked up on her...and she's wearin' an eye patch. I
dunno what they did to her, but her uncovered eye was blank
as a corpse. She was like Jack Nicholson, at the end of that one
movie. That goddamn place short-circuited my little girl's brain
in the name of the Lord."

Garcia was stunned. She wasn't sure what to say. Coffey
stepped up.

"What did you do then, Mr. Lusher?"

"What the hell you think? I took my boy's advice."

Before Jane walked into the prison, she'd been convinced that
she had a hard childhood. But as her dad spoke of exorcisms,
she understood how limited her definition of "hard" was. Now,
she grasped that human suffering could stretch far beyond the
limits of her meager imagination.

"When I regained consciousness," Harlan said, "Hazel
was alive. Her eye was bandaged, and her wounds eventually
healed...the physical ones. But not her mind. She was totally
detached. I started to wonder if she really *had* been possessed. It
took decades for me to learn that her temperament had changed
because the frontal lobe of her brain had been pierced. What
Sister Jolley did was tantamount to an ice pick lobotomy."

Jane opened her mouth to respond. Nothing came out. She
was too stunned.

"But the rest of the congregation claimed the exorcism was a success. They started asking Sister Jolley to exorcize them, too. They did it *willingly*, Janey. Lordsville was completely disconnected from reality. Things were getting worse...I knew we had to escape.

"So, I made a plan. We would leave during the summer solstice service, because it lasted well into the night. I spent weeks preparing. I quit taking the drugs. I squirreled away food and stole what money I could from Sister Jolley's cabin. I put our supplies in a potato sack and hid it near the creek we always played in. I went over the plan with Hazel a hundred times, but not once could I tell if she understood. I just had to hope she did and try to get us out."

Jane sensed what was coming next.

She could almost feel the heat. She could almost see the smoke.

"We made it to the day of the solstice without incident. But then they came. The big men and Momma. Hours before we were set to escape. Dean Jolley helped the men drag me to the chapel. I fought as hard as I could. Momma led Hazel behind us, and she didn't struggle at all.

"Sister Jolley was already in the middle of her sermon when they brought me inside. She told everyone that Hazel and I were intertwined—heart, life, soul—which meant the devil had tainted us both. Sister Jolley went out to get the calf as Momma filled the firepit with accelerant and Dean strapped my wrists to the cross.

"But I fought with everything I had. I kicked one man and broke his nose. I headbutted the other. Momma went on and lit the fire so she could help Dean hold me down.

"She ordered Hazel to try and calm me...and Hazel came down. But she *grabbed* Dean Jolley off me and threw him into the fire! Dean started screaming somethin' awful. The cross I was on tipped over, and I busted my head on the edge of the platform. It knocked me out cold.

"When I came to, Hazel was undoing my restraints. Smoke was everywhere. The firepit had toppled over, and the blaze was spreading fast. Brother Dean was flailing around the chapel like a human candlewick. Everyone else was too busy trying to save Dean to think about saving themselves. I could smell his skin melting as Hazel pulled me down the aisle toward the doors.

"Somehow, she got me out without being noticed...that's what I thought, at least. Then Momma stumbled through the smoke after us.

"When Hazel saw her, she ran up the stairs and *pushed* Momma back inside the church! Then Hazel, she...she smiled at me...before she walked back into the flames. Hazel shut the doors behind her as I passed out again...then screams and darkness...as I prayed for death."

33

Around the time Jane walked into Salem Hill and Lt. Garcia entered Ev Lusher's trailer, Henry was on the verge of reaching a harder-fought destination. The pain in his hip grew worse with every pedal, every push, and it was beginning to feel like he was grinding his bone to dust. But still, he pedaled forward, coasting when he could, letting the wind at his back propel him toward a culmination of fates.

The more prevalent his pain became, the more mental energy was necessary to ignore it. His focus grew so internal that he didn't notice the entrance gates of Lordsville on his right, where the road cut left. When he looked up to navigate, the faded sign—LORDSVILLE LOVES YOU!—slapped him back on task.

He hit the brakes, skidding to a stop on the shoulder, kicking up dust. It hurt like hell to dismount from the bike; he cursed his hip as he forced his leg over the frame. His feet wobbled on the gravel. He scanned the fence line, which was overgrown with dying foliage and coils of bare branch. He listened for signs of life. He heard none. He gripped the handlebars and walked the bike to the entrance gates. The weatherworn cabins beyond them looked abandoned.

Trinity of Light, my ass, Henry thought. *It doesn't even look like they have electricity. If the Jolley family's as rich at Otis says, they sure don't know how to spend their money.*

His theories about secret alliances and Trinity-allied Knights Templar felt childish now, nothing but high-flown fantasies of desperation. He leaned the bike against the gate. His original plan had been to sneak into the compound through the woods, but now all that cloak-and-dagger shit felt unnecessary. Henry limped to the center of the gate—it was unlocked.

Fuck it, I'll just go in and take some photos, then maybe—

"Can I help you, son?"

The voice hit Henry like a stun gun; he was immobilized except for his eyeballs, which spun in his skull until they found the man standing on the opposite side of the fence. He was big, bald, and middle-aged, rocking camo pants and a flannel shirt. He wore a genuinely friendly smile on his considerate face, and a genuinely deadly handgun on his considerable waist.

"Noticed your limp, there," the man said, moving toward the gate. "I'm happy to help ya inside if you like. I know we've got a wheelchair around here somewhere . . ."

"Uh, I, I, I, um, huh?"

"To get ya to the chapel," the man clarified. "You're here for a faith healin' ain't ya?"

"I, uh," he cleared his throat, "yep. Yes, sir, I am."

The man's smile widened. The rusty gate latches screamed to life as he pulled it open.

"I'm Brother Pine," the man said, offering his hand.

Henry accepted it nervously. "I'm Henry."

"Brother Henry! Come on in. Sister Jolley will fix ya right up. Should I get the chair?"

"I think, uh, I'm good to walk..." *The gun, you idiot!* "Let me just get my bike—"

Brother Pine gripped Henry's shoulder and drew him forward. The move didn't seem as aggressive as it felt. Henry looked back to where his gun was hidden as Brother Pine shut and latched the gate.

"It's safe right where it is," he said. "Welcome to Lordsville."

They walked. Brother Pine kept at Henry's pace, in lockstep, smiling all the while. As they passed the cabins, Henry realized *none* of them were abandoned. There were people all around him, hunched in the shadows. They had a dusted-over look that made them impossible to see from the road, which was now a few yards and a billion miles away.

A dead deer was strung up in one of the yards. A shirtless man was gutting it, slashing the flesh away angrily. He had prison tattoos on his chest and track marks on his arms. He wore an eye patch. Henry slid the camera out of his sleeve and into his shaking hand. He took two pictures of the man, and nearly shrieked when Bambi's entrails hit the ground.

"We don't get many congregants your age," Brother Pine said.

"I wasn't even sure this place was still a place," Henry said. "But nothing's helped my hip so far, and I'm desperate."

"That's why the Lord led ya here, Brother Henry."

On the right, an empty plot of land stood between two structures. Unlike the rest of the compound, the lawn was neatly kept. Three crosses stood in the center of it.

Three crosses...the sign of the trinity. "Is that where the fire was?"

"It is." Brother Pine nodded, then pointed farther down the

property. "New chapel's down yonder. Sister Jolley couldn't stand to build it here."

"I don't think I could either."

Brother Pine wrapped a heavy arm around his shoulders. The gun pressed into his side, but even Shooter Kane wouldn't be ballsy enough to go for the weapon. The smartest thing to do at this point was let things play out.

"Service doesn't start for twenty minutes," Brother Pine said. "How would ya like to go ahead and meet the woman who is gonna change your life?"

"I'd, uh, yeah. I'd like it a lot."

Brother Pine steered him toward a cabin set apart from the others. A long black sled of a Chevy was parked out front. Henry frantically rummaged through the cluttered notes of his mind.

What do I do? What do I ask? What would Otis do? What would Jane do?

But all he heard was his heart pounding in triple time. His reflection stretched across the hood of the Chevy as Brother Pine led him to the cabin door. He forced himself to take a picture of the front plate while Brother Pine knocked. There was no answer. Henry wound the film and took another photo. Brother Pine knocked again, harder.

"Free to enter," a high, raspy voice with a Southern twang called from inside.

Henry's everything clenched. He shoved the camera up his sleeve, adjusting the hoodie as he stepped forward. Brother Pine opened the door. He ushered Henry inside.

The single-room structure was sparse, and a large desk took up the bulk of the space. Two chairs faced the desk, which was covered in piles of scribbled-upon paper. Seated behind the desk was Sister Pearl Jolley. Her hair was long and white, patchy at the scalp. Track marks and liver spots covered the skeletal arms that jutted from her black frock.

She smiled. Henry could hear her dry lips crackling.

"Sister Jolley," Brother Pine said. "This is Brother Henry. He's in need of a healin'."

"Of course you are, dearie," she said with more life than Henry expected. "You came to the right place. It's no secret what the power of eternity can do!"

She extended an ancient finger and motioned him forward. Henry limped across the wooden planks. She stood and offered him her hand.

"Call me Sister Jolley," she said.

He took it. They shook. Flesh on flesh. It was surreal.

Brother Pine left the cabin, shutting the door behind him. Sister Jolley gave Henry the once-over. He tried not to flinch as her cold eyes creepy-crawled across his features.

She sat down, so he sat down.

"You're here as a free moral agent," she said, telling not asking. "You're here to be healed, to have your sins *ripped* away, drowned in the purifying blood of the Man Christ Jesus."

"Um, yes, ma'am," Henry stammered. "My hip. I came because my hip . . ."

"No," she spat, "it's not your hip, my hip, our hip, their hip, but *his* hip! As you stand on this side of eternity, tell me, tell him, tell the Man Christ what *truly* ails you."

Her voice grew faster and less coherent with every word. Henry tried not to panic.

Her eyes narrowed. She wanted an answer. He was scared enough to tell the truth.

"Uncertainty," he said. "That's what really ails me."

"Ah...then let me take away your pain...I can turn you into a Blood Bought Believer if you lay your uncertainty upon me." She opened her palms, signaling that the floor was his.

"OK...those three crosses outside," Henry said, "when I looked at them, I heard a voice inside my head. I don't wanna say it was *God* or something, but the voice said 'Trinity of Light' and something like 'Ennobled Ascent.' Does any of that mean anything to you—"

Her laugh sounded like a bag of drowning kittens.

"It means God is the dispensator of time and judgment who has seen fit to give *you* a glimpse of thrice mediations betwixt man and God...but that's not the question that cuts deep into the innards of your soul, is it, young Lusher?"

Henry's throat locked up. He couldn't speak.

"Don't you think *God* recognizes you?" Sister Jolley asked. "He who speaks directly through me? Don't you think he's shown me the burning question inside of your heart? Don't you think I know, deep down, you wonder if your father has a devil inside of him, a manifestation that I gave my only son to destroy? Well *praise* be, we will answer *all* tonight!"

Henry almost pissed himself. Outside, a bell tolled.

"Come," Sister Jolley said, turning toward it. "The Snake Pit beckons!"

His bladder let go, snapping him out of his daze. Henry jumped up and rushed to the door before Sister Jolley was on her feet. He pushed through it and went tripping into the cool autumn air, where dozens of zombified zealots were now lurching toward the chapel.

Henry caught his balance as Sister Jolley burst through the door behind him.

"The Snake Pit beckons!" she called to the others. "This boy accepts the Man Christ Jesus as his Lord and Master! He's ready to pay for that belief in blood!"

The zombie walkers hooted and cheered as Henry limped away. Tears stung his eyes.

He limped toward the gate as fast as he could.

He limped toward the bike as fast as he could.

He limped toward the gun as fast as he could.

Away from the Man Christ maniacs. Toward his six-cylinder savior.

Henry moved as fast as he could...but it wasn't fast enough.

"I got ya!" Brother Pine yelled.

Henry found himself being pulled backward, into the seat of an old wheelchair. He cried out as his elbows slammed against the metal armrests. Brother Pine tousled Henry's hair from behind. He spun the chair around and rolled Henry toward the chapel. Others reached out as they passed, fondling Henry's arms, face, hair, and neck with their grubby hands. Every single one of them was packing heat. Through the open doors of the chapel, Henry could hear those already inside singing an off-key version of a Beatles tune, copyright infringing for Christ: "Oh, I need your love, Lord, guess you know it's true, hope you need my love, Lord..."

Brother Pine rolled him to a woman standing sentry at the door. She held a silver tray of Dixie cups. Brother Pine took a cup and drank. She lowered the tray down to wheelchair level.

"I d-d-d-don't want any," Henry stammered, shaking his head.

"Take this," she droned. "Sanctify your eyes so they may close to this side of eternity. Blood is the great purifier. Take this and be washed clean."

"Amen." Brother Pine nodded. He took a cup. He handed it to Henry.

"Fffffuck," Henry whispered to himself.

He closed his eyes and drank. The effect was instantaneous. His throat burned. His ears rang. Brother Pine wheeled him into the chapel, right down the center aisle. Four rows of pews boxed them in. Sister Jolley waited at the podium. Her glare was no longer cold; it was burning.

Once they reached the front of the chapel, Brother Pine spun Henry around to face the congregation. Bruised arms, stained teeth, and hooded eyes stared back at him. Colors traced their movements as they clapped. The drugs had kicked in. Henry's world was psychedelicized.

"Sisters and Brothers," Sister Jolley preached, "free moral agents one breath away from eternity! We have with us a child pained by uncertainty, *hobbled* by fear of the devil!"

The crowd hooted and hollered. Their auras had colors. The colors had sounds.

"I don't mean the devil of yesterday," she went on. "I don't mean the devil of the evangelical liars or Christ crucifiers or bloodless deniers! I mean the devil *inside*, the devil pumping through his young, strong, tainted veins. Shout the savior's name if ya know it!"

"Man Christ Jesus!" someone yelled.

Sister Jolley moved to Henry's side and kneeled. "Are you ready for your pain to end, child? For your questions to be answered?"

"U-u-u-uh, um," he stammered. She gripped his wrist. Her nails cut skin. "Uh, y-y-yes."

She stood and turned back to the crowd. "Glory be! This child is a Blood Bought Believer! The sale of the century is happenin' right here at eternity's gate!"

The congregation went wild. It was junkie joy abound. Henry felt like he was floating and drowning simultaneously. Suddenly, Brother Pine was placing a wooden box beside the wheelchair. It was the size of a child's coffin. Sister Jolley pulled an unsheathed blade from behind the pulpit. It was long and thin and old. She kept it close to her side as she knelt again.

"There can be only one mediator betwixt God and man, which is the Man Christ," she said. "And there can be only one mediator betwixt man and Satan, which is the serpent. Those that crawl can see through our eyes like glass...straight into our souls."

Henry didn't understand until she opened the box. He looked down and saw three sickly copperheads slithering inside the coffin. He screamed. The congregation cheered. Sister Jolley reached into the coffin and grabbed the biggest snake. She wrapped it across Henry's neck. His shoulders shivered and slumped as the snake's tail slid across his forearm.

"Meet the eyes of the serpent," she ordered. "Let it claim you if you are his!"

Henry couldn't move. The snake weighed him down like an albatross. Sister Jolley took another snake from the coffin and lay it upon his lap. Henry experienced fear beyond fear.

"Meet the gaze of the serpent! Let it peer through your eyes like glass!"

Henry looked at the snake in his lap. The snake looked up. They locked eyes.

The snake struck with lightning speed. Henry didn't even see it move, just felt fangs stab into his left thigh before blood started seeping through his pants. Henry shrieked. The crowd screamed back. White-hot pain exploded in his bicep. The other snake had clenched on tight.

"Blood is the great purifier!" Sister Jolley yelled. "Let it bleed, let it bleed, let it bleed! Blood is the great purifier, child! You are pure! You are pure! Hallelujah, you are pure!"

The crowd cheered. Henry shot up from the chair and went flailing forward. Behind him, Sister Jolley overturned the coffin, freeing the final snake. Henry crawled desperately toward the chapel doors. Henry crawled until he felt fangs rip through the useless cotton of his socks, piercing those inept shields of skin until they settled into the meat of his ankle.

Henry looked back as the poison hit.

The serpent smiled.

The world went black.

34

They were Lordsville bound. Sgt. Coffey steered. Garcia fidgeted in the passenger seat; the old man's story frayed the few remaining nerves she had intact.

"Penny for your thoughts," Coffey said, eyes on the road.

"I'm thinking about the shit fit Sheriff Connors is gonna throw when we bring Pearl Jolley in for questioning."

"It'll be one for the books." He grinned. "That's for sure. But nothing Ev Lusher said makes Harlan seem any less guilty to me. That stuff about their momma...Jesus Christ. I think the psycho switch was flipped in his head from the jump. I ain't saying there isn't a copycat, but I still think the original batch of murders was all him."

The road got bad. Coffey slowed down. Garcia grew more impatient by the pothole.

"I don't know," she said. "The 'psycho switch' has been flipped on this whole case. Even my copycat angle doesn't seem feasible now. I'm trying not to think in worst-case scenarios."

"Which would be what?" he asked.

"That the Lusher kid is right. The Blind Spot Slasher was never caught in the first place."

He sighed. She rubbed her temples as he slowed to avoid another pothole.

"Hey," she said, "see your right foot, there? Kindly press it on the fucking gas so we get to Lordsville before the sun goes down. I can't deal with another haunted house."

He switched on the lights and siren. He kindly put the pedal to the metal.

What do you do when your dad tells you that your aunt burned twenty-nine people alive? Sit in stone-dumb silence with your eyes on the floor. Jane didn't flinch or blink. She was at a complete loss.

"Hazel did it to save me," Harlan muttered, as if to convince himself. "I know that doesn't make it right, but...intent has to count for something, doesn't it? Right?"

Jane gave a single, barely perceptible nod.

"I didn't, I *couldn't* tell the police what happened...and the other survivors wouldn't speak on it...the exorcism, the drugs, there was just no way to tell the story without implicating Sister Jolley. She alone came out with her version of the truth...casting blame on me, of course. But I understand. She wasn't inside the chapel. She couldn't know...and if she did, it didn't matter. The Jolley family covered it up, made it go away. It was amazing how quickly something so horrific drifted from the public's mind.

"But Sister Jolley didn't forget. No...I waited years for her to come after me, to impose some sick act of vengeance. But I never imaged it would be anything like . . . when I was arrested, when I learned those girls had been stabbed through the eyes, I knew Lordsville was responsible."

"Why didn't you tell the police *then*," she said, exasperated. "You weren't a kid anymore! You had a family, you had had *us*, you should've told them everything, you should've *made* them investigate—"

"I did, Janey. I swear, *I swear to God* that I did. They laughed it off. The sheriff, the DA, my own idiot lawyers . . . no one in Paradise wants to believe anything as crazy as the truth. I wanted to bring it into the trial, but my lawyers worried it would make me sound unstable. I couldn't prove any of it, after all, so they—"

BRAAAANNNNNKKK!

The alarm made both of them jump.

Harlan's escort guards stepped forward. He nodded to them, then turned back to Jane.

"I have to go," he said. "I'm sorry, Janey."

Her lip quivered. She quit recording and pocketed the Dictaphone. She felt so many things, *too* many things. She couldn't find the words or actions needed for the moment.

"What do you say when there's nothing to say?" Jane asked.

"I love you," he replied.

Jane found that it worked just fine.

Night teetered on falling. The world was more shadow than light. Garcia had Coffey kill the sirens when they were ten miles out. A few moments later, the vine-laced fence of Lordsville came into view. He slowed down as they neared the gate. Garcia recognized the bike instantly.

"Park over here," she said.

Coffey parked next to the bicycle. He killed the engine. They got out. Dread descended on Lt. Elena Garcia as she moved toward the rusty pink Huffy.

"That's Jane Lusher's bike," she said.

"Shit," Coffey groaned.

"Call for backup. 10-33, possibly a 10-61."

"Shit," he said louder. He opened the driver's side door and called dispatch. Garcia moved to the center of the gate. Coffey joined her a moment later.

"Do we wait for backup?" he asked.

She unholstered her weapon in response. He nodded, then did the same.

She unlatched the gate. It screeched open. They both got chills.

They moved forward.

Clock the footprints in the dirt...

Clock the sweeping marks of a limping leg...

Clock empty porches, closed doors...

She moved carefully, keeping to the shadows. Coffey followed in step.

Clock the smell of death...there!

She aimed her weapon—at a deer carcass, half-flayed, left in the open air.

She lowered her gun. She took a breath. Coffey wide-eyed her, relieved. They kept going. Shadows. Shadows. Nothing. Nothing. They kept going. They came to a long black car matching the description of the BSS-mobile.

Clock the blown tires, the rust, the overgrown grass...

Someone screamed in the distance.

They ran toward the sound, guns raised. They passed a clearing and veered left with the road, toward a windowless white chapel. A few yards out, she could hear voices inside the chapel. A few feet, she could hear what they were saying.

"Walk, child! You've been purified! Your broken body is healed!"

Her heart pounded. Her vision sharpened. She got adrenalized.

She posted on one side of the chapel door. Coffey posted on the other.

They locked eyes. She mouthed her words—*on three*. He nodded.

He gripped the door handle. She flipped her safety off.

One.

Two.

"Sheriff's Department!" she screamed as Coffey pulled the door open.

Her supersharpened senses surveyed the scene at maniacal speeds.

The old woman in the center aisle...

Henry Lusher on the floor, bloody and unconscious...

The big man on stage unholstering his handgun...

"Don't do it!" she screamed at Brother Pine.

His hand stopped midair, hovering over the butt of the gun. The congregation turned toward her with drug-drained expressions. She clocked gun after gun after gun after gun.

Garcia stepped forward. Coffey came in behind her. Once Coffey had Brother Pine covered, she focused on poor Henry Lusher. His skin was flush, like rotting lavender.

"Step away from the boy," she ordered Sister Jolley.

"Leave this place," she said. "God is the only law here."

"We just want to help," Garcia said. "So back away slowly."

"He *has* been helped!" Sister Jolley exclaimed, nudging Henry with her foot. "Blood is the great purifier! Go now, child! Get up and walk!"

"Back! Up! Now!" Garcia yelled, moving closer.

She had almost reached Henry. Then the zombies in the pews began chanting.

"Walk . . . walk . . . walk . . . walk . . . walk . . . "

Sister Jolley nodded to the rhythm. "The Man Christ commands you up! Walk! Walk!"

Garcia squatted, keeping her gun on Sister Jolley. She reached for Henry, determined to get him out before things got worse. But as her fingers grazed the boy's swollen hand, she saw a flash of movement on the floor by Coffey's feet. She turned just in time time see a sickly copperhead sink its fangs into the meat of his calf.

Coffey screamed, jerking backward. The sudden movement caused Brother Pine to draw his weapon and fire. Garcia heard the bullet meet the bone before firing five rounds into the gunman. Other congregants drew their arms. The church started its own personal apocalypse. Gunshots echoed off the walls. Blood splattered across the pews. Sister Jolley opened her mouth, as if to declare it God's will, but all she managed to do was laugh and laugh and laugh and laugh.

35

It was scary going to the scary places: rows of houses as destitute as a postwar scene, overpasses and alleyways where shadows possess a life of their own. But they went to every one of them that morning and afternoon, searching until the sun was nothing but a fading sliver of light.

They found no sign of his father anywhere. No sign of his car, either. Otis and his mom were at a loss. They'd been searching for seven hours, hours spent in awkward silence. They finally decided to get dinner and regroup. His mom suggested Wendy's. It was Otis's favorite.

Otis ate his Jr. Bacon Cheeseburger and watched the sunset across the parking lot. His mom called more emergency rooms and spoke to more receptionists. None had record of Fred Perkins in their care or their morgue. Otis wiped grease off his hands before checking his phone.

No missed calls. No messages.

He wondered what Henry had learned at the prison. He wondered why they hadn't called.

He flipped through the app store mindlessly to dull his senses. It gave him an idea.

"Mom," he said, rushed. "Give me his phone number."

She read off his father's number without question. He plugged the digits into a new app. He waited on Wendy's sluggish Wi-Fi... until his phone pinged. He looked up at his mom.

"I found him, let's go."

A sign came into view: RICKY JOE'S GOLD & PAWN: PAYDAY LOAN$! WE CA$H CHECK$!

"You're kidding," his mom sighed.

"No," Otis said, "this is the place."

His new Find-a-Phone app had successfully guided him to a broken heart.

She pulled into the parking lot. Otis scanned it—his father's Lincoln wasn't there. She parked near the blacked-out glass windows of the pawnshop.

Otis was out of the car before she unbuckled her seatbelt. He pushed through the heavy glass doors and charged inside. An electric bell chimed overhead, too chipper for the occasion.

Otis turned down the first aisle. He passed a PlayStation, a set of china, a stereo, a blender, a microwave, a case of watches, and countless other artifacts haunted by sad specters. He walked each desperate row, searching for a father he knew was no longer there.

Then he approached the front display counter where they kept the good stuff—jewelry, handguns, laptops, cell phones. A clerk emerged. His ponytail and silver skull rings clashed with the purple staff polo he wore.

"Can I help ya, young man?"

"Yes," Otis said. "I think my father pawned his cell phone earlier."

The door announced Otis's mother. She joined them at the counter.

"Android or iPhone?" the clerk asked.

"It's an iPhone," she said, taking the lead. "Fred Perkins. Fredrick."

The clerk looked over some paperwork and then nodded. He went to the storage shelves behind him and returned with a Tupperware container labeled APPLE IPHONES/IPADS/IPODS—HOLD. He sat it down in front of them on the counter.

"Should be in here," he said. "We put a forty-eight-hour hold on everything before it goes on display. He can buy it back if he wants to, just FYI."

Otis popped off the lid. It was packed with dozens of devices. Many were in cases. Some were decorated with stickers and plastic jewels, misplaced personal touches.

"How much do you buy these for?" his mom asked, while Otis searched.

"An iPhone? 'Bout forty bucks."

"Forty? That's it?" she seemed relieved. She turned to Otis. "Your app must've been wrong. He'd never..."

Otis found his father's iPhone. His mom's words trailed off until they were nothing but an inaudible mutter. A family portrait stared back at them from the lock screen—all smiles.

Jane spent the first half of their drive recounting her father's true-life horror story. The next quarter was reserved for

Mammaw's understandably mixed reaction—confusion, revulsion, and a sense that she still didn't know the half of it. They spent the home stretch sitting in silence.

Mammaw grumbled internally, aggravated by the spottiness of her memory. At some point in her life, she *must've* known Harlan's sister had her eye cut...or about the snakes...or his escape. She had the frustrating sense she'd heard most—if not all—of the information before. But now it felt like a revelation, an unwanted present she was forced to open twice.

She squinted into the sunset and steered onto Lockland. The house was as dark as an air-raid blackout. Mammaw scoffed. "Goddamn memory's worse than I thought. Must'a forgot to pay the electric again."

"No," Jane said, "look, my bike's gone. Henry must've went somewhere."

"Maybe," she said, "but don't ridin' a bike hurt his hip?"

Dread filled the car like carbon monoxide, and by the time Mammaw pulled into the yard she was woozy. She parked and Jane got out. The phone inside was ringing. The ringing stopped.

The ringing started again.

Jane turned to Mammaw. Mammaw tossed her the keys.

Jane ran for the house. The dog began to bark.

Garcia focused on her hands. She ignored the sounds and scuttle and screams and sirens of the ICU. Her hands were trembling, useless now. Less than an hour before, they had been steady enough to kill a man. She kept her eyes locked on them as she paced outside the operating room. She refused to sit down until

Sgt. Coffey was out of surgery. She ignored her own exhaustion. She ignored the blood on her uniform and the crusty splats of it in her hair.

Coffey had been shot twice—in the left shoulder and the right oblique. He'd been bitten by at least one snake. She wasn't sure how much blood he had lost, but it sure seemed like a lot.

Henry Lusher was down the hall, in an ICU isolation room. Deputy Kern stood guard outside. The boy was sedated, pumped full of antivenom and fluids. She had no clue how many times *he'd* been bitten—when they loaded him into the ambulance, he was swollen and purple.

Garcia struggled to grasp how things had gone so horribly wrong.

If I just would've noticed the snakes…

If she just. But she didn't.

When Coffey got bit, his reaction caused the big guy to fire in a panic. Two rounds hit Coffey before Garcia put the shooter down. That part she understood. But no cause-and-effect logic explained what happened when the rest of the congregation drew their weapons.

One woman fired around the room at random, hitting a congregant near Garcia in the neck. Then another man shot *her* before opening fire on the pew beside him. An older guy in the front row was shot in the face. A few others were shot as well. Pearl Jolley was unharmed.

"Excuse me, Officer…"

She looked up. A doctor stood before her, strong jawed and weary eyed.

"I wanted to give you an update on your partner," he said. "He's stable. We've set the scapula fractures displaced by the bullet and are repairing the muscle damage to his hip. We're being extra cautious because of the snakebite. The antivenom won't be as effective if he needs a blood transfusion, so it's a bit of a balancing act, but everything's going well. We'll have him patched up soon."

The slightest sigh of relief pursed her lips. "And the boy? Any updates on him?"

"He's stable," the doctor said. "Copperhead venom isn't usually fatal, but he sustained six bites, I believe. He's just lucky you got him here when you did. You saved his life."

She shivered and shook her head.

"His bloodwork shows traces of psilocybin, as well as some type of synthetic hallucinogen that isn't in our database. Our pathologist is trying to pin it down, but I want to keep the boy sedated until the effects wear off. Has anyone looked you over—"

"I'm fine," she said. "Thanks. For the update."

He nodded and hurried through the heavy doors of the OR.

Garcia felt helpless, useless, reckless, friendless, childless, and alone. She was going to have a panic attack if she didn't get some air. She felt the urge to curl up in a ball right there on the floor but willed herself down the hall to the ambulance bay and shoved through the doors.

The night was cool. The air was sharp and clean. She focused on her breathing.

Eventually, her heart rate slowed to a manageable beat.

She put her hands in her pockets. Her fingers stroked her old smoke break prop.

"The things we do to be alone," she mused, pulling the cigarette from her pocket.

"Need a light?" a voice rasped behind her.

She turned. A wisp of a man stood beneath the red neon cross. He wore a hospital gown and slippers. He had no hair or eyebrows. It was hard to tell his age. He held an IV stand with one hand and had a cigarette in the other. His smile was slight but genuine.

"Aren't you cold?" she asked, joining him.

"I'm all right." He shrugged. He put his cigarette between his lips and picked a Zippo off his IV monitor. He flipped the cap open and flicked the flame alive.

Garcia leaned forward. The tip of her cigarette singed.

"That your blood?" he asked.

She shook her head and stepped back. She took a long drag then hacked the smoke up in a coughing spasm. The man took a slow drag, James Dean cool. Garcia cleared her throat.

"First one," she explained.

"Don't worry, second time's a charm."

She took another hit. She got light-headed. It was a welcome sensation.

She exhaled. She only coughed twice. "Do your doctors know you're out here?"

"Yeah. But they quit naggin' about healthy living once the word 'terminal' comes up."

"I'm sorry," she said.

He shrugged and took a drag. She did the same.

"The world is a vampire," he mused, exhaling.

"What?"

"It's from some song. It was big when I was in high school, on the radio constantly. It's been comin' back to me lately, the way it starts... 'The world is a vampire, sent to drain.'"

"Smashing Pumpkins." She nodded.

"Huh?"

"The band. Smashing Pumpkins."

"That sounds about right," he said.

He flicked the cigarette into the darkness. He lit another.

Otis saw his father's Lincoln before they'd pulled up their driveway. It was parked crooked, next to the house. The porch light reflected off the long hood like an oil slick. Both rear doors of the car were open, and the interior dome light was on.

"He's home!" his mom yelled with unbridled relief.

Otis rolled his eyes. She parked next to the Lincoln. Through the window, Otis watched his father come down from the porch. He was waving, smiling a goofy smile, dressed in the cutoff sweatshirt he donned whenever he did housework. A rag hung from his waistband.

His mom smiled as she got out.

"Fred!" she yelled. His father went to her. They embraced.

Otis waited until their barf-worthy lovefest was over before getting out. The crisp fall night was pierced by the overwhelming stench of bleach. Otis spotted a spray bottle on the ground beneath the passenger door of the Lincoln.

"We looked everywhere for you," his mom was saying. "When Mr. Fiorello called, I—"

"I know," his father said, "I'm sorry, I'm sure you were scared silly. But I had the most ridiculous—"

"Oh yeah?" Otis snapped, as he stomped across the gravel. "What happened?"

"Not what you think," his father said, turning to him. "I

swear. Last night, my pain was too bad to sleep. So, I went driving, the seat warmer and the movement helps...so, yeah, I went driving, right? But I, well, I wasn't paying attention to how *long* I was driving, and I, I ran out of gas! Can you believe that? I sure couldn't. I tried to call you, but my phone died and my car charger doesn't work and so, so, I spent *hours* trying to hitch a ride but no one would give me a ride, so I ended up sleeping in the car! *Then*, this morning, I *still* couldn't get a ride! I ended up having to *pawn* my darn phone just to buy enough gas to get home! Can, can you believe that?"

Otis's jaw clenched. His mom rubbed his father's neck consolingly.

"Oh, honey," she sighed. "I'm so sorry. Talk about one thing after another!"

"What's the bleach for?" Otis asked.

"Oh," his father said, a little off-guard. "I forgot that part. When I finally got gas, I accidentally sprayed some on my clothes! I've been having a terrible time getting rid of the smell. Plus, I ate McDonald's yesterday, and you *know* how bad it stinks up the car..."

Otis sighed. "This, right here. This is the worse part. Because this part's all you."

"Otis," his mom snapped, "he just explained—"

"You can't change the past," Otis said, ignoring her. His eyes were fixed on his father. "You can't help that you were attacked, or that it left you in all this pain, or that you got hooked on those pills the docs gave you...but you can help this. You can help the lying." His voice rose as sloppy tears rolled down his face. "You could *ask* us for help, but you don't! You just *keep* telling lie, after lie, after lie, ones too *stupid* for anyone with half a brain to believe! You aren't a *victim* when you're lying to your family—you're just a, a, another *fucking* junkie!"

"But it's not *me*!" his father cried, shocking Otis to silence.

Otis took a step back. His mom did too.

"I would never lie to you," his father stammered. "It's like I turn into someone, *something* else. I don't know, I don't know, I don't *know*! I would *never* do anything to hurt you. I'm sorry, *I'm sorry, I'm sorry*! It makes me, it, it, I become someone else!"

"Then fuck you," Otis said, "and fuck the *other* you too!"

Then he ran. Ran without thinking, ran like kids run when there's nothing left to do or say. He ran to where his bike was parked. He ignored his mother's cries. He kicked the kickstand up. He ignored his father's pleas. He jumped on the bike and pedaled. Tears blinded his vision. He could barely see well enough to steer. He didn't care. He made it to the driveway. He was going too fast. He didn't care. He had nowhere to go. He didn't care.

The dark swallowed him whole.

He didn't care.

When Garcia walked back into the hospital, she found Sheriff Connors outside Henry's isolation room speaking to Deputy Kern. The florescent lights didn't do the sheriff any favors; he looked like he'd aged twenty years in the last two hours. He nodded hello as she approached.

"What's the word on Coffey?" he asked her.

"Still in surgery, but he's gonna be all right."

"Good," he said, "that's good." He opened the door and looked in on Henry.

Garcia joined him. The kid was "sleeping." IVs pumped numerous medications into his bloodstream. The swelling hadn't gone down much, but his color was back to normal. Sheriff Connors shut the door as quietly as he could.

"Pearl Jolley deserves a slow death for this twisted shit," he muttered.

They took a few steps back to keep the noise down. Kern stayed beside the door.

"Is she talking?" Garcia asked.

"Not a peep. Mayor Jolley put a muzzle on his long-lost cousin right quick. Family's sending down a team of lawyers from Richmond. I don't expect a word from her until then."

And what idiot informed the mayor of her arrest? Garcia thought.

"We've been interrogating the others," he continued, "but their brains are as fried as a fairground Oreo. Litton's driving their DNA swabs to Charleston as we speak, so maybe it'll give us something. CPD is fast-trackin' the results. Hope to have some answers by tomorrow."

She nodded. "Have they found anything on the property?"

"More drugs than a Tijuana titty bar," he said. "No offense meant."

"Offense taken."

"And noted. Sorry 'bout that...long night. Jimbo's got his cadaver dogs over at the compound right now, but there's a lotta ground to cover. None of the vehicles on the property actually *run*, as far as we can tell. It looks like they get their food air-dropped as if they're Doctors Without Borders. Doesn't seem like they've left the grounds for who knows how long."

"Which means what?" she asked.

"It means, crazy as they are, I don't make the Lordsville crew for Carrie Clemmons. Hard to imagine them acid-heads pulling off a murder and successful body dump without a vehicle."

"You wouldn't be so quick to write 'em off if you'd seen them in action," she said. "They're all psychotic. I could see any one of them killing with no hesitation. Plus, Harlan Lusher's father is willing to testify that Pearl Jolley stabbed his daughter through the eye, just like BSS. I think she's obsessed with the Lusher family and getting revenge for the fire of '84."

"Harlan Lusher's daddy told you that?"

"Right before I found Pearl Jolley torturing his grandson."

"Goddamn," he groaned. "I don't know what to think no more. Maybe she *was* involved. Maybe…goddamn…goddamn. OK, when Jolley's lawyers arrive, I want you in charge of the interrogation. Go at her hard. Bleed it out of her if need be. But for now, go home and—"

"I'm not leaving until Coffey's out of surgery," she said. "I'm fine. Really."

"Fair enough." He shrugged. "I need to get back to it. Call me when he's out?"

"Yes, sir."

"Hell of a job, Lieutenant," he said. "I hope you know you're a…hell of…yeah." He tipped his hat to her, something she'd never seen him do. Then Sheriff Connors shuffled away. She stood there a moment before leaning on the wall beside Kern.

"I threw the kid's bike in my cruiser," he said. "I hope that's OK. It woulda been tied up for months in processing, and I figure a kid needs a bike. Kids like him, more than most."

"Agreed," she said.

His eyes drifted past her. She followed them. Jane and her grandmother were rushing down the hallway, checking every room number they passed. Garcia stepped out from the wall and waved them down—when they saw her, their expressions morphed from panicked to terrified. It took a moment for Garcia to remember she had blood all over her uniform.

"It's not his," she called out as they ran toward her. "He's OK! He's OK!"

Jane and her grandmother shared a look of doubtful relief.

"Where's Henry?" Jane panted when they reached her.

"In here," she said. "He's sleeping. Come on, I'll fill you in."

Kern opened the door for the women. Mammaw and Jane entered. Garcia shared a look with Kern as she followed them into the hospital room. Kern grinned slightly and shrugged.

"Silver lining for ya, Lieutenant...compared to you, the kid don't look too bad at all."

36

Jane was too anxious to weep. All she could do was squeeze Henry's hand. She sat at one corner of his hospital bed. Mammaw sat at the other. Lt. Garcia recounted the evening as gently as she could. There would be time for gory details later, and the sanitized version of the story was bad enough for one night.

"But she's in jail?" Mammaw asked once Garcia had finished.

"Yes, ma'am, Pearl Jolley and all of her cronies are in custody."

"Was anyone else hurt?" Jane asked, keeping her eyes on Henry.

"Unfortunately," Garcia said. "One officer was shot. He's in surgery now and expected to recover. Three members of Lordsville were killed."

Jane's eyes clenched shut. She teetered on a panic attack of immeasurable proportions.

"I'm sorry about your comrade," Mammaw said.

"I'm sorry about your grandson."

Jane forced her eyes open. Henry's hand was turning red from how hard she was squeezing. She let go. She searched her pockets, but she didn't have her pill carrier. No buspirone or Valium. She didn't have her pills. She needed her pills. Her anxiety compounded.

Mammaw registered the movement. "What is it, honey? Your meds?"

"Yeah I, shit, shit, I can't find them," she said, checking her back pocket. "I didn't think to grab my carrier when...everything happened so fast..."

"My deputy can run her home if you want to stay here," Garcia said to Mammaw.

"Thank ya," she said, then turned to Jane. "Go on back to the house, baby. Gravy needs his dinner anyway."

"But what if—"

"Your brother's stable," Garcia reminded her, "and sedated enough to sleep through the night. Why don't you get some sleep yourself? I'll have an officer bring you back first thing in the morning."

She didn't want to go. She didn't want to leave him.

"I'll call ya as soon as Henry's up," Mammaw promised.

She knew she had to go. She knew she had to leave him.

"OK," Jane said, her voice shaky. She lifted Henry's hand off the bed and kissed it.

Mammaw sighed. They both bowed their heads. Two devotionals. One sad liturgy.

Otis was exhausted. He'd been riding aimlessly, angrily, not pacing himself at all. He finally pulled onto a bare patch of grass to catch his breath and figure out his next move. It was hard to concentrate. All his mind would focus on was his father standing in the driveway. He thought *at* his father, as if he could continue lambasting him via telepathy: *You're too smart to make up such stupid lies...or is it that you think I'm so young and dumb I'll believe anything?*

The possibility was insulting enough to get him back on task.

"I'll show *you* who's dumb," he growled. "I'll show this whole freakin' town."

It was settled. He would finally take his BSS theories to the sheriff and the press. Soon, Paradise would be beholden to the boy genius, the adolescent avenger that was about to blow the doors off their legendary sealed-shut case.

But first, he had to speak to Henry. He needed an update on the prison interview.

He got out his phone and dialed their house—no service.

"Stupid freaking phone!" he screamed.

He jerked his arm back to launch the phone into the woods but caught himself before he could. Instead, he shook the phone angrily before putting it back in his pocket.

Then he was off, pedaling toward Henry. Henry would have the answers. Henry would make everything OK. He was too upset to muse on how desperation makes the best of friends.

Mammaw watched over Henry, lost in the ebbing tide of his shallow breath. Lt. Garcia saw Jane out, and Mammaw was thankful for that. Her angel baby was strong but emotionally fragile—Mammaw worried she might crack if she sat with Henry much longer. She hoped Jane would take a Valium and blur the events of the day. The last thing her girl needed right now was clarity.

The door opened a crack. Lt. Garcia looked in to see if she

was interrupting. Mammaw motioned her inside. She shut the door quietly and took the seat Jane so recently occupied.

"I'm sorry, kid," Garcia whispered. "I should've listened to you and your PI."

"Who?" Mammaw asked.

"Your private investigator. Henry told me about him earlier, when we were going through shirt orders. Perkins, I think the name was."

"Ah, Otis." Mammaw grinned. She looked back to Henry. "Poor baby. He always did think Lordsville framed his daddy. But he don't even know the half of it . . . "

"What do you mean?" Garcia asked.

"Jane visited Harlan today. He told her things . . . about that place, about Pearl Jolley."

"Like what?"

"Nothin' he ain't already told the sheriff—"

"I'm not Sheriff Connors," Garcia urged. "Please. It could be important."

"It's stranger than fiction, that's for damn sure," Mammaw said. "Pearl Jolley went so far off the deep end, she started doin' exorcisms on her church flock. Only she wasn't splashin' 'em with holy water—she was killing animals and sticking knives through their goddamn eyes. Harlan's momma was in on it too. She even let Pearl Jolley do it to his sister—"

"Hazel?" Garcia asked.

Mammaw nodded.

"Do you think Harlan would be willing to testify against Pearl Jolley in court?"

"I think he'd like nothin' more."

"I need to step out and make some calls," Garcia said. "Will you two be OK?"

Mammaw nodded. Garcia got up and went back into the hall. Mammaw looked down at Henry. She sensed something significant coming together in the back of her mind. A stage was being set, masked by the heavy curtain of age. There was no point tugging at the pulleys and levers. The curtain would open or it wouldn't. The spotlight would shine or remain dark.

She petted her grandson's hair. She had never felt so old.

"Did you know most lemurs spend their *whole* lives in trees?" Deputy Kern asked, keeping his eyes on the road. "Their feet don't touch the ground *once*. Ain't that something?"

"Yeah." Jane nodded. "It is."

The whole ride had been that way. Jane sitting shotgun with her hands clasped together, Kern rambling off random facts about random things like a flesh-and-blood Snapple cap. But the odd trivia distracted her enough for her nerves to even out. Her muscles were still tense, but her breathing had gone back to normal and her heart rate had started to slow.

"I gotta say," he said, "to go to Lordsville alone the way he did… your little brother must be one bad mother-shut-your-mouth!"

She laughed. She couldn't believe it, but she laughed. "He is. He really is."

Kern steered onto Lockland Street. She turned to look at him.

"Do you know when the press conference is gonna be?"

He cocked his eyebrow, confused.

"Sheriff Connors," Jane clarified. "When's he gonna announce that Pearl Jolley murdered Carrie? I was thinking maybe Henry should be there."

"Maybe," he muttered. His face clenched up.

"What?" she asked. "What is it? Something about Lordsville?"

"I can't talk to civilians ab—"

"I deserve to know," she snapped.

He sighed. "You didn't get this from me. But I heard the sheriff talkin' earlier...he doesn't think Jolley killed that girl."

"But how's that, h-h-how is that possible?"

"Don't get me wrong," Kern said, "she'll rot in jail for what she did to your brother—"

"But she's the Blind Spot Slasher!" Jane yelled, anxiety back in full force. "She framed my dad! Doesn't this prove that? What the hell else do you need?"

"I don't know...all I heard him mention was the Clemmons girl. I could be wrong."

Jane couldn't respond. Her jaw clenched shut. Her muscles turned to stone.

The cruiser pulled into the yard. Kern shifted into park but kept the engine running. He popped the trunk and got out. Jane forced her stiff fingers to unbuckle her seatbelt and pull the door latch, pushing the door and stepping onto the grass in one rigid movement.

Kern already had the bike on the ground. "Want me to wheel it to the house?"

"No," she mumbled, "thank you." She took the handlebars and pushed the bike through the yard. Dry leaves were crushed to dust beneath the rolling rubber tires.

"Give us a call when ya need a ride to the hospital," he hollered. "OK?"

She waved back, noncommittal. Kern sighed, mumbling to himself as he climbed back into the cruiser. Then he pulled out of the yard. When his headlights veered back on the road, Jane realized how dark it was. She struggled to get her keys in the door. Little claws began scratching on the other side.

Dog Mom first, she ordered herself as she turned the key. *Take care of Gravyboat before you take a Valium and veg out. No time to be selfish—Gravy'd do it for you.* She opened the door.

The dog wasted no time with hellos. He charged through the screen door and into the yard to pee. Jane leaned inside and flipped the porch light on.

That's when she saw Henry's note.

She read it. Then she noticed her belongings scattered on the ground. Makeup. Tampons. Gum. It didn't make sense. She grabbed the bike's handlebars and unzipped the fanny pack.

"Holy shit," she gasped.

Gravy trotted back onto the porch as Jane reached inside the fanny pack. Awestruck, she slowly removed the revolver as if she were pulling Excalibur from the stone. The light caught the silver barrel of the gun when she opened the chamber. It was loaded. The gun was loaded.

"Holy shit," she said again, louder.

She opened the door, followed the dog in, and locked it behind them. She turned on a lamp and sat the gun on the kitchen table. She fed the dog. She chugged two glasses of water.

She looked at the gun. She paced. She looked at the gun. She paced.

If Pearl Jolley isn't the killer, did Henry risk his life for nothing?

No. It wasn't for nothing. It was for her. Henry did it for the family.

"You crazy asshole," she said.

Gravy looked up, realized that she didn't mean him, and went back to his dinner. Jane walked into the bathroom and flipped on the light. She grabbed the Valium and twisted the cap.

Henry went there with a loaded gun. He was willing to go all the way. Hazel saved Dad from the exorcism. She was willing to go all the way.

What was Jane willing to do? Medicate? Disassociate? Numb herself to uselessness?

She caught her reflection in the mirror. She stared herself down.

Doesn't their blood run through your veins? Aren't you still a Lusher? Aren't you still—

"Calamity Jane."

Jane put the lid back on the pill bottle, twisted it, and set it aside. She set Lordsville aside too. If Pearl Jolley wasn't the Blind Spot Slasher, then that meant the killer was still out there. Lordsville was to blame for much of their suffering, but the killer was to blame for it all.

The killer took her father. Her family.

The killer took her childhood. Took her place in the world. Took her little brother.

She had to find him. Whoever he was. Wherever he was.

She had to put it all on the line. For Henry. For Hazel.

She had to go all the way.

She flipped off the bathroom light and went back into the kitchen. She found Otis's cell number magnetized to the fridge. Once she gave him the rundown, he would know how to fit the pieces together. She grabbed the phone and dialed.

She waited. No answer.

"It's Jane. Call me back ASAP," she ordered his voice mail.

She hung up. She tried again. Still no answer. She hung up.

The anxiety that had crippled her now propelled her forward. She went back into the bathroom and opened the drawer beneath the sink. She applied her war paint: foundation, mascara, blood-red lipstick, twice as much eyeliner as usual. She rubbed some lipstick between her fingers and used it as blush. In a matter of minutes Jane Lusher looked cheap and alive.

She went into her bedroom to change clothes. She slid into her shortest pair of shorts and a pullover sweatshirt. She laced up her running shoes, then went into Henry's room.

Music. Comics. Ridiculous pulp mysteries that now felt spot-on with their ridiculous lives.

Jane opened his closet and got what she needed: Orgasmatron.

She put the jean jacket on over her sweatshirt, popping the collar like her brother did as she walked back into the kitchen. She slid the .357 Magnum into the interior jacket pocket.

It was scary how well it fit.

Jane stood there for five minutes, willing Otis to call her back.

He didn't. She tried him again. He didn't answer.

It was all on her. She looked down at the dog. His little tail wagged. His little eyes had that love-light gleam. She petted him before going to the front door and ripping off the note.

She crossed out Henry's message. In its place, she wrote the most plausible lie she could think of for Mammaw, not wanting her to worry if she came back to an empty house.

Jane took one more look around, grabbed her keys, taped the note to the door, and split. She mounted her bike, death-gripped the handlebars, and sharpened her eyes. The wind picked up, and leaves scattered. Calamity Jane rode into the darkness. Orgasmatron was her battle flag, and it beat against the night sky harder than any black sail ever could.

37

Sgt. Coffey's surgery was a success; he would be moved to the ICU after his blood pressure settled. When Deputy Dernt arrived for guard duty, Garcia went to the ICU waiting room. She had to see her unofficial partner with her own two eyes before going home for the night.

The chaos of the ward had dulled to a muted panic. Her shock had dulled as well, and it was replaced by crushing exhaustion. The post-shock fatigue had her mind playing tricks. She tried watching the TV, but all the cable news talking heads reminded her of Pearl Jolley. She was so zonked out that when she saw Craig and Ruby, she assumed it was a hallucination.

Her fiancé and little girl walked down the hallway, looking lost.

"Craig?" she called out hesitantly, convinced it was a trick of the mind.

But Craig stopped. When he saw her, his broad shoulders collapsed with relief. Then he got Ruby's attention and pointed to the waiting room. Ruby lit up. She ran to her mother. Garcia dropped to one knee and opened her arms. Ruby gave her the most necessary hug of her life.

"What are you doing here, chiqui?" she asked, still squeezing.

"Daddy let me stay up past my bedtime to give you the super-hero prize!"

"What?" she laughed.

Craig was smiling when he reached them, but there were tears in his eyes. "Your superhero membership card," he said. "I told her you earned one tonight, but it won't be official until you get your super-secret reward. That's why we had to *sneak* up, right?"

"It's secret, 'cause it's dark out," Ruby explained.

Garcia just kept smiling. It was all she could do.

"Well, go on," Craig said. "Give Mommy her reward."

Ruby took a deep breath, making a show of it, then plastered a thousand kisses all over her mother's face. Garcia burst out laughing. Craig did too. He wiped his eyes.

"I think...it *worked*!" Garcia yelled suddenly. She picked Ruby up and spun her around in the air. Now Ruby was the one laughing, still giggling when she came back to earth.

Craig slid the gym bag off his shoulder and placed it on the ground. He reached into his wallet and got some dollar bills. "Why don't you go to the vending machine and get Mommy a snack? If you pick something good, she might even share it. It's right over there, see?"

"Sugar this late?" Garcia whispered to him.

"We're screwed either way," he whispered back.

She shrugged. He handed the money to Ruby.

"Straight to the machine," Garcia ordered. "Stay where we can see you."

Ruby nodded and stepped back, then noticed the stains on her mother's uniform.

"Ketchup," Garcia said. "Mommy spilt it all over herself."

"Mommy's sloppy," she giggled, before trotting over to the vending machine.

Her parents sat down and watched her.

"What are you doing here?" Garcia asked.

"Sheriff Connors called. He told me what happened...some of it, anyway. Said you needed a change of clothes. There weren't a lot of options left at the house, but at least there's no *ketchup* on these. Elena, when I got that call, I thought..." He couldn't finish.

She took his hands. She'd missed them.

"I'm OK," she said softly. "Everything is OK."

"No, it isn't," he muttered. "This distance between us is my fault. I should—*we* should— already be living here with you. I know I've been slacking on the remodel, but...screw the remodel. I'm calling a realtor tomorrow. We—"

"Don't need to talk about it now," she said.

"I just can't stop thinking about it."

"Well," she said, "compartmentalization's my superpower."

"Yeah...guess it is. I just hope I'm still worthy of being your damsel in distress."

They both smiled. She squeezed his hand.

"Still have a key to the new house?" Garcia asked.

"Of course."

"Why don't you two stay with me tonight? I'm still living out of boxes, but her room's pretty much set up."

"Yeah," he nodded. "That's a great idea."

Ruby came back, cradling junk food in her arms. The girl

could barely walk straight, and Garcia knew she was running out of gas. She picked Ruby up and sat her on her lap.

"Look at all these snacks!" she said, feigning amazement.

"I got bunches," Ruby yawned.

"How about we save them for breakfast," Craig said. "We're gonna stay at the new house tonight with Mommy. How's that sound?"

Ruby nodded sleepily. Garcia took the packets of junk food from Ruby and placed them in the seat beside her. They both stood, and Garcia handed off their daughter. Ruby was snoozing within seconds, drooling on his shoulder. Garcia kissed Ruby goodbye. She hesitated then, but Craig did not. He planted a serious kiss on her lips. It was long. Familiar. Right.

"You're definitely still my damsel," Garcia said, swooning a little. "Lois Lane's got nothin' on *my* man."

"Damn right." He smiled and kissed her again.

Otis bore down on Lockland. He didn't slow as he neared the house. He didn't care that he was sweat-soaked and disheveled. Insecurities are secondary when you're a man on a mission. He noted their grandmother's car was missing. He rode through her usual parking space, struggling for balance as he rumbled across the front yard and eased down the brakes.

Jane's bike is gone too, he thought as he came to a stop.

He dismounted. He walked onto the porch. He saw the note:

I went to help do inventory at work. I know it's late, but if I don't keep busy, I'll lose it. Love you. Jane.

Otis knocked on the door.

No answer, besides the dog scratching at the other side. He got out his phone. It was back in service. He had nine missed calls from home and three from Jane. He knocked again. No answer. Just the dog. *Do I really have to ride all the way downtown to find out what's going on?*

He huffed and puffed. He didn't know if he could stand to bike any farther.

He re-examined the note: an earlier message had been scribbled out.

He pulled the slip of paper off the door, flipped it over, and held it up to the porch light.

"Went to Lordsville..." he read aloud. "Henry."

Otis slapped the note back on the door and whirled around. He was so flummoxed that, when he mounted the bike, he lost his balance and went tumbling into the leaves. But he didn't whine like he usually would. He simply got up, wiped himself off, picked up the bike, and got back on. Because pain and humiliation are secondary when you're a man on a mission.

Fresh energy buzzed through his legs as he started toward the bookstore. There were answers waiting for him in the dark.

He pedaled as fast as he could.

Small-town customs rarely change, even in the bleakest of times. Paradise was no exception. Those who could buy gas still bought it to burn, and they spent their nights cruising the main drags and backroads of town. "Joyriding" wasn't the word. They were pacing restlessly, desperately combing the roads in search of *something*— some event, some change, some reminder that they were alive.

Jane watched the cars drive beneath the I-64 overpass. For the most part, the passengers ignored the clusters of people huddled by the support beams and the women walking the road. But, once in a while, a car would pull over to buy and/or sell something and/or someone.

She hid her bike behind a tree with a highway cross fastened to it and watched the nocturnal world until she got a handle on things. Then Jane unbuttoned the jean jacket and did a practice draw. The gun got snagged on the pocket. She tried again, with a higher arc.

It worked.

She drew and holstered five more times to make sure she had the technique down. The gun didn't give her a sense of security, but it did clarify matters. She was playing with life-and-death stakes, and she needed to keep her wits about her if she wanted to live through the night.

Her plan was simple enough: take down the license plate numbers of every car that stopped. If she spotted a possible BSS-mobile, she would approach the car and get a physical description of the driver. She was determined to do whatever she had to, besides get in the car. It was common knowledge that once you got into the car you were as good as dead.

She pulled the gun again. She holstered it again.

She stretched her neck and arms. She shook out her heebie-jeebies.

Shit. She was ready.

Calamity Jane emerged from the woods. She kept near the trees as she and made her way to the overpass. She studied the other women walking the road, imitating their stop-motion silhouettes; she moved slow, hunching her shoulders while simultaneously shaking her hips. She made a point not to look at anyone or anything for too long.

A truck pulled up to one of the women. Jane closed in, walking diagonally to the gravel shoulder. She knelt down and crept behind the truck. She took the pen from her pocket as the woman approached the driver's side window.

"Whaddaya need? Whaddaya got?" she heard the woman ask the driver.

Jane couldn't hear his reply. She wrote the license number on her wrist then went back into her *Night of the Living Dead* act. The truck pulled away. The woman put a handful of cash down the front of her jeans. She nodded hello. Jane nodded back. She headed for the overpass.

Other cars stopped at other points in the road. Each did some type of drug transaction, as if the bridge was an after-hours pharmacy drive-thru. Jane realized there were cars parked deep in the shadows, hour-rate motels on wheels. She would need to get their plate numbers, too.

Calamity Jane began her lap around the overpass. Once her eyes adjusted to the darker darkness, it wasn't as scary as she'd expected. The highway overhead rumbled. Those beneath it were sad and lost. They seemed to huddle into each other there in the shadows of love, imitating what genuine human connection their augmented states would not allow. An acoustic guitar echoed off the concrete, cutting through the ebbing growl of the interstate. The guitarist sat against a support beam. She didn't look much older than Jane. An emaciated pit bull lay beside her. With an in-tune guitar and an out-of-tune voice, the girl began to sing:

I say, Americans of all races and creeds
banded and bonded by their cripplin' need,

I know it's a shame and I know it's a sin
but all I wanna do is get high again...

Jane listened, transfixed. Soon, the singer had an audience of half a dozen or more. It reminded Jane of a book she'd read in Ms. Egerton's English class called *The Grapes of Wrath*. It was a sad—yet hopeful—book. But in Paradise, the milk of human kindness curdled long ago.

"Love that jacket," a voice behind her rasped.

She tensed up. She turned.

A man in a leather vest with a gray beard smiled approvingly. "Lemmy is God."

"My brother says that all the time," she told him, smiling back.

He nodded and continued on. Four or five cars passed. She watched them go, amazed that they were able to ignore the scene. The last of the vehicles slowed and pulled beside her.

It was a Silverado pickup covered in mud. Pop country blared from the cab and then switched off. The window lowered. Jane approached slowly. Her trigger finger itched. There were two men inside, both in their twenties. They wore jumpsuits and were covered in coal dust. The red dashboard lights made their eyes looked predatory, hungry.

"Hop in, legs," the driver said. "We got forty-seven bucks between us."

"And a bottle of Jim," the passenger added.

These guys aren't BSS. They aren't smart enough. "Hey, thanks guys, but I'm OK—"

"Crack whore bitch," the driver spat. The music kicked back on as they peeled away.

Guitar girl went into a bluesy version of Steve Earle's "Cocaine Cannot Kill My Pain." Jane stood and listened.

Something about the chord progression sent a chill down her bare legs. Then, from the corner of her eye, she saw one of the cars parked across the road pull forward. The tires rolled slowly—creeping—barely noticeable, and stopped once it was parallel to her.

The car was a black sled of a thing, almost as long as a limousine. The driver was outlined by a faint green dashboard glow. Jane sensed him looking at her. She felt exposed.

The Blind Spot Slasher. It had to be him. The chill spread throughout her body.

A few cars cut between them. Jane stared at the car. The driver stared back.

The road cleared. She stepped from the gravel to the blacktop and crossed the road at an angle, as if she weren't walking to the car but somewhere behind it. She removed the pen from her pocket, determined to get the plate number, nerves be damned. She reached the other side of the overpass. She knelt down, focused on her breath, and copied the license plate number.

That's when she heard it—*click*.

She looked up to see the back door of the car open slightly. It was an invitation.

Once you get in the car, you're as good as dead, she reminded herself.

She stood up. The gun was heavy at her side. She walked down the length of the frame to the driver's side door. She gestured for him to lower the window. He didn't.

Once you get in the car, you're as good as dead, she told herself again.

She leaned into the open door.

"What do you need? What do you got?" she asked, as steady as she could.

"Please," the driver said, "get in so we can talk."

Once you get in the car...

Jane got in the car. She shut the door. Her hand was tense, ready to quick draw if necessary. The driver didn't look at her. He kept his eyes forward and down.

"What can forty buy me?" he asked. "Oxy or hydro, vikes, even..."

As he spoke, another car passed. Headlights illuminated the interior, and Jane saw his eyes dart up to get a glimpse of her in the rearview mirror. They were the eyes of a rabid animal.

"It's you," he whispered. The car darkened again.

"I, um, I have Oxys," she stammered, pretending she hadn't heard. "Let me just, uh, go get my stash—" Jane reached for the door handle. The locks snapped shut before she pulled it.

"You shouldn't be here," he said.

"Open the door," she demanded, voice shaking. She kept pulling at the handle.

He turned around as another car passed. Jane realized she wasn't looking at an animal, a boogeyman, or a monster—she was face-to-face with Fred Perkins, whom she'd met days before.

"Open the door," she screamed.

She fumbled for the gun. The barrel got caught on the pocket. She yanked at it.

"No, no, no," he said, sobbing madly. "We can't, we, we must—"

She got the gun free and raised it, aiming at his face. He reeled, hitting the horn with his back, alerting everyone dwelling at the overpass that some serious shit was going down.

"Open the door, or I'll blow your fucking head off!" she ordered.

"OK, OK, OK, OK," he sputtered, fumbling with buttons until the locks popped open.

Jane pushed at the door with such force that she tripped over the doorframe and flailed face-first onto the gravel. She cried out in pain, clinging to the gun. Her knees were cut to shreds. Her ankles were still in the car, feet hooked on the interior frame.

She heard the driver's side door open. The guitar stopped playing. People on the other side of the overpass were walking over. Jane used her elbows to crawl backward across the gravel. The pain was excruciating. The fear all-consuming. Yet she would not stop.

Jane was bathed in headlights almost as soon as she reached the blacktop. A Honda Civic slammed on its brakes less than five feet from her head. Jane yelled even louder than before. Other cars squealed to a stop behind the Honda as Fred Perkins stumbled into the road after her.

Jane aimed the gun. She cocked the hammer back.

"We can help you," he pleaded, raising his shaking hands. "Please! Come on—"

BAM!

Jane fired a warning shot into the bridge above them. There was a ricochet. People screamed. The cars stopped honking. Fred Perkins backed away quickly, eyes still focused on her, trembling hands raised to the heavens. Jane brought the smoking barrel back to earth.

"Jane?" a familiar voice called.

Jane kept her gun on the monster as she looked around, trying to find the voice. A woman from one of the backed-up cars was waving her down. It was Ms. Summers. Jane had never seen her look so scared and confused.

"Try to follow me and I'll fucking kill you!" she yelled at Otis's father.

"I'm s-s-sorry," he muttered. "I'm, I'm not m-m-me anymore . . ."

Jane stumbled toward Ms. Summers's car.

"Oh, honey!" Ms. Summers exclaimed, flabbergasted. "What are—"

"Quick," Jane snapped. "We've gotta get out of here!"

Ms. Summers nodded. They both got in the car. She gunned it and pulled a U-turn before Jane had even shut her door. They raced away from the overpass. The shock, rage, horror, and exhaustion of the moment hit Jane all at once. She screamed at the top of her lungs.

Ms. Summers flinched but kept her eyes on the road.

Jane began to weep. Ms. Summers stayed silent until her tears ran dry.

"Jane," she said softly. "Why don't you, um, let me hold on to that for now."

Jane looked down. She was still holding the gun. Her finger was still on the trigger. Her hands were no longer steady, and the firearm shook wildly. Her badass levels were depleted.

Jane reeled, disgusted. She let go of the gun as if it were covered in raw sewage. Ms. Summers reached over—slowly, carefully—and took the gun from Jane's lap. She put it in the side compartment of her door and then reached back to take Jane's shaking hands into her own.

"I have to ask you something," she said, "and please be honest with me, because I just want to help. Were you buying drugs down there?"

"Drugs?" Jane scoffed, almost laughing. "Oh God, no! Nothing like that. I . . . it's a long story. I'll explain everything. But can you take me to the sheriff's station?"

She nodded. She picked up speed.

Jane's subconscious played connect the dots.

The sheriff's station...the night it all started...

"Otis," Jane gasped.

"What is it?" Ms. Summers asked.

"I need your cell phone, quick!"

"It's there, in the drink holder."

Jane grabbed the iPhone. She couldn't figure out the touch screen, so she hit the square with a phone logo and prepared to dial Otis's number. She realized she didn't know it. It was written down at the house.

"Shit!" she yelled, gripping the phone. "I, I...we need to stop at my house. It's an emergency, my friend's in danger. Can you take me—"

"I'm on it." Ms. Summers hit her blinker. She changed course.

Jane was close to hyperventilating. She did Lamaze breathing. Ms. Summers looked over.

"Honey, you need to tell me what's going on."

"I know," Jane panted, "I'm just, ugh, I...I feel like all hell's breaking loose."

"Well, yes," Ms. Summers said. "I've gathered that much already."

38

Sgt. Sean Coffey opened his eyes. His color was better, considering, and his vital signs were stable. Garcia tried not to flinch when she noticed the flecks of dried blood in his mustache.

"Hey, partner," she said. "Welcome back to existence."

"Whitn-n-n-ney...Houston?" he croaked, referencing the T-shirt Garcia changed into after shedding her bloody uniform.

"Wrong diva," she said. "How you feeling?"

"The b-boy?" he asked weakly, ignoring her. She could tell he was fading again.

"He's OK. You saved his life, you know that?"

Whatever he tried to say next came out as incoherent mumbles, which soon morphed into snores. She picked the blood out of his mustache and flicked it into the trash can. Then she grabbed her duffel of bloody clothes and slowly walked into the hall.

She'd never been so eager to get home.

Home. To her family. She liked the sound of that.

Suddenly, she clocked footfalls behind her. Heavy breathing. Running.

"Lieutenant!" Deputy Dernt called to her from farther down the hall. When he reached her, he was breathing harder than a triathlete. Her tired mind absently wondered how he'd passed his last fitness exam. "The kid . . . " He panted, bracing the wall.

"What? What about him?"

"He's awake."

Garcia pushed past her wheezing deputy and rushed down the hall, surprised by her burst of energy. She rounded the corner as the graveyard shift doctor was leaving Henry's room. When she reached him, he stopped to block the door.

"Family only," he said.

She was about to give him the riot act but then remembered she wasn't in uniform. She scoffed at herself and pulled the badge from her pocket.

"Lt. Garcia, Sheriff's Department."

"Oh, I'm sorry. I'm Dr. Baker." They shook hands.

"I need to talk to him."

"He still has psychedelics in his system," Dr. Baker said. "You won't get anything coherent from him. He needs to rest. I've administered a sedative—"

"More reason to move your ass," Mammaw said from behind him.

Dr. Baker huffed, aggravated, but continued on to finish his rounds.

Mammaw took Garcia's arm and led her to Henry. The kid was woozy but awake.

"He's drugged, but that don't mean he ain't coherent," Mammaw whispered. "I shacked up with enough musicians in my day to know. Just gotta listen to the words *between* the words."

Garcia smiled politely. The old woman sounded a bit psychedelicized herself. When Garcia reached the bed, she was shocked to see how dilated Henry's pupils still were.

"Detect-t-t-tive," he muttered. "Officer, Sheriff, I have to tell you, I have to tell you..." He broke into a coughing fit. "It's the eyes! The devil is in the eyes look for the eyes the serpent the eyes like glass they see the devil see the devil see the devil through eyes like...glass..."

"Whose eyes?" Garcia urged, shaken by his words, though she didn't understand them.

"The Blood Bought Believer! *Blood is the great purifier! Blood is t*—"

Henry passed out midsentence.

Mammaw gently reached over and closed his mouth for him.

The women looked at each other from across the bed.

"I didn't make heads or tails of that," said Garcia.

"Blood is the great purifier," Mammaw mused. "Why does that sound familiar?"

"Ever watch *The 700 Club*?"

Mammaw scoffed. "Gimme a moment to marinate on it."

Garcia stepped back and watched Mammaw pace the room. The duffel bag felt almost as heavy as her eyelids. She was about to say her goodbyes when the old woman's body stiffened and she stopped dead in her tracks.

"The eyes," Mammaw muttered. "The eyes like..." she turned to Garcia.

"What?"

"Harlan's sister," Mammaw said rapidly. "Were they identical twins?"

"I'm not sure..."

Mammaw grabbed the bedside phone. She dialed in a panic. She waited.

"What is it?" Garcia urged.

Mammaw hung up and looked back to Garcia. "You still got your gun on ya?"

"I...yes, but—"

"Come on! If I'm right..."

She ran into the hall without finishing the statement. Garcia followed the old lady out.

Henry's eyelids twitched. Alone, he dreamed.

Spilling her guts made Jane feel better. Saying it out loud, telling it as one story—starting with the podcast and ending at the overpass—made it feel like nothing *but* a story. Her words were gravitational; the more she talked, the more grounded she felt. Word by word, her heart rate steadied. Sentence by sentence, her tear ducts closed. Jane's hands were hardly even shaking by the time she finished purging herself.

"I'm so, so sorry," Ms. Summers sighed. "I don't quite know what to say."

"I don't think I would either."

A car passed them going the opposite direction. Something in Jane's peripheral vision glimmered. She looked at Ms. Summers, who was fully focused on the road. Ms. Summers was crying. The headlights must have reflected off the tears.

"But your brother will be all right?" she asked.

"Yeah, I think." Jane nodded. "We'll have a better idea in the morning."

"Lordsville," Ms. Summers said, her voice sharpening to a

point. "A den of false prophets. Their tongues should be ripped out and fed to pigs. They should all be burned at the stake for what they've done to him."

"Uh, totally," Jane said, not sure how else to respond. She had never seen Ms. Summers get angry before. She found she didn't like it.

"What are you doin' out so late?" Jane asked, trying to change the subject.

"Oh," she said, her tone perking, "you won't believe it. I found a first edition of *Dracula* at an estate sale in Clarksville. They only wanted five thousand for it. It resells for *ten times* that much! But the seller couldn't meet me until he got off work."

"Awesome," Jane said. She turned to the back seat, assuming the book would be there. But no book. No anything.

"Where is it?" Jane asked. "I'd love to see it."

"Where's what, dear?"

"The book."

"It's in the trunk," Ms. Summers said.

"Oh. OK." Jane shrugged and faced forward. They passed Cupid's Playground—an XXX video store—which meant the next turn was Lockland. Jane mentally prepared for the call she had to make. She hoped she was wrong about the monster in the road, hoped it wasn't Otis's dad.

Ms. Summers passed the turn.

"That was my street," Jane said. "I've gotta call my friend, remember?"

Five seconds passed.

Ten seconds. Twenty.

"*Truly there is no such thing as finality,*" Ms. Summers whispered, still focused on the road. "That's my favorite line from the book. It's so beautiful, so...apt."

"Um, Ms. Summers?" Jane tried to sound calm. "Do you need directions?"

"No, dear. I know this road well. I've found her out here many times."

Jane gulped. "Found who?"

"Momma."

39

Garcia never imagined someone so round and old could move so fast, but Mammaw sped through the halls of the hospital like a boulder rolling through the Temple of Doom. Garcia matched her speed but still lagged on any details.

"What was it?" she kept asking. "What don't I get?"

"Blood's the purifier," Mammaw huffed, rationing her breath. "She said it yesterday." She cut a sharp left, nearly running over a male nurse. They reached the exit leading to the parking lot. The automatic doors took a billion years to open.

"Who said it?" Garcia panted.

"The bookstore bitch...no wonder she's so nice to Janey—"

The doors opened. Mammaw ran out and searched frantically for the car.

"The Book Nook?" Garcia asked, following. "Summers? The owner? Is that who you mean?"

"Yeah," she panted, "but I don't think that's her name. I think her name's Hazel Lusher."

"What?" Garcia scoffed. "You think his sister came back from the dead?" She hadn't meant to sound dismissive, but the idea was like something from a soap opera.

"Who says she really died? Far as I know, they didn't find no body. She coulda been the Slasher all along!"

"But why would she go on a killing spree? Why would she frame Harlan?"

"You can ask her yourself, if I find my goddamn car." Mammaw huffed, frustrated.

"Come on, my cruiser's right there."

Mammaw nodded. They jogged over to it.

"Gotta hit my house first," Mammaw panted. "Jane ain't answering the phone."

Garcia unlocked the car. "You think she's in trouble?"

Mammaw got in without answering. Garcia understood. She hit the lights.

It was the longest ride ever. Every uphill slope validated Otis's lifelong aversion to exercise. Halloween decorations were out in full tilt, and each porch he passed was lit vampire red or Frankenstein green. The streets and sidewalks were empty. Paradise was Spook City, USA.

When he heard the music and drunken clamor, he smiled.

Downtown. Finally.

He knew the bookstore was somewhere around there. It couldn't be that hard to find.

Jane was never going to believe the hell ride he'd just been on.

They cut the night. Ms. Summers kept her eyes straight and both hands on the wheel.

Jane was nervous. *There's no reason to be nervous!* Jane was scared. *There's no reason to be scared!* Jane argued against her own instincts. She was desperate to believe everything was fine.

"Where are we going?" she finally asked.

"We're traveling the road to salvation," Ms. Summers said with a smile.

That smile was cold clarity. It turned Jane's insides to ice.

Six years, it took six *years for you to see it...*

"You and my dad have the same smile," Jane said.

The smile broadened. Ten seconds passed. Thirty. Ninety. A hundred.

"Momma said it was the only thing identical about us," she finally replied.

Jane almost threw up. Her senses struggled to compute the fact that she was sitting beside a ghost. But she held in the bile, held in the shakes, held in the tears, held in the screams. She went into survival mode, and her anxiety became secondary. She had to play it cool. The less fear she showed, the greater her chances of getting away.

"I always felt like we could be related," Jane made herself say. "You're my aunt, aren't you? You're...your real name's Hazel, isn't it?"

"I've wanted to tell you for so long," Hazel said, "but it wasn't safe as long as Sister Jolley walked free. She would've had me killed as soon as I surfaced."

"Does Dad know?" *Please tell me Dad doesn't know.*

"Some of it," she said. "He knows that I wasn't in control on the night of the fire. I swear, I was as surprised as he was when

I...I was so confused, so out of sorts, all I knew was I had to save him...and stop Momma from hurting us ever again."

"Then he didn't really take the ritual knives, like they accused him of?"

"I took them before I slipped out the window, in case I had to fight my way free. But I didn't. No one tried to stop me. No one even noticed. I made it to our supplies, made it to the woods, to the highway...then I hitchhiked all the way to Toledo. I lived on the street for a year or so, until I was committed to a psychiatric hospital.

"That hospital was a blessing. Without those doctors' help, I never would have recovered from what they did to me. It took *eighteen* years to get back to life...to get back to Paradise."

"But no one recognized you?" Jane asked.

"Well, I dyed my hair," Hazel said, "and the hospital gave me this to help my dissociation." She took off her glasses and sat them in her lap, then arched her thumb and forefinger. She clawed into her eye socket until her glass eye came loose with a soggy *pop*!

A black hole stared out the windshield.

From where Jane sat, it looked like the car was being driven by a skeleton.

"Harlan recognized me, of course. He was very successful by then, easy for me to find. When I went to his office, he nearly fainted...it was the most beautiful moment of our lives."

"Then why didn't he tell us?" Jane asked. "Why didn't *you* tell me?"

"It was too dangerous," she said. "The Jolleys have too much pull around here. We couldn't trust the police, couldn't trust anyone but each other. Everything would have been easier if I went back on the road...maybe I should've. But I couldn't bear to leave Harlan again. So, I hid in one of his model homes while he used his connections to set me up with a new identity. Once I established myself around town, he gave me the money to open the store."

"Model home?" Jane muttered. "Not the one that...not the Love Shack?"

"That name *disgusts* me. What happened there had nothing to do with s-e-x."

Jane didn't know what to say. Hazel put her eye back in and her glasses back on.

"Your father knows I'm not a murderer," she finally said.

"You're right." Jane nodded. "He knows you saved him. He told me so."

"But he doesn't know the *harder* truth." She sighed. "It's too much for him to accept."

"What's the harder truth?" Jane asked, though she didn't want to know.

"Sister Jolley was half right...the devil really *was* inside of me. She just didn't know how to get him out."

Jane's mind went light as a feather. Her body snapped stiff as a board.

The car was silent for an eternity. Silence. Dark. Silence. Dark.

"For years, I refused to believe it." Hazel finally said. "Then one night, on a road just like this...I saw her. The marks on her arms. The death in her movements. Momma had come back for me and Harlan. A voice in my head screamed, 'Stop her! Don't let her get away! *Stop her!*'

"So, I did what I had to. I stopped her. But then she changed, like magic. She wasn't Momma anymore, just a dead girl. It was a silly, stupid mistake. We *all* make mistakes, right?"

"Right," Jane muttered. "Did Dad know about the mistake?"

"No," she said. "I almost told him...but before I could, it happened again. That's when I knew the devil really was inside me, tricking me, he *had* to be! So, I couldn't tell Harlan. It would've broken his heart...but it's the only plausible explanation, because I am *not* a killer."

"I know you're not," Jane said. "You're the sweetest person in the world."

"I knew you'd understand...after all, you have the same devil inside you."

40

Otis gave up. He couldn't ride anymore. His back hurt from hunching over. His thighs burned from rubbing together. So, he walked the final blocks of his journey, relishing the night air as his mind buzzed with curious energy.

Did Henry really go to Lordsville? What did he find? What did they learn from their dad?

Jane would have the pieces. He would put them together.

Otis pushed his bike onto State Street. He noticed the awning of the Book Nook just as a dark car pulled to the sidewalk directly across from it. The car parked. The driver got out, and the passenger followed. They kept in step as they walked across the road and beneath the awning of the shop. The short shorts threw Otis off, but when he saw the jacket, he knew it was Jane.

"Hey!" Otis shouted, unable to hide his excitement.

But Jane didn't react. He jumped on his bike and pedaled as hard as he could.

"Jane!" Otis yelled.

She wouldn't look at him. She was focused on unlocking the door, which she hadn't managed to do by the time Otis reached the two of them.

"Jane," he panted, "I've been looking for you everywhere!"

"Well, hello." The woman with Jane smiled. "Who's your friend, Jane?"

Jane still couldn't get the door unlocked.

Otis smiled back. "I'm—"

"He's nobody," Jane said coldly, then turned to him. "Don't you have your own bullshit to deal with? Get the hell outta here. *Seriously.*"

"B-b-but I've *got* to know what happened!" Otis stammered.

Jane looked at him intently. "*Listen to me*, you fucking loser, all you've gotta know is that we don't need your help, we don't *want* your help, so stay away from us. Go obsess over someone else—"

"Jane!" the woman gasped. "That's no way to talk to a friend."

The woman offered Otis her free hand. She grasped something else in her other hand, but Otis couldn't see what it was. *Probably a book*, he thought. He shook hands with the woman. Her grip was firm.

Jane's gaze had intensified. Otis didn't notice.

"I'm Suzie Summers, this bookshop's humble proprietor."

"Otis Perkins," he said. He turned to Jane. "I'm sorry if I...maybe I *am* obsessed, OK? But I've *got* to know what happened at Lordsville. Please..."

"Jane's due for a break. Why don't you come in? We'll share some tea and tell some tales."

Jane shook her head emphatically—*NO!* Then the woman nudged her, hard. Jane opened the door.

"Thanks," Otis said, entering. "Sorry again for bugging you."

Jane didn't respond. Neither did the woman. They followed Otis inside.

With the siren on and the hour late, they reached the house in record time. Mammaw spent the drive telling Lt. Garcia everything Harlan had divulged to Jane. Garcia was still processing the information when she pulled up to their front yard.

"Is that a note on the door?" Garcia asked.

"Aw hell," Mammaw said. "I'll run up and check it."

Mammaw was out of the car before Garcia shifted into park. She watched the old woman waddle through the yard. The rational part of her mind attributed Mammaw's theory to decades spent at home reading cheap crime novels. But exhaustion made the *other* part of her brain more elastic than usual— and the theory was no more far-fetched than anything else she'd witnessed over the past two days. She'd seen a fallen faith healer call down mass murder, seen a ghost speak through the rubber mask of a madman; if those forty-eight hours had taught her anything, it was that the poison soil of Appalachia sustained death long after the harvest of life.

Mammaw reached the porch and tore the note from the door. Garcia rolled down her window to gauge the reaction. The dog inside began barking.

"SHIT!" Mammaw screamed. She threw the note and ran back through the yard.

Garcia's heart revved up. She radioed the station. "This is Lt. Garcia, code eight at the Book Nook, downtown Paradise, not sure of the address . . . repeat, requesting backup."

Dispatch radioed back immediately. "Be advised, Lieutenant, all available officers are at the Lordsville compound. May take them a moment to respond."

"Be advised, tell 'em to haul ass."

The shop that once felt like a home to Jane now felt like the set of a play. The books, register, tables, and chairs were props. She had no stage directions, no script. All she could do was improvise, let her fellow cast members guide the performance until inspiration struck.

They were only a few feet inside the store when Otis started playing his part.

"So did Henry go to Lordsville?" he nearly begged.

She nodded—*yes*. Hazel stood behind her, gun in hand.

"Holy shoot!" Otis gasped. "That's so...but where is he now?"

"The hospital," Jane said. It was all she could manage.

The excitement drained from his face. "What? *Why?* What do you mean?"

Jane tried to answer but couldn't. She tried to hatch a plan but didn't.

"I'm afraid he was bitten by a snake," Hazel said, "but he'll survive, won't he, dear?"

Jane nodded again. She tried not to cry. She'd never seen Otis so speechless.

"You should go see him," Jane snapped, her mouth suddenly working. "Go, like, *right now*. He's in the ICU at St. Mary's, room 140. Hurry. *Seriously.* It'll mean the world to him."

Otis nodded wildly. He turned to the door to do as she asked.

But when he pulled the handle, it wouldn't open. He tried again. It refused.

"Henry's wounds will heal, but Jane's suffering is urgent. She needs your help."

Otis turned, confused, and looked at the lady in the dark glasses.

"This medicine she takes . . . *anti*depression, *anti*anxiety, *anti-, anti-, antiCHRIST!* All just Band-Aids. But you can't put a Band-Aid on a *soul* . . . can you, Otis?"

"I, um, I don't kn—"

"I don't know why we're susceptible," Hazel mused, speaking to herself more than anyone. "Maybe it goes back to the tree of life. But I see the rest so clearly. The drugs may have clouded Sister Jolley's interpretation of the Lord's directive, but I'm not clouded. No, no, no, no, no . . . I've got it all worked out. I can fix this, I can save her . . . and you showing up the way you did is proof! You were guided here by *his* hand. You were brought by divine intervention."

Jane opened her mouth to speak. That's when Hazel showed Otis the gun.

Henry never dreamed of murder.

As he lay alone in the hospital room, Henry dreamed of his sister. He dreamed of the creek behind Mammaw's house. They spent entire summers on the bank of that shallow water when they were little—wading with the minnows, listening to music, lazing on the hot, dirty rocks.

In his dream they sat on their favorite rock, the longest one on the embankment. He watched his sister skip stones. Every stone she tossed bounced across the brown water. But they didn't sink; they just chased the current until they were out of sight. Henry knew they kept going on and on and on, forever and ever. Her magical ability filled him with a deep sense of dread.

They were standing too close to eternity. It was just a skip away.

Otis recognized the gun. It had been aimed at him before.

But this time, he didn't fall backward. He froze completely.

"Won't you properly introduce me, dear?" Hazel asked Jane.

"Um, OK," she managed. "Otis this is m-my aunt...Hazel."

Otis wide-eyed the smiling woman. The Rolodex of his mind spun.

Hazel Lusher...Harlan Lusher's twin sister...it could have been her DNA at the Love Shack...but if she were at the crime scene...

"Did you do it together?" Otis asked, before he could stop himself.

Hazel gave him a curious look.

"The murders," Otis clarified. "Was it you and Harlan, or you alone?"

Jane winced.

Hazel simply scoffed. "There's no time to retell that tale. The Lord has sent us a message, and we must act upon it *now*. We must go, children. Walk. Quickly." She nodded to the back of the store.

Jane went first, moving slow. Otis watched her head subtly swivel, scanning the room. Otis followed her.

"There's nothing to be afraid of, Otis," Hazel said. "This is a *happy* occasion!"

"If there's nothing to be afraid of," he said, "will you put the gun away?"

"The Lord *provided* me with this gun. I don't want to seem ungrateful."

They reached the back office. Hazel motioned Jane inside. The small room wasn't much more than a desk, a filing cabinet, and a locked display of rare books. Otis watched Jane's eyes crawl over the room and knew she was looking for a weapon. But there were none—no baseball bats, no chain saws, no sledgehammers, no nothing.

"Grab the benediction off my desk, Otis," Hazel said. "I wrote it from memory."

A scribble-covered piece of paper sat upon the desk. Otis picked it up. He glanced at it. Words were spelled backward. Some were upside down. It said so much. He felt like crying.

"What now?" Jane asked, turning to her aunt.

"The basement."

Jane looked at the small door on the opposite side of the office. She opened it, and they were greeted by the smell of old books and chemicals. She flipped on the light. Without thinking, Otis reached out and took Jane's hand. He squeezed. She squeezed back. They entered the basement that way, hand in shaking hand, with Hazel following.

Three dead children, all in a row.

"To your left," she ordered.

Jane turned left, down a row of shelving units filled with unsold books. A bare cement wall lay beyond them. Two pairs of handcuffs dangled from the corners of a folding chair that was covered in rust or oil or blood. A third set of cuffs was wrapped around the lower support rod of the chair legs. A fourth pair hung from the ceiling—one claw gripping a pipe while the other was open, salivating for flesh.

"The restraints are for your own protection," Hazel said. "You'll see. Go on."

Otis took a cue from Jane and scanned the basement for weapons.

No tanks. No bombs. No machine guns. No nothing.

"Jane," Hazel said, "please go to the cuff on the ceiling and close it around your wrist."

"No way—"

CLICK.

Hazel cocked the gun and pressed it to Otis's head. He started crying.

"That's the devil talking," Hazel said to her. "*My* Jane knows the Lord placed Otis here to taste of his glory. But if you insist on being difficult, there will have to be a price. We can replace this boy if we must...so, must we?"

"No," Jane blubbered. "Please, n-n-no."

Hazel nodded forward. Jane went to the pipe. She had to stand on her tiptoes to get the cuff around her wrist. She *cl-cl-cl-cl*-clicked the handcuff shut.

Hazel nodded, satisfied. "Otis, please hand me the benediction."

Otis did so without looking at her.

"Now sit down in the chair."

Otis did.

"Cross your ankles, and cuff them around the bar."

He bent over. He crossed his ankles. He snapped a cuff around one of them.

"Hey," Jane stammered, "he d-doesn't need to be locked up.

Not to be a witness. We'll do it, OK? Whatever you want. But you don't need to chain him too. You d-d-don't."

"The other ankle please," Hazel said to Otis.

He was trembling. Blubbering. Stammering. Stuttering something inaudibly sad.

"What was that?" Hazel asked.

"I, I, I want," Otis said, louder, "I said I want my d-daddy, I just want my daddy . . ."

"Soon," Hazel cooed. "Now, please, the ankle."

Otis cuffed his legs to the chair. Then she made him cuff his wrists. He searched the room, searched his mind, searched his memory, searched through every book he'd ever read, but he couldn't think of anything to do or say that would do a damn bit of good.

Otis finished cuffing himself. He was hog-tied in steel.

"There," Hazel smiled, "all done. You'll be happy you're secured in just a moment."

She turned around and disappeared beneath the basement stairs.

"Sister Jolley was able to blind the devil," her voice said from the darkness, "but she couldn't get him out. No devil will *ever* be lured from their host by a meager sacrificial calf."

Hazel returned from the darkness carrying a hunting knife sheathed in brown leather. Otis felt the color drain from his face. She sat the knife on a bookshelf, just out of Jane's reach.

Hazel went back under the stairs. Clamors and clatters came from the dark.

"Jane," Otis whispered, "on three, I'm gonna toss myself into that bookshelf. Grab the knife if it falls toward you. If it doesn't . . . well, it won't matter. This is our only chance."

"No," Jane hissed, turning to him. "There has to be another way."

He ignored her. "One. Two. Th—"

His voice caught. His eyes bulged out. Hazel emerged holding two tins of Kingsford lighter fluid and set the containers next to the knife. The blade. The flame. The benediction.

"The Lord has spoken," Hazel said. "It is time for an exorcism."

"You crazy fuck!" Jane screamed. "If you hurt him, I'll kill you!"

"So much rage." Hazel sighed. "Don't worry, your demons will be gone soon—"

KNOCK-KNOCK! KNOCK-KNOCK-KNOCK-KNOCK-KNOCK!

KNOCK-KNOCK-KNOCK KNOCK-KNOCK-KNOCK-KNOCK-KNOCK-KNOCK!

All three of them froze.

Someone was pounding on the door upstairs.

Hazel put the gun to Otis's forehead before he or Jane made a sound.

"This is Lt. Garcia, Sheriff's Department! Open the door, Ms. Summers!"

"Jane? It's Mammaw, baby! Are you here? Hello? Hello?"

"If you make a sound," Hazel said, "I'll bring your grandmother down here and burn *her* next. I'll kill the sheriff and carve out her eyes. I'm more than happy to do it. They aren't blood."

"Please open the door, Ms. Summers!" Garcia yelled. *"It's an emergency!"*

Hazel looked at Jane. Hazel looked at Otis.

"Say you understand."

"I u-underst-st-stand," Otis mumbled.

"I understand," Jane whispered.

She put her finger to her mouth and lowered the gun. A nickel-size bruise began forming in the center of Otis's forehead. Hazel hurried through the basement and up the stairs. The ceiling pounded footfalls as she walked through the office and into the store.

Otis looked at Jane. Jane looked at Otis.

Otis looked at the knife. He began to count.

Garcia pounded on the door. The center glass shook, and the SORRY, WE'RE CLOSED sign bounced mockingly. Mammaw stood to her left and peered through the display window. Garcia wasn't sure what that vantage offered, but what she could see made her uneasy.

Clock every light on after hours . . .

But no one in sight. No one doing inventory . . .

Worse than the sight of the place was the silence. Either someone was in there and not responding, someone was in there and *couldn't* respond, or someone had left in a hurry.

"Is there a back entrance?" Garcia asked the old woman.

Mammaw shrugged.

"Screw this," she said. "There's a pry bar in the cruiser."

"I'll get it. You keep banging."

Garcia tossed her the keys. "Driver's side compartment."

Mammaw ran to the cruiser. Garcia knocked again. Mammaw opened the door and grabbed the pry bar. Then, through the glass, Garcia saw the shop owner emerge from the back office, smiling and waving apologetically as she walked toward the front door.

"Help! Please! Help! Help us! She's crazy!"

"We're down here! Help! She has a gun!"

Garcia's eyes followed the screams to a ventilation window on the corner of the building.

The rest happened in slow motion.

Garcia looked back up. Hazel stood in the center of the shop, still smiling, gun raised. Garcia pulled her weapon, knowing she was late on the draw. Hazel pulled the trigger. Garcia braced for the coming warmth of death ...

Suddenly, the cruiser crashed into the store like a wrecking ball.

Twisting metal grated Garcia's ears. Shards of glass cut her skin.

The bullet hit the engine block. The engine revved with rage, plowing down bookshelves and smashing into Hazel as she fired again. This shot went high and blew out the glass door. The car shattered Hazel in a similar fashion, demolishing her hip and pelvis before ramming her into the wall of spirituality books at full speed, apparently breaking her back and bursting most of her insides to muck. Blood sprayed from her mouth as she screamed, soaking the hood of the cruiser.

Her glasses were knocked from her face. Her glass eye popped out of the socket.

Then Hazel Lusher's skull hit the hood of the cruiser with a dead thud.

Garcia steadied herself on the doorframe. The sign greeted her from the floor: OPEN! COME IN! She stepped inside. The ground crunched beneath her boots. She walked across the wreckage, too amazed she hadn't been shot to notice the cuts she'd sustained from the glass. The car began smoking. The engine died. Mammaw climbed out, wincing and rubbing her back.

"Are you OK?" Garcia asked.

"Better than her," she said, nodding to the corpse.

Garcia looked at the body. The blood Hazel spat out was now running back down the hood of the car, shrouding her head like a veil. Garcia stepped forward to check her pulse.

Mammaw stopped her. "Come on, let's find my baby. Leave this bitch for the worms."

Otis was in a tremendous amount of pain. He was trapped beneath the shelf he'd launched himself into. He was double trapped. Double screwed. But he didn't care—because it had worked.

Jane had caught the knife. She held it at the ready.

Otis held his breath. The outcome of the commotion upstairs meant life or death for him. Minutes passed. Lifetimes. Stars were born and burned to dust while he waited to learn his fate.

"Jane?" Lt. Garcia called out from the silence.

Jane and Otis locked eyes and then let off like a firing squad.

"*Here!*"

"Down *here!*"

"The basement!"

"*Hurry!*"

"The *basement!*"

Otis could hear the door at the top of the stairs fling open, followed by a thunder of footsteps as Lt. Garcia ran into the basement. She was followed by Mammaw, who ran straight to Jane with outstretched arms.

"Baby!" Mammaw sang as she hugged her.

Garcia focused on Otis. It took her three tries to move the shelf off of him.

"Jesus Christ," she gasped, when she realized he was chained to the seat. "Are you OK?"

He couldn't answer. He was stunned. He was safe. He was saved.

"Keys? Where are the keys?" Mammaw asked.

"Check her office," Jane said.

"Mine should work," Garcia said. She reached for her utility belt, then remembered it was in the duffel bag with her bloody uniform. "They're in the car, hold ti—"

Garcia raised her gun to the stairs.

Otis squirmed on the ground. He couldn't tell what was happening. He saw Mammaw and Jane turn to the staircase, and whatever they saw standing there made them rigor-mortified.

Step by creaking step, the mangled body of Hazel Usher came into view. She slumped against the wall for support. Her empty eye socket glared. Her hair, face, and clothes were drenched in blood.

She still held the gun.

"I saw her," Hazel rasped. "Momma. Waiting in the darkness-s-s, I saw . . ."

"Please," Garcia said, "lower the gun. Let us get you help."

"Momma's in the darkness," she kept muttering, "holding a baby . . . a little blue girl . . . waiting . . . and l-laughing . . . oh, Jane, I'm so sorry, now I finally understand . . ."

Hazel looked at Jane. Jane looked at her.

Hazel's eye grew eerily clear. "Once you get the devil in the blood, he never leaves."

Hazel smiled as she brought the gun to her temple.

Jane shrieked as she pulled the trigger.

41

Brutal hours passed. The street was cut off from the press. Sheriff Connors demanded it. Government vehicles jockeyed for position along the block. Cruisers from the county and state police. CPD's CSI van. The coroner. Numerous ambulances.

Garcia hung around after giving her initial statement. There would be more questions later—she'd racked up two official inquests in less than twenty-four hours—but right now the four of them were offered mercy and rest. Deputy Kern drove Jane and her grandmother home.

Garcia stood with Sheriff Connors and watched them pull away.

"That girl will be asleep before they clear the block," the sheriff said.

"I hope so." Garcia sighed.

"Time you get home and do the same."

She nodded and walked away, stumbling a little, still in a daze. People were working and lights were flashing, so she kept to the middle of the street. A lab tech from CPD waved at her.

She waved back. She saw a few other officers she knew. She saw Levi Sutter and Mayor Jolley. She saw genuine journalists and rat fink reporters arriving on scene. She saw the boy from the basement sitting on the bumper of an ambulance, all alone.

"Hey!" she called, walking over. "What are you still doing here?"

"Oh." He shrugged. "The EMT went somewhere. I wasn't sure if I should wait."

She pointed to his bandaged wrists. "That from the cuffs?"

"Yeah." He nodded. "What are yours from?"

"The glass," she said, touching one of the dozen Band-Aids on her arms and face. "I'm Elena Garcia, by the way. We didn't have much time for introductions." She extended her hand.

"Otis Perkins," he said, shaking it.

"Wait," she laughed, "*you're* Otis Perkins? The investigator?"

"Uh, yeah. Why is that funny?"

"Because," she said, sitting beside him, "the PI who cracked this case is just a kid! Incredible... Christ, is that why you were here tonight?"

"Sort of," he said, blushing. "And I didn't really crack anything. I just looked at old leads and applied as much logic as possible... but I never saw *this* coming. Not until it was too late."

"That's how it goes," she sighed. "Want some advice? One gumshoe to another?"

He nodded.

"In this gig, you've gotta be willing to take logic *out* of the equation."

"What do you mean?"

"I mean curveballs are the norm," she mused, "and sometimes

they curve in patterns that no amount of experience prepares you for. I think Lenny Bruce said it best—in a world where carpenters get resurrected, *anything* is fucking possible."

Otis started laughing. She did too. She patted his back.

"But you're off the clock now, kid. Call your parents. It's too late, or early, for you to be out."

"I lost my phone down there," Otis said, nodding to the bookshop.

"Oh. Come on, then, I'll give you a lift."

Otis pointed to her cruiser, which was currently residing indoors.

"Right," she scoffed. "Do your parents have any idea where you are?"

"No," he admitted. "We got into a fight and...long story."

"I know that look," she said. "They must have messed up pretty bad."

"Really bad," he sighed.

"When I had my little girl, I learned there's a lot of stuff that all those parenting books don't mention. The main one being how *consistently* I mess things up. Take tonight, for instance— my daughter called me a superhero. But you know how it made me feel? *Anxious*. Because I know next time I screw up, I'm gonna have even further to fall."

"I used to think my father was a superhero," Otis mumbled after a moment.

"I thought mine was too," Garcia said. "It fucks you up when you realize your parents are human. But if you can find a way to forgive them for *that*...you can forgive 'em for anything."

Otis nodded. They sat in silence as the other investigators bustled about.

Across the street, the neon sign in the window of Tudor's Café flickered to life.

"Otis Perkins," Garcia said, "if I had the power to deputize you, I'd do it right here and now. But in lieu of that, how about I buy you some chocolate chip pancakes? Maybe some grateful citizen will even offer to give us a lift home."

She stood up. Otis hesitated for a moment, then joined her.

They walked side by side down the center of the street toward the café.

"What's going to happen to Harlan Lusher?" Otis asked.

"I'm not sure," she admitted. "We need to piece together what happened here first."

"That's not going to be easy."

"No, kid, it won't. But if you and I put our heads together, I bet we can figure it out."

Otis smiled and looked away. It seemed for a moment that morning had broken. But it was only the flashing of sirens, lighting the lingering night.

EXODOS

August was hot as all hell. Jane sat on the edge of their favorite rock with her feet submerged in the creek. She hadn't ventured down the embankment all summer and was pleased to find nothing had changed. The water still warmed in the dog days, and the mossy rocks still felt slimy and ancient when she ran her toes across them. Sandstone still broke apart easily, and the flat edges of their favorite rock still made the best skipping stones in the business. Jane had a good-size pile of them gathered there beside her. She picked another rock up, whirled it into the water, and counted—*one, two, three, four, five!*

Five skips!

She felt a childish sense of accomplishment, though she hadn't come for that. Jane was there to say goodbye. In eight days, she was moving into the freshmen dorms at WVU. She knew there was a chance she would never come back to Paradise again.

Eight days left, but this was the only one she had to herself.

The rest of the days were for her dad.

It took seven months for the state to clear him of murder, and another six weeks to schedule his release. The process had been maddening, but in seventeen hours Harlan Lusher would finally be a free man.

Public opinions on the matter varied. The Lushers were still the most hated family in Barkley County, and Jane prayed the court would award them enough wrongful conviction compensation to move somewhere else and get fresh start. She dreaded the thought of Henry being stuck in Paradise without her, especially now that Otis was gone.

Her brother's best bud had left for Duke the week before. Henry loaned Otis his entire collection of Shooter Kane paperbacks for the drive. Otis made Henry swear he would visit him. There was no talk of Otis ever returning to West Virginia.

Jane felt guilty for leaving. She even briefly considered turning down the scholarship she'd worked so hard to attain. But Henry wouldn't hear of it, and neither would Mammaw. Her father was just as emphatic: "One thing I learned in prison is that there's no making up for lost time. Lost time is lost. The clock keeps moving forward, and we've gotta keep moving with it."

Behind her, a door slammed.

She heard Henry's feet trample across the porch. It was a joyful noise that Otis Perkins was to thank for. Otis had shown how much he cared for Henry by showing that others could, too. When the violence of last October made national news, Otis did something they never would've considered—set up a GoFundMe page to raise money for their medical and legal expenses. The page raised more than expected, and they ended up with enough cash to fund Henry's ICU stay *and* the corrective surgery on his hip, as well as therapists for them both.

"Hey!" Henry called, his shadow stretching over the embankment. "Which cake does Dad like? Double chocolate or funfetti?" He and Mammaw were prepping the welcome home party.

"Funfetti," Jane said. "It was Mom who liked chocolate."

She waved him down to the rock. Henry didn't hesitate. His denim flew behind him as he maneuvered the incline to where she sat. He'd cut the sleeves off his jacket so he wouldn't have to take it off in the blistering summer months.

"It's fuckin' hot," he said, hopping onto their rock.

"Yeah, but check *this* out. I can beat my old record."

She picked up another stone and let it fly. It hopped across the surface of the water *six* times before sinking. She cheered for herself. Henry clapped, too, but his expression was odd.

"Oh"—she huffed—"not impressed?"

"Sorry, I...you just gave me déjà vu."

"You dreamed about me skipping stones?"

"I dunno." He shrugged. "Maybe, I guess."

"Awwww," she teased, "it's because you're gonna miss me. How sweet!"

Henry rolled his eyes, but he didn't refute her. He sat down cross-legged and picked a stone from her pile. Then, suddenly, he asked, "Why didn't Dad ever tell us she was alive?"

"Because he promised he wouldn't. I don't think we woulda told either, do you?"

"Guess not," he said. "I've never told anyone ya pluck your nose hairs twice a week."

"Well, I've never told anyone that you secretly like Justin Bieber," she shot back.

"Hey!" he snapped. "That one goes to the fuckin' grave."

She smiled and nodded. He smiled back.

"Love you, Ass Face."

"Love you, Butt Breath."

He tossed his chip of their stone into the creek. It cut along the surface of the water. They sat together and watched the currents of eternity carry it away.

ACKNOWLEDGMENTS

Indulge me whilo I wax poetic for a minute:

Much of the work on *Paradise, WV* was done during the pandemic. THANK YOU from the bottom of my heart for supporting my work—if I couldn't continue creating while locked down, I would've lost my mind . . . and I don't have much left to spare.

Secondly, I'd like to acknowledge the victims of violent crime and those working to bring perpetrators to some semblance of justice. It's natural to be enamored by the abnormal (serial killings included), and I'm more drawn to it than most. But I challenge myself and all of you to hold tight to our empathy—none of us should have a favorite murder or murderer.

Endless thanks to my brother and artistic collaborator for your help on all my projects. My parents and family for the endless support. Liz, my Wild One, for helping, encouraging, and generally putting up with my crazy ass. Kristin, benevolent artist and friend, for showing me how to actually outline a book. Thanks to all my homies and bandmates worldwide for keeping me going, keeping me creative, and keeping me laughing through the shitshow that is life.

Thank you, Shannon, my first and most dependable advocate. Thank you, Leslie, for keeping me going with your tireless encouragement. Thank you, Ben, for always having my back. Much thanks to Stephanie, Heather, Carey, Jessica, and everyone at Keylight/Turner Publishing.

Lastly, I'd like to thank my grandparents. Mammaw Rufus very much comes alive on these pages, and I'm eternally grateful she passed on her love of cheap pulp thrills and lowbrow living. I'm equally thankful for my more pious Grandad and Grandmother—two Blood Bought Believers from Barboursville, WV, who never showed nothing but love to a sinner like me.

ABOUT THE AUTHOR

Rob Rufus is an author, musician, and screenwriter. His literary debut, *Die Young With Me*, received an American Library Association Award. It was named one of the "Best Books of the Year" by Hudson Booksellers and is currently being developed for the screen. His first book of fiction, *The Vinyl Underground*, was chosen as a Junior Library Guild gold-star selection. He now has multiple screenplays and TV pilots in the works. His musical projects—Blacklist Royals/The Bad Signs—have released numerous full-length albums and toured in over a dozen countries. He is a cancer survivor and works closely with many advocacy groups and nonprofits. When he isn't on the road rock-n-rolling, you can find him in East Nashville, TN.